Fool Me Once

By

Linnhe McCarron

Fool Me Once

Second edition December 1, 2020
Paperback ISBN: 978-1-7330443-6-3

Contact information: linnhemccarron@gmail.com

Cover design by *Marcy Norwood*
www.dandmequinedesign.com
Editing by *Rita M. Reali,*
https://persnicketyproofreader.wordpress.com/
Formatting by *Debby Johnson*
https://nippi1.wixsite.com/nacauldron/formatting-services)

Published in the United States of America

Also By Linnhe McCarron

The Riverwood Series
Fool Me Once (2018)
A Bitter Wind Blows (2019)
Signs of Life (2019)
Ride A Pale Horse (2020)
Far And Away (2020)
The Hand of Fate (2021)

DEDICATION

For Anhi

Chapter One

Ronnie Chandler pulled into the Jones Bones BBQ parking lot right on time. Her stomach had been in a knot for the past hour. She needed to eat soon, but she was exceptionally nervous. She and her partners would be meeting with their potential investors, and she wanted it to go well.

She had dressed carefully to make a good first impression. Ronnie was one of the lucky few whose hair had turned not gray, but silver, and she spent good money to have it cut every six weeks. The shiny strands grazed her collar in back and framed her oval face with two long graceful curves that ended in precise points. She always looked sleek and elegant, even in the faded jeans that were part of her signature look.

Today, she wore faded, straight-legged Levis with a cashmere turtleneck in a color that could only be called wisteria. She'd never particularly liked purples but had changed her palette to add dramatic contrast to her striking hair. Her violet eyes were courtesy of tinted contacts, and she had an entire wardrobe of those.

A navy belt circled her waist, and its simple silver buckle was mirrored by the wide silver bangle on her wrist. She wore smooth gray leather western-style boots and pulled it all together with a densely-woven Harris Tweed jacket in shades of deep purple, burgundy, navy, and pale gray. When she'd looked into her full-length mirror earlier that morning, she was pleased with what she saw, satisfied that she'd achieved what she'd intended, which was to have dressed up more than usual without appearing to have tried too hard.

She pushed her sunglasses onto the top of her head, taking a moment to let her eyes adjust to the restaurant's interior after coming in from the strong noontime sun. Rickie and Andee were already seated at a table with three men. Two had their backs to her, but all three stood as she approached.

Ronnie pulled the navy leather glove off her right hand and extended it, sucking in a breath as she stood facing the handsomest man she'd ever seen. Of the group, she recognized Charles Walker Westlake immediately because he was the older of the three. She knew one of the others was his son, Chip, and quickly identified him as well by the unmistakable likeness to his father.

Shaking hands with the senior Mr. Westlake, she gave her name as Veronica Chandler but told him everyone called her Ronnie. He grinned and responded, "And everyone calls me CW." As introductions were made, she learned that the third man, the one whose extraordinary good looks almost took her breath away, was Luc Deschaines.

Charles Walker Westlake had a patrician profile, and both his appearance and his demeanor telegraphed the power he possessed in the real estate world. He had carefully mentored his son, Chip, and the in-joke in financial circles was that Chip was indeed a 'chip off the old block.' The Westlake Group's reputation preceded them, and the three realtors understood that investors worked with facts and analyses; in their business, it all came down to the numbers.

The twelve hundred acres was too extensive to cover in the few hours between driving up from Nashville and the BBQ lunch. Once or twice, Ronnie caught a look that flashed between father and son and again between the two younger men. Ronnie was confident that Andee had planned the tour to give the would-be investors the best sample of the property's geographic features—the deep gorges and ravines, panoramic views from high bluffs, clear creeks, hidden ponds and endless rolling terrain prime for pasture. Andee had said the day before that she intended to let the land 'sell itself' as she was sure it would and now, listening to the lively discussion that had begun as soon as their party was seated, Ronnie was gratified to learn that Andee's exuberance for the scenery had the investors assessing the possibilities for a lucrative return.

As agents at Horse Country Real Estate, Ronnie and her partners made it a point to keep up with new listings or for-sale-by-owner properties and to be knowledgeable well beyond the often-meager description in the Multiple Listing Service. Ronnie, in particular, hated it when agents blatted that everything was pristine, everything was unique. Those words just about made her blood boil when she heard them or saw them in ads. Her pet peeve was agents who thought that any piece of land was a horse property. Who wasted space in the description by saying, "Build your dream home" or "Bring your horses!" Her partners had often heard her rail against them.

Sometimes gates were too narrow, and trying to get a horse trailer through them would be like threading a needle. Or they were set too close to the road, so there wasn't enough distance to straighten a big rig before getting through the gates. Or there was nowhere to park a horse trailer, or to turn a flatbed loaded with hay around so it could back in. Ronnie had a long list of pitfalls that they would avoid in creating their equestrian community.

Knowing Andee as she did, Ronnie was sure that she had replayed the site visit in her mind over and over as she drove to the restaurant, examining each sentence, each expression, reading between the lines, and getting a sense of the trio's group dynamic.

"We saw a selection of the property's features, a good representation," Charles had offered, noncommittally, as soon as the entire group was seated. Ronnie suspected that he played his cards close to the proverbial vest, and they shouldn't expect much more from him at this point.

Now, as the group waited to place their orders, Ronnie turned to study the men. The relationship between two of the three, father and son, was pretty clear, but what about the third guy? Was he an equal partner? Junior partner?

Sitting diagonally across from him, Ronnie found Luc's good looks extremely appealing. Smooth black eyebrows drew her attention to his dark blue eyes and long sooty eyelashes. With his thick ebony hair, she guessed that his lineage was Black Irish, although his name sounded French. His worn jeans had clearly been ironed, and she guessed that his western boots were handmade. She bit her lip to keep herself from grinning because she had already assessed his tweed jacket and pegged it as perfectly tailored, had already approved of the crisp white shirt, the good belt, and the huge Breitling chronometer on his wrist.

His eyes followed her gaze, and he held out his arm. "This watch was a gift from Charles and his wife, Julia, when I graduated from Horvath Business School and joined the firm," he told her. "He gave one to Chip and one to me. It's my most treasured possession, and I only take it off to have it cleaned once in a while."

Ronnie heard the pride and affection in his voice and knew that these three men shared a bond a lot like hers with her partners. She liked that and hoped this venture went forward. It wasn't if she reminded herself—it was when.

Ronnie quickly eyed Luc's left hand, noting the absence of a wedding ring. Andee was happily married, and Rickie had been in a relationship for the past several years. But her partners often accused her of having shadows in her eyes and hiding her loneliness. *Stop speculating and concentrate.*

Ronnie forced her attention back to the conversation. "It's all good, but my preference is the baby back ribs," she heard Rickie telling Chip. "We've got about an hour and a half before we need to meet the helicopter, so take your time."

"You're flying back tonight?" Ronnie asked, a little embarrassed to have let her thoughts wander. She struggled now to re-engage.

"Well, it all depends on what we see today," Charles said as he motioned to the waiter that he was paying for the whole table. "My pilot is in Nashville with our corporate plane; we were there on another potential venture yesterday. We have far more flexibility with our schedule than if we were flying commercial. Flexibility is crucial in our business."

The afternoon's overflight should provide all the information the investors needed to make a decision, but there was so much that could make or break the presentation. If this venture were successful, it would put Horse Country Real Estate on the map. Creating an equestrian development from a vision and a raw piece of land was a real departure from selling tiny cabins to weekend riders or one-acre or two-acre lots where commuters could set up a crude horse camp. If it went forward, this project would require an enormous commitment of time.

It was a project that would earn the Horse Country agents both the admiration and enmity of their peers. Not that they needed any more animosity. This was an aspect the three realtors had discussed at length. Ronnie had laid their trepidation out on the table when the concept was first broached. In a profession where any high-school graduate could get a license, there was too little competence, too little oversight, and too much back-stabbing.

Two servers approached the table, one carrying the drinks and the other a large tray. There's no graceful way to eat barbecue, and the ice was soon broken as everyone shared the side dishes and enjoyed the meal.

"Is the barbecue sauce-tomato or vinegar-based?" Chip had asked a short while later.

"Does it matter?" Luc asked.

"I've spent a fair amount of time in North Carolina, and the state considers itself 'the cradle of 'cue,' the Barbecue Capital of the World—and I've certainly eaten my fair share of barbecue along the way," Chip said.

"Vinegar is the secret ingredient of Carolina barbecue," he told the group, "but, curiously, North Carolina is divided on the issue of sauce and as you travel farther west, barbecue sauce moves from the thin vinegar-based variety particular to the eastern part of the state to the thicker tomato-based sauces in western North Carolina.

"You could say that the North Carolina Barbecue Sauce Feud has been—smokin'—since the early 1800s," he joked.

He'd successfully put everyone at ease with his barbecue trivia.

"Aren't words great?" Ronnie contributed. "Look at the word 'barbecue.' It's both a noun and a verb; you barbecue the meat to produce barbecue, and you invite friends over for a barbecue. There's a barbecue joint in every town, usually more than one, where you can grab a side of ribs or a pulled-pork sandwich."

Barbecue wasn't a New England specialty, so Ronnie didn't pass up many opportunities to enjoy it once she'd sampled both varieties and discovered that she liked them equally. "The best way of summing up the experience is this," she continued, "your fingers are your fork!" Ronnie herself wanted the investors relaxed and enjoying themselves because not only were she, Rickie, and Andee selling the concept, they were selling the area.

She and her partners had been together for six years. She and Rickie had worked in large general-practice real estate agencies. Although they were considered independent contractors, they were nonetheless bound by the management style practiced by each managing broker. They had learned what they liked—and didn't like—and what they themselves would do differently, given the opportunity. Changing agencies is difficult because so many loose ends refuse to be tied up simultaneously, but realtors do often change agencies. The grass isn't greener on the other side of the fence—until, one day, it is.

Ronnie had worked long and hard to get a doctorate in English Literature, a prerequisite for a serious career in academia, and had never—not for an instant—envisioned herself as a real estate agent. She'd never imagined her marriage shattering or leaving New England, but both had happened, and she was living proof that when one door closes, another opens. The past was firmly where it belonged—in the past—and Ronnie found that she enjoyed the myriad facets of listing and selling property.

Rickie and she had had a number of closings together and always appreciated each other's similar work ethic. One day, when the attorney conducting the closing was detained in court, and the buyers and sellers were waiting in the conference room, desultorily making small talk, Rickie suggested that she and Ronnie step outside. "What would you think about opening an office together?" Rickie proposed to Ronnie.

Andee was the newcomer to real estate. She was a professional landscape architect and had worked in an architect's office, where she felt valued and fulfilled.

Rickie and Andee had met at a trailhead several years earlier and stood for a few minutes, discussing the recent rains and the possibility of trail washouts ahead. They'd ridden together that day and many times again over the next few years. After Rickie introduced Ronnie to Andee, the three women had enjoyed many hours on horseback together. When Ronnie and Rickie decided the time had come to throw in together and open an office, they persuaded Andee to get a real estate license.

Andee's forte was selling land, and she shied away from residential listings. She was, more often than not, engaged by buyers to work up a site plan for their purchase because she was so knowledgeable about things like drainage, or how and where to build a retaining wall. When her expertise and ideas saved hundreds and thousands of dollars in site prep, she compiled an impressive list of satisfied customers who were only too happy to recommend her services.

Each woman brought talents to the table that complemented the others. They were, for the most part, on the proverbial same page and pulled in the same direction. They had agreed early on that they would list and sell only horse properties. All three were avid riders, and they knew that the Big South Fork was a natural draw for horsemen. On their website, In the Heart of Horse Country, they culled all of the mobile homes, little brick ranchers, and anything that didn't have enough land to make it viable for horse ownership, leaving a comprehensive collection of equestrian properties.

Their plans for the tract of land in Emery Pond were an ambitious project by anyone's standards. There were a number of equestrian communities in Tennessee, and they intended to combine the best features of each. They'd done their homework, looking at the layout and style of each, the trails and stabling, the common areas and amenities. In particular, they intended to utilize several of the features they'd found appealing at Trail's End.

Ronnie took two fliers out of her portfolio and handed them to CW. "Split Rock and Seven Oaks are two of our local equestrian communities," she explained. "The entrances to both subdivisions are so dramatic that the fliers are a great sales tool. The developer has cleverly used a huge cracked-open boulder instead of trying to move it, and he called the development Split Rock. Once people see it, it sells itself!" She was pleased to see CW nodding approvingly as he passed the two fliers to Chip. "It looks like he did the same with those huge trees in Seven Oaks," Charles noted. "I'm guessing the same developer did both subdivisions." At that moment, Charles pulled his cell phone from his breast pocket and held it to his ear.

He must have had it set to vibrate, but he wouldn't have taken the call if it wasn't important. Glancing over, Ronnie saw that Andee was literally holding her breath, and she shot her gaze toward Andee's plate, silently signaling that she should just continue eating. *But what if they just bagged the whole idea and flew back later this afternoon?* So much effort had gone into this showing. Long hours of planning, scouting, scheduling the time, checking with the seller. So many times that was the scenario in real estate. Eager buyers often came and 'kicked the tires,' used up time, gas, and energy, leaving the realtor with nothing to show for it.

"I understand," Charles said, succinctly. "No, tomorrow. Well, let's give it until close of business." Chip raised an eyebrow, but Charles shook his head slightly from side to side, indicating that there was no immediate crisis.

When the meal ended, Charles had taken the bill, calculated the tip, and laid the exact amount on the table. In the parking lot, Andee directed the three men into Ronnie's SUV because her truck was still towing the small flatbed trailer with the ATVs and would be left behind with Ronnie and Rickie until they returned. Arrangements had been made to meet the helicopter in a field a short distance from the restaurant.

Rickie and Ronnie waited in Rickie's vehicle for the hour the overflight would take. The civilian helicopter they'd chartered was not only very comfortable but well suited for this task. Though it could accommodate six, only Andee went up with the three investors and the pilot. Thoroughly prepared as always, she carried her topo's and was easily able to help the other passengers correlate what they had seen on the ground with this magnificent bird's-eye view.

When Andee and the three investors re-joined Ronnie and Rickie, the group walked slowly over to Charles' rental car. "That was very informative. I'm thinking I'd like to stay over," Charles said to Chip.

Luc had spread one of Andee's topo's on the hood of the vehicle and asked, "Is it okay if I write on this?"

Andee had a marker pen ready and handed it to him.

"How'd it go?" Ronnie, her lips barely moving, whispered to Andee.

Andee's expression didn't change, and she replied in a low voice, "I think it went really well. Charles sat up front with the pilot and kept asking him to circle. A couple of times, he seemed to want to get a better look at a particular feature or see it from a different angle, so he asked him to descend. Charles had a notebook on his knee, and he sure scribbled a lot of notes!"

Charles shook hands with each of the three women. "I want to drive through those two equestrian communities and then drive around the area some." He saw that Rickie was about to reply, and he held up his palm. "We'll find a place to stay in Cookeville and have dinner there. Something pressing has come up, and I've got to get back so we'll have early departure in the morning."

It was a given that if CW wasn't interested at all, they'd be back in Virginia that evening. It was a positive sign he wanted to discuss his impressions with the others, without a further tour. Backing a project was a combination of determining that the concept was sound, being in the right place at the right time, and crunching the numbers, as well as an understanding and cooperation among the partners.

"I'd love to sink my teeth into a project like this," Chip was telling Rickie. "And I'm already making mental lists of all the things we would need to do to get this project underway. It sounds easy enough but, believe me, it's incredibly complex, and we'd all need to be thoroughly prepared from the first minute of the first hour of the first day. I can tell you from experience, in a rural area, venture capitalists are often considered *vulture capitalists!"*

As the investors prepared to leave, Ronnie's knees almost went weak when she heard Chip say, "This would be an exciting project in a lot of respects. This is a beautiful area, and I'd look forward to spending some time here. I'd like to bring my wife and boys and let them see what it's about. I'm sure my wife would enjoy a horseback ride, and the boys are kayakers—although I'm not so sure I want to introduce them to Big South Fork's Class V rapids!"

"You'd probably want to rent a cabin in Creekside," Ronnie told him smoothly, careful to keep her emotions from showing on her face. "Let me write down the web address. It's centrally located, and all of the log cabins are tucked into the woods and very well appointed. I'm sure you'd be really comfortable, and you'd enjoy it."

"When you get on the website, each cabin has a calendar that shows what dates are already booked and what dates are available."

"What about you, Luc?" she asked. "Will you be bringing your family, too?"

"I've been divorced for several years," Luc replied. "I have a teenage daughter, but I'm not sure she's an outdoor enthusiast." Most people would assume that his daughter was too involved with girlfriends, boyfriends, shopping or sports to be interested in coming to such a rural area and he usually let it go at that. Chip knew the truth, but he was Luc's best friend, as well as his business partner, and he would never provide any personal details. However much Luc chose to share was entirely up to him. "What about you?" Luc asked Ronnie.

Luc had glanced at Ronnie's left hand even before they were introduced. The fact that she wore no wedding band indicated she wasn't married. But you had to have a certain focus to be a successful venture capitalist, and he wanted to know how much time and energy she would be devoting to this project if it came to fruition.

Before getting into Charles' rental, Luc hung back, his eyes meeting Ronnie's. "We could be seeing a lot of each other over the next year or so," he said, his tone casual. *Oh, God*, he moaned inwardly. *She probably thinks I'm hitting on her, which I surely am not! What an idiot!*

"I've been divorced for eleven years," she said flatly. She smiled slightly to offset her tone, but he sensed the bitterness she obviously had to suppress. That was a feeling he could relate to. "I married a law student right after he graduated. While I expected he would practically live at the office for the first several years, it became apparent that there was no end in sight, and I would always be number two on his list." She didn't elaborate further, and Luc steered the conversation in a different direction.

"Chip's dad is the senior partner, but you've probably figured that out. Once the three of us get a project underway, he leaves the day-to-day to Chip and me. We're very selective about what we get involved in for that very reason; there's money to be made, but all of us would like to have a life."

"CW lives on the Eastern Shore, as you might expect," he explained. "He's got a nice power boat, and he's a golfer, so Bayside is just the place for him. There's plenty for his wife to do, and he can take the grandkids water skiing or crabbing. He's really the one with the connections, and he can capitalize our projects with a few phone calls. Then Chip and I do the legwork."

Ronnie had momentarily tuned out of the conversation. She was wondering how Luc's black hair might feel in her hands. The collar of his shirt was unbuttoned, and the hair on his chest just barely showed. She thought she'd like to undo that second button—and the third—and the fourth! She thought about how strong his hands looked. It had been a long time—too long. She had to pinch herself mentally to stop the inappropriate appraisal of his body.

Although she had been immediately attracted to him and acknowledged that there might be some degree of chemistry between them, Ronnie realized he was simply collecting data, and she got the message loud and clear. He wanted a working relationship, and no more.

Not wanting to be rude, she turned to Chip, but it was Luc who answered. "How did you all meet?"

"It was my very great good fortune to be in the right place at the right time," Luc said. "Chip and I were fraternity brothers at Daniels College, and we shared an apartment when we went to business school at Horvath University. There was no question he would be going into business with his father; he'd been groomed for it all his life. CW took a liking to me when he and Mrs. Westlake—Julia—came up for parents' weekend our freshman year, and he's treated me like a son since the day we met."

"Wow," Ronnie said, impressed. "You were lucky!"

"Yes, I was. But I've worked hard, too. Still do."

"What about your daughter?" Ronnie asked.

"What about her?" Luc asked cautiously. Ronnie was puzzled by his hesitation. Most parents would be eager to talk about their offspring.

"How old is she?" *This is like pulling teeth; something's not right.*

"She's fourteen," Luc said. "Stephanie lives with her mother, who has re-married. Now that she's occupied, we don't struggle over custody. In fact, she all but ignores Steffi and seems pretty determined not to have any more children."

"So, will your daughter be coming with you when you do come here?" Ronnie persisted.

"I'm sure she will, and you'll meet her. But I doubt that it will go well. She'll take one look at you, and it will be hate at first sight."

"Why?" Ronnie gasped. "Because she'll feel threatened?"

"That, and more." Luc sighed. "She's morbidly obese. I'm sure she eats because she's so unhappy, but I'm at a complete loss. She hides food; it's almost impossible to insist on healthy meals and snacks."

"What about her mother?" Ronnie asked, genuinely interested.

"Kelli is embarrassed by her daughter, and has chosen to turn a blind eye, as she does to everything that displeases her."

"How sad," Ronnie said. "You must feel terrible about that."

"I do!" Luc exclaimed. "Stephanie is so sullen that nothing I say or do seems to get through to her."

"Sounds like you have a lot on your plate," Ronnie observed.

"You must be surprised that I've told you all this," Luc said slowly. "This is a painful issue that I never discuss with near strangers. I've dated some, but it always seems to end in disaster. Not many women want to hang around when they realize Steffi is part of the package."

Ronnie could see that CW was becoming impatient, ready to dispense with small talk, and get on with the remainder of his day.

"We passed by Cookeville on our way up from Nashville," CW said, "but we'll want to go back and take a look at the town itself. The area's demographic will certainly be a factor in our decision; it's all part of the proverbial big picture."

"Cookeville is growing very rapidly and has a large medical community," Ronnie told him. "It's also a big college town. You'll want to look at Crossville and Jamestown too if you're trying to get a feel for the area."

"Jamestown looks like the town that time forgot," Andee said. "It reminds me of that movie, the one that was shot in black and white, in the early 70s."

"Right—right," Chip said. "I remember that!"

"Part of the problem in Jamestown is that all the downtown storefronts are empty," Rickie told the investors. "You-Know-Who had a lot to do with that, of course, but the streets are too narrow, and there's no on-street parking, which makes it hard to patronize shops or offices downtown."

"No urban renewal?" Luc asked. "No widening the streets?"

"Most of the buildings in Jamestown are constructed from local sandstone, that's a major constraint," Rickie replied. "But Big South Fork is the big draw," she clarified. "People come to Jamestown specifically for the trail riding, hiking, and mountain biking that a national park offers, and it pumps a lot of revenue into a sleepy small town."

Andee picked up next, offering, "After you drive through Split Rock and Seven Oaks, you should go through Jamestown and then straight down Highway 127 to Crossville. You can pick up the interstate there. When you're ready for dinner, there are quite a few dependable choices. There's seafood and Italian, as you'd expect, but there's also Cajun if you want something with more ambiance."

Several days earlier, Ronnie had reminded Rickie to tell Chip, as they finalized their plans for the trip, that parts of Tennessee are dry, and they might want to bring whatever alcoholic beverages they enjoyed. Since they were traveling in a private jet, they weren't limited in carrying liquids, and he made sure to include a bottle of his father's favorite single-malt scotch in his bag.

"Fentress is dry," Ronnie clarified now. "And the surrounding counties were too, but now all of the surrounding counties aren't. You'll be able to have a drink with dinner in Putnam County."

Ronnie pulled her cell out of the side pocket on her shoulder bag and thumbed the Do Not Disturb feature from off to on. The phone responded with a series of tones. "I love this smartphone!" Her mouth quirked into a smile. "I can see my emails and texts as they come in, and I can keep prioritizing, rather than being blindsided when I do get to the office," Ronnie spoke passionately since this was another of her pet peeves.

"Real estate has changed so much," she told Luc. "The days of doing floor duty and having customers come in are over. Half the time, they do their own research online, and, with an online mapping app and a GPS, the first time I hear from them is when they're in the driveway of a property that interests them."

"I'd hate that, too," Luc commiserated. "I like to know what's what and keep things organized in their own little compartments."

That was subtle. I get it, fella. Don't worry; my compartment is local realtor and potential business partner—there'll be no more, no less.

She wanted to set him straight right now.

"I only have two compartments: work and home," she said lightly. "I've had a few relationships here and there, but, right now, the main men in my life all have four legs."

"Men?" he joked, touching her arm.

"Two Tennessee Walker geldings. My cat is a female."

"I see," he said slowly. There was a glint of amusement in Luc's eyes, but he obviously got her message loud and clear as well.

Chapter Two

A day later, the investors were long gone, and they were back to business as usual. "I. Will. Not. Do. This!" Ronnie glared at Rickie and Andee.

"Whoa! Hold the phone," Rickie protested. "I'm not the enemy here. What's the problem?" Ronnie's posture was rigid, and her face was set in a mask of fury. "No! This is not negotiable. I don't care about the commission. I will not have another closing with that asshole."

"Which asshole?" Andee snickered. "Ya gotta narrow it down some." The tension in the room was so thick you could cut it with the proverbial knife.

Ronnie made eye contact with Andee and burst into rueful laughter. "Shit!" she muttered, sagging into her office chair. She slapped the pink 'While You Were Out' slip on the desk and glared at Rickie again. "I'm serious; I can't do it. I won't do it."

Ronnie was clearly upset, and it was apparent that the three of them would have to talk it out—whatever *it* was.

"What? Who?" Rickie prompted.

"It's just not right," Ronnie said. "You've heard me say this a million times. They flap their lips about this being a self-policing profession and raising the bar, but they never do anything about anything. What's the point? If they don't care, why should I care?" she demanded, although the questions were rhetorical.

They'd had this discussion before, more than once. Rickie and Andee still didn't know the cause of this particular issue, but they'd heard enough to know what the general irritant was. "Any ignorant, lazy, sloppy, short-sighted, self-serving asshole who wants to be a realtor can get a license." Ronnie was on a rant, and there was no point in interrupting, attempting to reason with her, or trying to mollify her; this was just one of those things that had to run its course.

"Continuing education is a joke; the answers are right in the back of the book, so what purpose does that serve, except to generate some revenue and fill the square?" Another rhetorical question. "Do you know how many people I know personally who have taken the real estate exam more than five times?" Ronnie's voice rose as she vented her frustration. "It's multiple choice, for God's sake, the law of averages says a monkey could pass it, given enough tries."

"At least three," she continued. "No wonder people don't respect realtors. For every good one, there are nine who can't grab their own ass with both hands. And Marcia is one of them!"

Andee and Rickie exchanged looks. They understood the problem all too well. Ronnie didn't have to say another word; empathy among the partners was always taken for granted when this topic was discussed. "I hear you," Rickie said. "What's going on?"

"She has no listings of her own!" Ronnie continued angrily. "She lets everyone else do all the work of filling out paperwork, taking pictures, promoting the listings, mollifying the sellers and then, like a blind pig occasionally finding a truffle, some poor unsuspecting prospect falls right into her web and she gets a sale."

“You're mixing your metaphors," Andee pointed out. "Also, pigs actually use their noses to smell truffles, not their eyes to identify them, so that aphorism doesn't even make sense."

"You know what your problem is?" Ronnie turned to her, still furious. "You're such a linear thinker!"

"Okay," Rickie interrupted, holding up her hand before the argument escalated. "Marcia has somehow snagged a poor, unsuspecting client who has made an offer on one of your listings, Ronnie," she guessed. "Did I get that right?"

"Exactly!" Ronnie told her. "I simply cannot drag myself through this again. She doesn't have a clue about pulling up a plat; she has no relationship with the septic inspector and can never seem to get a copy of the permit. She's not conversant with the correct forms and, when you ask, she just gets defensive—etc. etc."

"Working with her is a frigging nightmare," she added vehemently.

"Yes; it is," Rickie agreed. "What property is it?"

"The seller's name is Shillen; it's that cute cabin on Red Fox Road," Ronnie said.

"I can't place it," Rickie replied.

"You know what I mean," Ronnie insisted. "They call that whole area 'Hoofbeat Hill.'

"Gotcha. Is that the one with the black metal roof?"

"Yes," Ronnie said. "Almost all of the cabins have green roofs or that copper color that was so popular for a while, but this one really stands out."

"That's because black is your favorite color," Andee said, teasing Ronnie as she often did. "From an architectural standpoint, I would think a black roof would hold the heat."

"Black used to be my favorite color, but purple is the new black," Ronnie informed her.

Andee eyed Ronnie's clothing and said, "You might be right. You look pretty elegant today, girlfriend. What's the occasion?"

Ronnie was wearing a pair of velveteen jeans, the color of concord grapes, and a fitted quilted jacket in the exact same shade. Under it, she wore a soft silvery-gray turtleneck sweater. Her accessories were simple, as always, and included the silver bangle she usually wore on her right wrist, a gray leather belt, her favorite gray cowboy boots, and the silver hoop earrings she wore almost every day. With her prematurely silver hair, the combination was stunning.

"I went to pitch the listing for Valley View, and I needed to impersonate rich people," Ronnie explained. "You know how they feel more comfortable when they think you're one of them, and you understand what they need."

"That's something you'll have to get used to. If we get into this project with those boys in Virginia, we'll have a steady stream of rich people in our lives!" she advised Andee.

"We haven't heard from them, have we?" Andee asked. "The 4-wheeling and the flyover seemed to go very well. We should have heard back by now."

"I'm sure they're doing due diligence," Rickie said. "The longer it takes, the better. If they didn't see it as viable or it's an interesting project but not for them, we'd probably have heard not long after they were here."

"So, anyway…" Rickie attempted to steer the discussion back on track. "Ronnie, you don't want to have to work with Marcia on a closing for the Shillen cabin, is that right?"

Ronnie nodded forcefully.

"Can't blame you, but we'll get through this. When the time comes, we'll schedule a mail-out closing on the sellers' side. We'll eat the cost of overnighting the docs, and the seller will probably be delighted not to have to spend half a day driving into town and attending a closing," Rickie told Ronnie.

"Let's get Jackie in on this," Ronnie suggested. "I can handle all of the paperwork behind the scenes, but Jackie can make or receive any of the inevitable phone calls with Marcia. If she wants to speak with me, Jackie can tell her I'm not available and put her through to you. Ha! Ha!"

Each office had a managing broker who assumed responsibility and accountability for all transactions. Ronnie and Rickie held brokers' licenses and were equally qualified, but between them, they had decided that, since diplomacy was Rickie's strong suit, she was the stronger candidate. Ronnie and Rickie trusted each other implicitly and knew that they were pulling in the same direction. There was no attempt on Rickie's part to oversee Ronnie's work, and, more often than not, Ronnie made and implemented decisions without the constraint of having to run it by the managing broker for approval.

As a relative newcomer to real estate, Andee held an affiliate broker's license. She could pass the broker's exam with her eyes closed but had to fulfill the requirement of gaining experience for three years, mandated by the Tennessee Real Estate Commission.

"You know, this will be good experience for Jackie," Ronnie said. She's been halfheartedly studying to take the real estate exam but, if we're involved in a major project, we're going to need her to handle most of what I do now with the residential properties." She nodded, still formulating a strategy. "Jackie may need to take that exam sooner rather later."

"She won't even have to change her name," Andee joked. "She fits right in here—Rickie, Ronnie, Andee, Jackie. What are the odds?"

"I'm not New Age or anything, but it does seem like some sort of a sign, doesn't it?" Ronnie said.

"You feel better now?" Rickie asked.

"Yep." Ronnie grinned. "A day without Marcia is a day full of sunshine!"

Later that day, Ronnie was sprawled in a rocker on her neighbor's front porch. An opened bottle of Merlot sat on the railing between them, only an inch left in the bottom. "I shouldn't drink any more this evening. I have a really busy day tomorrow showing property, but I've missed you, and I'm so glad to see you," Ronnie confided.

"Well, I've been right here, for the most part," Melinda Morrison-Myers said. "You're the one who blasts out at daybreak and comes dragging in at dark. You're my nearest neighbor, and I never see you anymore. Let's have one more glass of wine," she urged. "Who knows when I'll see you again?"

"You might have to carry me home," Ronnie told her. "I'm about ready to fall asleep in this chair."

"Have you eaten?" Mindy asked Ronnie. "I can throw something together in a few minutes." She picked up the wooden cutting board, empty now except for a few stray crumbs. "A few crackers and a little hunk of cheese aren't enough for supper if you haven't." When Ronnie didn't answer, she asked, "How about a piece of leftover lasagna? I can zap that in just a few minutes."

"I haven't eaten," Ronnie admitted. "Homemade lasagna sounds really good. Thanks."

"Who said it was homemade?" Mindy laughed. "It is homemade, actually, but not in this home, and not by me. Caroline Jamieson brought it the last time she was here, and I stuck a few pieces in the freezer. I just had one for dinner, and there's one piece left. You're welcome to it."

A few minutes later, Mindy bumped the screen door open with her hip and stepped out onto the porch with a plate, steaming and redolent, in one hand and an unopened bottle of wine in the other. After setting the bottle down, she handed Ronnie a fork and put the plate on a small side table. "Just pull that table over in front of you." She produced a corkscrew from her back pocket and expertly levered the cork out of the bottle.

Soon words were flowing out of Ronnie's mouth as easily as the wine out of the bottle. Before she realized it, she had unloaded all her thoughts and feelings.

"That's some story," Mindy acknowledged, flopping back in her oversized rocker and stretching her long legs out. "There's a *whole* lot goin' on there." She blew out a long breath. "How are you ever going to find enough hours in the day for a project of that magnitude and keep up with all of your listings?"

"I'm not," Ronnie told her. "There's just no way, it's impossible. Jackie is taking those practice exams online, and she's got a date for the realtor's exam. She ordered the real estate correspondence course, but it sat on her desk, practically untouched, for the last few months. It's the sixty-hour course where you're supposed to take the quiz at the end of each chapter and send it in. I think you have to get seventy percent to pass the damned thing, and then you're eligible to apply to take the exam.

Ronnie sipped her wine appreciatively, then continued. "I didn't do the self-study course. I took one of those two-nights-a-week things for eight weeks and let someone spoon feed the important parts. Anyway, the three of us are going to be overwhelmed and overloaded and maybe in over our heads with this project, so Jackie will inherit the normal daily workload once she gets her license. She's really excited and has thrown herself into it now."

"Good thing too," Ronnie added. "Can't come soon enough for me."

Jackie had finished the sixty-hour course in eighteen hours, astonishing herself and everyone else. "She ripped through three chapters a day for six days," Ronnie told Mindy. "No joke! When she couldn't get a date to sit the exam in Knoxville quick enough to suit her, she made an appointment to take it in Chattanooga."

"Don't a lot of people fail that exam?" Mindy asked.

"You'd be surprised," Ronnie told her. "It's rote learning, and you just have to regurgitate the exact answers that are in the book. There's no independent thinking, but it's shocking how many people do fail it. I mean, test anxiety is one thing, but people fail it several times. I guess they just tense up. The test isn't hard, but knowing you only have a certain amount of time puts a lot of pressure on you, and then you see people who have finished start to stand up and walk out."

"What about Jackie?" Mindy wanted to know. "You think she'll be one of those, or you think she'll sail right through it?"

"She's no dummy," Ronnie told her. "She sees what an opportunity this is to literally take over the office. I think she'll be fine."

"Will Rickie still be the broker?" Mindy asked.

"For a while," Ronnie replied slowly. "Someone has to be the managing broker, and right now, it's Rickie. If we open an office in conjunction with the project, my guess is that she'll hang her broker's license there, and I'll become the managing broker here. Whether we open an on-site office hinges on how much advertising is done and how much excitement it generates. Obviously, investors would like to see properties pre-sold and use those funds in the start-up phase.

"The scope is mind-boggling," Ronnie said and then stopped. After a moment, she continued, "I just can't get my mind around it, and I'm having trouble sleeping. It's so exciting; I just can't stop thinking about it."

"Maybe that's not all that's exciting," Mindy teased.

Ronnie narrowed her eyes and gave her a mock glare.

"Sounds like you need a sympathetic ear, someone who is distanced and can be more objective," Mindy said.

"That's it exactly," Ronnie agreed, relieved. She felt so lucky to have such a wonderful neighbor and good friend.

With her innate sensitivity, Mindy tactfully changed the subject. "Well, it should take some pressure off of you to start transitioning your workload to Jackie. I don't know how you do it, trying to keep all those sellers mollified. Don't they get discouraged if there aren't many showings or any offers?"

"You don't know the half of it," Ronnie groaned. "Jackie thinks that what she does in the office is mundane and boring and that what I do is glamorous and rewarding. She's in for a rude awakening."

"In fact," Ronnie said, gleeful in spite of herself, "she's about to be thrown into the deep end. You know I point-blank refuse to endure another closing with Marcia Szczepanski? Well, she has a buyer who's made an offer on Shillens' and Rickie agrees that would be a good way for Jackie to get her feet wet."

"Oh, *no*!" Mindy hooted. "Marcia Szcze-Pain-In-The-Ass-Ski?!"

"It's funny, but it's really not funny," Ronnie replied. "There are so many tenth-rate realtors out there, and on a scale of 1-10, with one being the best and ten being the worst, Marcia's about a twenty. I don't know why anyone would go near her. The magnetic signs on her car look like someone's eighth-grader designed them. Oh my God, those awful colors! All you have to do is to look around and see that her real estate signs are always dirty or falling over—usually both—and it doesn't seem to occur to her to straighten them. I mean, she's so cheap, she gets another one of those crappy pay-for-minutes cellphones she uses, then crosses out the old phone number on her riders and hand writes the new one with a black marker. Don't get me started!" Ronnie tsked in disgust. "I could go on and on."

"You know what I always say—water seeks its own level. You don't want to work with the kind of people she attracts, anyway." Mindy continued, "Speaking of buyers, did I tell you that I talked to Asha last week, and she told me Theo's getting married?"

"How can he?" Ronnie demanded, horrified. "He's still married to Caroline!"

"Not for long, apparently," Mindy said. "The ink won't be dry on the divorce decree before we'll be seeing a notice of the upcoming nuptials in the Washington newspaper. And that gold standard of society wedding announcements, the New York paper." Mindy's dry-witted sarcasm always amused Ronnie.

"Wow!" Ronnie was stunned. "How's Caroline taking it?"

"That's my point," Mindy said. "Apparently, the bride-to-be has her sights set on the North Carolina cabin, and it's not as much about having a getaway as ousting Caroline."

"Theo wouldn't do that!" Ronnie was aghast.

"No, I don't think he would," Mindy agreed. "He cares for Caroline, in his own peculiar way, but the riding sucks where she is. She was just here for about a week with two horses, and we rode the legs off them. I think she's going to need a clean break, so why don't you entice her with a few prospects?"

"It's an interesting idea. You know this is totally confidential, what we just talked about?"

"You don't even have to ask," Mindy assured her. "Of course, it is!"

"I have to go. Thank you for dinner."

"You need any help?" Mindy asked as the two women walked to the driveway. Ronnie opened her car door, and they faced each other in the pool of light from the interior. "Any time you're going to be late getting home, I can feed your horses, you know. Just call me."

"I really appreciate that," Ronnie said, putting her hand on Mindy's arm. "You're the best!"

Chapter Three

"Horse Country Real Estate, can you hold?" Jackie was finishing up a call on line one, had someone already on hold on line two, and had just answered line three. The day had absolutely flown by.

She was scheduled to take the real estate exam in Chattanooga first thing in the morning, so she was planning to leave the office by two, run home to feed her cat, grab her suitcase and pick up her best friend. Lea was going along for moral support, but Jackie knew that she was a shopper through and through and couldn't resist the lure of the nearby mall.

Rickie had advised Jackie not to over-prepare, to go into the test feeling relaxed and expecting to do well. In fact, she'd advised her to go to the mall with Lea and spend the evening hours enjoying herself and not stressing about the exam. Jackie loved clothes and was a pretty enthusiastic shopper herself, so it didn't take much to convince her to follow Rickie's advice.

Rickie was her role model in all respects and a wonderful mentor. Jackie admired Rickie's sense of style and picked up a lot of tips from her, especially now, when Rickie was helping her compose a particular look for herself.

"There's business casual," Rickie had told Jackie. "But even that's too formal here. What you need is country casual. You want to look businesslike and give your customers a feeling of confidence in you, but you also want to look like you're a horse person, and you understand country life. My advice is to find a brand of jeans that fits really well and buy them in a couple of colors you like. Coordinate some shirts, sweaters, a tweed jacket, or something similar. Get some good accessories. A couple of good-quality leather belts, a few pieces of everyday jewelry, a couple of scarves, and comfortable shoes."

Rickie's standards were high, and everyone at Horse Country Real Estate followed her lead. "I try to wear shoes that I can easily slip off at the door because a lot of times when you go to show a residential property, it's occupied, and it's respectful to the seller not to track mud in," Rickie added.

Jackie had seen how Rickie and Ronnie never seemed to wear an 'outfit.' They wore a dozen pieces that they just kept combining in different ways. "Keep checking back at that re-sale shop in Crossville," Rickie had suggested. "You can pick up some very nice things very inexpensively to get you started."

Rickie had showed Jackie how to put together a tote bag to keep in the car, so she'd never be caught unaware. "If you have to walk land, you'll want a pair of boots and socks to go with them. Put in a baseball cap, head net for bugs, a can of insect repellent for ticks and chiggers, an umbrella for yourself and a couple of extras for customers, a jacket in case the temperature drops, a slicker in case it rains unexpectedly."

"Put a pair of gloves in there, too," Rickie had advised. "People will tell you where they've hidden a house key, but you don't ever want to stick your bare hand somewhere you can't see and find that there's a snake or a spider in there, especially a Brown Recluse." She shuddered. "Put a small fold-up ladder in your car and a good flashlight and know exactly what you're reaching for. Put in an atlas for both Tennessee and Kentucky, people will tell you where they're going next and will ask you how to get there. You just want to be as prepared as you can be. Most people use a mapping program or GPS to navigate from one place to another, but an atlas will show you the whole state in an easy-to-see format. You may never need it, but it doesn't take up much space."

Rickie shook her head. "These days, people work the internet and, unknown to you, they're emailing with three or four other realtors. You need to do everything you can to seem as knowledgeable and as competent as possible, so they'll decide to work with you." Rickie spoke as if it was a foregone conclusion that Jackie would pass the realtor's exam. Jackie felt a surge of anxiety but squashed it. If Rickie believed in her, she knew she wouldn't disappoint.

Jackie felt herself very fortunate to have gotten this job as receptionist with Horse Country Real Estate. The prospect of becoming a realtor herself thrilled her; she couldn't think of any job where she stood to make as much money with just a high-school education. Rickie was a believer in profit sharing, and she had explained to Jackie the day she'd interviewed as receptionist that she would receive a fraction of each sale in the office, in addition to her wages. She would have a vested interest in doing the best job she could and would not feel like a lowly outsider, but a member of the team.

The call on line one was the Fentress County Chamber of Commerce, asking about advertising in the program for the annual Pleasure Horse Show held at the county fairgrounds. Jackie scribbled a message on a pink 'While You Were Out' slip and placed it in the center of Rickie's desk where she'd see it as soon as she came in. Jackie was expecting Ronnie back in the office within the next hour or so, but it occurred to her that she hadn't seen or heard from either Rickie or Andee all morning. There was a growing pile of pink message slips on Rickie's desk, and it would take her hours to plow through them. That was one of the downsides of being a realtor, Jackie knew, you had all those calls to return, even when you were tired.

The caller on line two was a man who said he and his wife were thinking about retiring to the area, so Jackie directed him to their website, intheheartofhorsecountry.com, and told him that he'd get quite a bit of information there. She picked up line three. "Sorry to keep you waiting," Jackie apologized to the caller.

"That's quite all right. I'm glad you're busy, it must go with the territory," the caller said. "This is Lucinda Westlake."

Jackie didn't recognize the name and assumed it was yet another inquiry about the area or about one of their listings.

"Chip Westlake's wife," the caller clarified, after a moment.

That didn't ring any bells either.

"Whom are you calling to speak with?" Jackie asked. She once would have said, "Who are you calling to talk to?" but Rickie had very tactfully helped her polish her speech.

"Well, whoever's available," the caller said.

"This is Jackie. I'm the only one here at the moment. Rickie, Ronnie, and Andee are all out of the office. I'm not sure when any of them is expected back."

After taking care of the customer, Jackie judiciously laid that message slip on Ronnie's desk so Rickie wouldn't be totally overloaded.

About an hour later, Ronnie came in. "Hey, girlfriend," she greeted Jackie, grinning broadly. "Big day tomorrow! I brought you something to wish you good luck." Ronnie put a small package wrapped in teal blue tissue paper and tied with a curly teal blue ribbon on Jackie's desk. Jackie loved all shades of blue, and teal was her favorite.

"For me?" Jackie was surprised and delighted. "Thank you!" She pulled the ribbon loose and peeled back the paper. Inside lay a pretty, lace-trimmed pair of teal-blue bikini underpants. Jackie looked at Ronnie uncomprehendingly, but said, "They're beautiful. I love this color!"

"They're lucky underpants," Ronnie explained. "You can't take the test without them. You won't fail—guaranteed. Then you'll have them for other momentous occasions when you need all the help you can get. We all have them, even Andee. Although hers are cotton," she added wickedly.

Jackie's eyes glimmered with tears. She treasured the friendship the three had offered. This was so much more than just a job.

Ronnie flopped down in her office chair and picked up the small stack of pink message slips. The one on top read simply, "Please call when convenient." She reached for the notebook she kept with names and contact info for real estate prospects. She turned to a clean page and prepared to make notes during the upcoming conversation. Then she frowned, looking at the message. Lucinda Westlake. This wasn't someone wanting to buy a small cabin or an acre of land.

Unclipping her phone from her belt, she quickly texted Rickie. It was premature to tell Jackie what was in the wind—if it was—and she didn't want to be overheard. So far, the upcoming deal was a closely-held secret just among the three of them. Except for Mindy, she added mentally, guiltily remembering the bottle of wine she'd shared with her neighbor a few nights earlier.

Rickie texted back a few minutes later.

—U call. Dying of curiosity but stuck here 4 another hour at least—

Ronnie heard Jackie gathering up her things, getting ready to leave for the day. She picked up the second slip and punched out the number. When Jackie stuck her head in the door for a moment and mouthed, "Goodbye," Ronnie gave her a big smile and a thumbs-up.

Ten minutes later, the phone was ringing in Reston, Virginia.

"Hello." The woman's voice was low and pleasing.

"Lucinda Westlake?" Ronnie inquired. "This is Veronica Chandler, returning your call."

"Yes, thanks for calling back so quickly," Lucinda said. “You met my husband, Chip, last week, and he's told me all about your beautiful part of the country. He and CW have spoken almost of nothing else.

"CW is very thorough," Lucinda continued. "If he decides to move forward, he'll want to be sure that everyone will be comfortable with such a time-consuming and long-range project. He's very family-oriented, and he wouldn't feel comfortable if the boys and I weren't also involved, to some small degree. He likes us to have a good sense of what Chip's working on, so Chip suggested we come to Tennessee for a few days to get a feel for the place and to meet you all."

Ronnie understood this was not a suggestion. "That's a wonderful idea," she agreed. "Chip mentioned when he was here that he'd love for you to see it, and I recommended that you stay in one of the cabins at Creekside. They're in a very rustic, wooded setting, but they're immaculate and very well appointed. They got a write up in a well-known national magazine a few years ago, and it sure put them on the map. I know you'd be comfortable there."

"You're a rider?" Lucinda asked, skillfully establishing a rapport.

"Yes," Ronnie told her. "I have two Tennessee Walkers, and I ride whenever I can. This area is known as The Trailriding Capital of the Southeast."

"I rode some, years ago," Lucinda said. "I've never ridden a gaited horse, but I'd love to give it a try. Is there somewhere there that rents horses?"

"Yes, there's an outfitter, Big South Fork Pack Trips, that I can recommend," Ronnie told Lucinda. "Will Chip and your sons want to ride as well?"

"Not on this trip, I don't think. They're eager to do some kayaking," Lucinda said.

Ronnie was nobody's fool; she could read between the lines. Chip was setting the scene for his wife to spend some time alone with her, Rickie, and Andee and provide her own feedback.

"If it's just you, I have a quiet second horse that you can use," Ronnie offered. "We all love to ride, so Rickie and Andee will want to go. We'll pack a lunch to eat on the trail, and we can show you some of our favorite places." They talked for a few minutes more, about the weather and what clothing to bring. No mention was made of Luc, and Ronnie couldn't bring herself to ask if he would be coming as well. Ronnie gave Lucinda Creekside's web address. They exchanged email addresses, and Lucinda said she'd let Ronnie know what Creekside's availability was so they could agree on a date that was good for all of them.

A lot had transpired since that initial meeting. Emails had flown back and forth between the three realtors at Horse Country Real Estate and the three investors at The Westlake Group in the ensuing two weeks as questions were posed and the concept refined. Satisfied with what he'd heard so far and intrigued to learn more, CW was increasingly impressed with the ladies in Tennessee. Each had certain strengths and talents and they certainly worked well together; it was quite a package.

He and Julia had accepted an invitation to a golden jubilee anniversary celebration in Naples in late April and plans fell into place for Chip and Lucinda with their two boys, as well as Luc and his daughter to fly from Washington in the company plane, stopping en route to Florida to drop them off at the regional airport in Crossville. They would rent a car and drive up to Jamestown on Friday afternoon, returning on Sunday afternoon to turn the car in and meet the return flight.

When the appointed day arrived, Ronnie pulled up in front of Southern Comfort and commented, "Holy Moly! That's a lot of windows to wash!" The V-shaped wall of the cabin was almost entirely glass, soaring two stories. She, Rickie, and Andee were right on time. The front door opened immediately and Chip stepped out. He greeted them warmly and turned to the woman right behind him. Putting his arm around her waist affectionately, he introduced her.

Lucinda was petite with frosted blonde hair pulled youthfully into a high ponytail. She was dressed for a cool spring evening in faded jeans with wool socks, a turtleneck sweater, and a fleece-lined quilted vest. Her dark eyes shone with warmth and good humor. *Oh, she's cute!* Ronnie liked her immediately.

The day was sunny and had been quite pleasant, but with the sun going down, there was a definite chill in the air. "Come on in and meet the boys," Lucinda said. "Chip asked them to get a fire going in the fire pit. I thought we could sit outside for a little while and have a beer or a glass of wine. Dinner's just steak and baked potato, with apple pie for dessert, so there's no elaborate prep. This is a wonderful cabin," she added enthusiastically. "Thank you so much for recommending Creekside. We've all been looking forward to coming."

"All of the cabins are delightful," Andee told her. "Almost all have hot tubs and either an outdoor fireplace or a fire pit. We knew you'd be comfortable here."

"I looked at the website and chose this one when I saw a picture of the rec room. With two teenage boys, that's a strong selling point," Lucinda said. "Also, some of the cabins had two or three bedrooms, and we needed four."

"You can really spread out since you each have your own room." Rickie picked up the conversational ball.

"Well…" Lucinda hesitated. "Actually, Chip and I are in the main bedroom, and the boys are bunking in together. Luc's got a room, and there's a room for Steffi."

"Oh, I'm glad Luc and his daughter could come. I thought it was just your family," Ronnie chimed in.

"Well…" Lucinda hesitated again. "They haven't actually come. I mean, they were supposed to but—there's no good way to say this so I might as well just say it. Luc's daughter has some problems, and she's difficult. She's angry about the divorce, and although her mother's remarried, she plays her parents against each other. Luc really has his hands full."

Ronnie took a sip of her wine, listening intently.

"She pitched a fit just before we were supposed to leave and refused to come. Short of picking her up and putting her bodily on the plane, there was nothing Luc could do."

"This isn't the first time she's tried to spoil our plans," Lucinda added. "She's a very unhappy child and does everything she can to punish her parents."

"We're all set out there, Lulu." Chip came into the kitchen, opened the fridge, and snagged a beer from the fridge. "You all have something to drink?" he asked, glancing around.

"You're a very attentive host, Mr. Westlake," Rickie complimented him. "Very kind of you to learn our preferences and stock our favorites. I'm sure Andee is impressed that you've laid in a supply of her favorite beer." Ronnie, Rickie, and Andee relaxed around the outdoor fire with Lucinda and Chip Westlake, after having been introduced to the couple's two handsome sons.

The night air was pleasantly cool, and the adults began the unhurried process of getting acquainted while the boys put the cabin's pool table to good use.

The weekend is off to a good start. Ronnie's initial reaction was disappointment that Luc hadn't come, but she liked the Westlakes so much that she was glad she could just be herself, without any undercurrents. Dinner was equally relaxing and enjoyable, with a lot of laughter. It was clear that they were a close, loving family. The boys, Charlie and

Chase, were knowledgeable about or interested in every topic that was discussed and proved as socially adept as their parents.

The plan for the coming two days was that Ronnie would host breakfast for everyone at her house the next morning, then Chip and the boys would take off with their kayaks for a Class II section of the Clear Fork River below Gatewood Ford, leaving Lucinda to spend the day riding with Ronnie, Rickie, and Andee. Dinner would be a simple affair and an early evening at Rickie's, with everyone tired from the day's exertions. The Westlakes wanted to do a short hike together on Sunday morning, and Andee advised them not to miss Twin Arches. That would give them just enough time to meet up again for soup and sandwiches at her house before driving back to Crossville to meet CW's plane.

It would defeat the purpose to meet at Creekside or to eat out. CW wanted Chip to see each of them interacting in her own environment before reporting back to his father. The old man was very fond of his daughter-in-law and always eager for her input. Lucinda's discerning eye would pick up styles and nuances that Chip, in typical male fashion, would be oblivious to. CW prided himself on leaving no stone unturned, and his entrepreneurial successes over the years attested to his financial acumen. After speaking with Lucinda the first time, Ronnie understood the purpose of the visit and it was she who suggested that each of them host a meal.

Breakfast was a big hit. There was plenty of food, and the boys ate voraciously. Ronnie had made a breakfast casserole the day before, layering hash browns in the bottom of a rectangular dish and pouring in scrambled eggs, spicy sausage bits, and cheese. It was bubbling when she pulled on oven mitts and took it out of the oven. She set the dish on a trivet in the center of the table, and everyone helped themselves. She had already poured glasses of orange juice and had plenty of hot coffee ready. She'd made rugelach ahead of time, using both store-bought apricot and some of her own homemade blueberry jam.

"This is *so* good," Lucinda complimented her. "What a treat!"

"I have to confess that I cheated." Ronnie laughed. "I just use frozen pie crust dough. My theory is, if I can't do it as well or better, why try?" she confided.

It had been quite chilly when the Westlakes arrived, but the day was warming up nicely, with temps expected to be in the low 70s. Chip, Charlie, and Chase couldn't wait to get going on their day's adventure, so Ronnie sent them on their way while she and Lucinda loaded the dishwasher and tidied the kitchen.

"Rickie and Andee should be here any minute," Ronnie said. "We all trailer tacked-up, so when we get there, we're ready to go."

"I didn't know you could do that," Lucinda said. "Where I come from, horses wear padded shipping boots over the knees and hocks, and head bumpers."

"It took a little while for me to get used to it," Ronnie replied. "Things are very low-key here, you'll see three or four tacked-up horses in a stock trailer."

The horses had their breakfast earlier and now looked up from their hay as the two women approached.

"You'll be riding Cash," Ronnie said, handing Lucinda a long cotton lead rope. "He's a six-year-old Tennessee Walker. There's nothing special you have to know about him. He's calm and amenable, and I think you'll really enjoy him. I can't wait to see your face when we start gaiting."

Ronnie's barn was a simple affair. It wasn't actually a cabarn, a local style combining a cabin and barn favored by weekenders for its inexpensive construction and ease of maintenance, because Ronnie's stalls were separated from the cabin by an open carport. This clever design kept odor and noise from her living space, provided shelter for Ronnie's vehicle, and allowed her to walk from the cabin to the stalls under cover. She had two stalls, a tack/feed room, and an open bay for hay and some wood shavings baled in clear plastic bags that were used for bedding. A broken-back roof on the backside housed two additional stalls that could accommodate visiting horses, and a sliding door concealed her lawnmower and an assortment of small equipment.

"This is wonderful," Lucinda told her sincerely. "Your whole life seems pretty wonderful, actually."

Ronnie wondered if she was fishing, waiting for her response. "It's as simple as I can make it."

"But that will change if this project goes forward," Lucinda observed.

Ronnie was saved from responding when Rickie's trailer pulled into the yard, a rooster tail of dust behind it. "Wait until you see Rickie's horse," Ronnie said to Lucinda as Rickie and Andee got out of the truck and came toward them. "She has a blue roan and a buckskin. I don't know which one she brought today, but they are both absolutely gorgeous."

They had agreed to take Lucinda down to the O&W, the old Olsen and Westcott rail bed. It wasn't part of the national rails-to-trails program, but it was the same idea, with the old rails removed and the stretch of level terrain available for recreation. Riding beside the North White Oak Creek for several miles was one of the most dramatic and interesting rides they could provide and afforded an opportunity to gait almost the whole way.

Then they would pull sandwiches, chips, and brownies out of their saddlebags at Coyle Branch, tie the horses up at the hitching rails, and sit on the wooden bench or on a 'lunch log' with the stream babbling in the background. They'd take an old tote road up the hill, a rock face on one side and a deep ravine on the other, and detour to the Leatherwood Overlook for the breathtaking view of the ford at the bottom of the gorge. If that didn't sell Mrs. Westlake on Big South Fork, nothing would.

They had planned to trailer in tandem to the Cumberland Trailhead and unload the four horses, leaving them with Andee and Lucinda while Ronnie and Rickie moved their trailers ahead to Burgess Field. They needed someone to follow them and give them a ride back to Cumberland, so Ronnie had enlisted Mindy to lend a hand because it would take only a few minutes and wouldn't be too big an imposition on her day. That would cut the last eight miles off the ride; they didn't want their guest to end up tired and sore.

Ronnie felt bad that she hadn't invited Mindy to go along, but she knew it was paramount that the time spent with Lucinda Westlake be quality time with just the four of them. She knew instinctively that Lucinda was making mental notes and could be a key factor in the decision to proceed—or not. The project was exciting, and the numbers would tell the tale as to its viability but, without the human element, it had the potential for disaster.

There would be enough to contend with once they started dealing with government agencies, municipal offices, environmentalists, and conservationists to say nothing of architects, contractors, subcontractors, and would-be buyers. They needed to know that they were not only ideologically sound but equally committed, that they would function in concert with mutual respect and trust. This weekend could well be the keystone for that complicated six-way relationship—not counting family members.

The day had proceeded as if scripted. Ronnie had helped Lucinda with unfamiliar tack, showing her how to cinch up a western girth. She'd given her a horn bag so she could carry her lunch, a water bottle, and a set of lightweight cross ties. She'd also given her a cantle bag so she could tie a jacket behind the saddle in case the temperature dropped unexpectedly. It gave Ronnie great satisfaction and pleasure to see Lucinda so enthralled with the scenery and delighted with the pace. Like almost everyone else, Lucinda carried a smartphone, and they stopped often so she could take pictures, knowing that she would be eager to share them not only with Chip and the boys but also with CW and Julia.

They'd gotten back to the trailers at about three-fifteen. Lucinda watched as the other riders stripped the horses' headstalls and bits off, leaving them wearing just the halter component of their trail bridles.

"You weren't kidding when you said you like things simple."

"Oh, my days of saddle soaping leather tack are over," Ronnie said. "I did a little competitive trail at one time, and it didn't take me long to appreciate biothane endurance-type tack that all hooks together. I just have to dunk it in a bucket to get the sweat off. After several uses or a particularly long ride, when it's really nasty, I give it a power wash with hot water and dish detergent." She laughed.

Ronnie waited until she saw that Rickie's horses were loaded, and her truck had started before pulling out. Lucinda commented on how thoughtful they all were.

"Actually, that's just good trail etiquette," Ronnie told her. "You may have noticed any time you have to cross a stream or go through a gully or over a log, the first horses will go up the trail a little way and wait. That's because horses are herd animals, and you don't want the horses in the back to get anxious and rush the obstacle, trying to catch up with the others. "

When they got back, they hosed both horses with warm water. Most barns had a wash rack with water coming from a frost-proof hydrant but Ronnie had a Y-connector from hot and cold spigots on the side of the cabin.

"I'm not a fan of cold showers, why would they be? My boys look so sleek when they're wet, but wait thirty seconds and they'll both roll in the dirt," she told Lucinda, shaking her head ruefully. "It's a lot harder than you'd think to keep black horses clean."

Lucinda had thoroughly enjoyed the day and thanked Ronnie effusively as Ronnie prepared to drop her back at Creekside. When they pulled up, there was an unfamiliar car in the driveway and Ronnie noted the South Carolina plates. But neither woman gave it more than a passing interest.

Chapter Four

Lucinda burst enthusiastically into the kitchen but stopped in her tracks when she found Luc sitting at the breakfast bar with Chip and the two boys. "Hey!" she greeted him.

"Hey, yourself," he responded with a grin, noting her wide smile, windburned face, and tousled hair. "Are you hooked?"

"Hooked on what?" she teased. "Tennessee, Big South Fork, gaited horses, or the blue roan I want for my birthday?"

"I saw that coming," Chip moaned, joining in on the teasing.

Luc tried not to let his personal problems interfere with business, so he had flown commercial to Knoxville and rented a car at the airport. It hadn't been possible to get a flight on Friday evening, and getting to Jamestown had, unfortunately, eaten up most of the day on Saturday.

Stephanie's behavior was mortifying, and he had to face the fact that it was getting worse. It left him at a complete loss as to what to do. It would certainly be helpful if Kelli handled their daughter's adolescent issues, but his ex-wife was completely wrapped up in her new life with her new house and her new husband and had essentially dumped the problem in his lap. He put that out of his mind for now; there was nothing he could do at the moment.

As was usual for this time of year, the warmth of the day had dissipated as the sun began to set. Charlie and Chase had built another fire in the fire pit, so Chip and Luc got themselves a cold beer and sat across from each other, as completely at ease in each other's company as they had always been.

"Whaddya' think?" Luc asked Chip.

"This weekend has been a lot of fun," Chip replied. "Kayaking was fabulous; too bad you missed it. The boys had a blast!" He turned serious for a moment, continuing, "And, as fact-finding missions go, it's time well spent. Those three haven't put a foot wrong. From what I've seen, it's a big thumbs-up."

"You had breakfast at Ronnie's?" Luc asked rhetorically.

"Cute place," Chip replied. "Small, simple—it suits her."

Lucinda had excused herself to take a quick shower and reappeared a short time later. She had on a pair of wheat-colored jeans, a rust-colored cotton turtleneck, an oversized plaid flannel shirt in a mélange of earth tones, and her quilted vest. Chip had dated his share of high-maintenance women and thoroughly appreciated his wife's unassuming style. She was a chameleon, never missing the mark, as she blended easily into whatever social setting the occasion demanded. In their line of work, she was certainly an asset, functioning as another set of eyes and ears, and Luc knew his friend was always proud to have her by his side.

Lucinda joined them, coming in at the end of their conversation.

"What a ride you missed, Luc!" she said. "One down, two to go."

She was referring to having a look at Ronnie in her own environment, with some time spent at Rickie's and Andee's houses yet to come.

"I never knew trail riding could be so much fun, and the scenery was spectacular," she continued. "I hate to leave tomorrow. This weekend is flying by."

"No pun intended," Luc finished for her. "Glass of wine?" He rose and went to get it for her.

When Luc was out of sight, Lucinda turned to Chip. "How's Steffi?"

"Don't ask," he replied.

"God, you just have to feel sorry for that girl," Lucinda said. "Steffi must hate Kelli, deep down."

Chip nodded.

"This project will be good for Luc," he told his wife. "When he got here, he told me what happened and said he was half relieved and half sorry Steffi didn't come this weekend. He knows she needs to get out of Kelli's orbit." They both fell silent when the screen door slammed.

"I'd be depressed too if I had Kelli radiating disappointment and disgust all day every day," Luc said. "I caught the tail end of that conversation. I don't know what else I can do. I've tried doctors, nutritionists, and therapists. Stephanie's learned to use her weight as a weapon, and it's pretty effective."

"No kidding," Lucinda said. "Still, as much satisfaction as that gives her short term, it must be torture for her to be surrounded by all those size-zero lacrosse players and assorted high achievers at school."

"I know they make fun of her. She gets it on all sides," Luc said. "But let's not dwell on that tonight."

Luc pulled his chair closer to the fire pit and sat back down. He took a pull on his beer and turned to Lucinda.

"So, Lulu, what's this about a blue roan?" He smiled wide, communicating his delight with her enthusiasm for the day's exploits. The success of this project would help to ensure their families' financial futures and open a world of new adventures in the process.

No starry-eyed optimist, he himself was well aware that it would be a rocky road once the environmentalists reared their ugly and entitled heads. That was all they talked about over dinner, and long into the night.

They'd planned an early evening, and Rickie had a molten lasagna ready to serve soon after they arrived at her house. Everyone was ravenous and tore into the crusty garlic bread. A big green salad accompanied the meal, and Rickie had balanced what might have been a heavy meal with mint chocolate chip ice cream for dessert. The three Tennessee realtors made everything seem so effortless. As methodical and prepared as he liked to be, Luc was well aware of the pre-planning that ensured the weekend went smoothly and knew they'd found their ideal partners.

If Ronnie was startled by Luc's unannounced arrival, she gave no sign. It was gratifying to have found a way to honor his commitment to the weekend, which boded well for a future alliance. Chip's boys were restless and left soon after dinner. When Andee suggested they take the rental car, she said she would run the three adults back to Creekside later.

Luc and Chip voiced their concerns about potential roadblocks from environmental extremists once they learned greedy developers were lurking, about to pounce, and the six adults batted that topic back and forth in a lively and sometimes heated discussion, sprawled in Rickie's small but comfortable living room. Rickie proved to be a wealth of historical and anecdotal information because she was native to the area, and they were considerably enlightened as the evening wound down. Luc knew Chip and Lucinda had intended to leave by nine, but all were surprised when he looked at his watch and saw it was nearly eleven.

Lucinda seemed enchanted with Rickie's little dollhouse.

"Victorian and Queen Anne have always appealed to me," Rickie told her, in response to Lucinda's compliments. "This house was actually a kit. When I was looking for a place, it was between this and a small cabin. It was the colors that convinced me, though, because it certainly is a departure from the local style. It was actually Ronnie's palette when I first saw it, architecturally-accurate hues like aubergine, pomegranate, periwinkle, and dusty pink, but she convinced me we could modify it. She helped me choose my favorites—olive, this creamy yellow, black, and rust to make it pop."

"The chintzes really work in this room," Lucinda said. "The Prince of Chintz himself couldn't have done it better! Did you hire him?”

"Unfortunately not," Rickie scoffed. "I certainly couldn't afford him and doubt I could have pried him out of Manhattan, in any case. I lived there for a few years and am well aware of his expertise, but I just had to rely on magazine spreads featuring his work and my own instincts."

"You did a wonderful job," Lucinda said.

"They're slipcovers," Rickie told her. "I swap them out for pale solid colors in the summer, with accent pillows."

"If she'd left the original colors, the blue roan would have matched, but now the buckskin does.

Matching is just *so* important," Andee teased, joining them as they headed outside.

The group migrated to the barn to see Rickie's horses, before saying, "Goodnight."

"So, this is the famous blue roan! Your reputation precedes you, fella," Chip told the horse solemnly. "What's your name?"

"Once in a Blue Moon," Rickie supplied.

"And who's your friend?" Chip addressed the horse again.

"Starbuck. He's a buckskin, and he has a small white star." Rickie held up his forelock for Chip's inspection. "I didn't name him," she added quickly. "I just call them Blue and Buck, it's almost too easy."

Rickie drew both horses out of their stalls at Luc's request and put them into cross ties in the aisle so he could see their conformation. He knew quality horseflesh when he saw it.

"What are you doing tomorrow morning, Luc? Are you going hiking?" Rickie asked as the group walked out to the vehicles clustered in the driveway.

Ronnie saw immediately where this conversation was headed; it wasn't a casual question. Rickie had a long-standing appointment to show a property first thing in the morning, and Andee would be busy getting lunch ready. Rickie was engineering an opportunity for Ronnie to be alone with Luc. Rickie had observed that she and Luc had seemed to gravitate toward each other and was undoubtedly thinking that Luc might open up if he and Ronnie had some time alone. Knowing Rickie as she did, Ronnie had no doubt about that. Rickie didn't miss much, and she would welcome any and all 'intel' before taking the plunge.

Plans were made accordingly. Luc would arrive at Ronnie's at nine in the morning, and she would trailer her two horses to Burgess Field, backtracking for an abbreviated version of the ride along the O&W. Ronnie called Mindy from her cell on the way home and left a voicemail, asking to borrow a saddle pad. She had noticed that the rolled edge on her new pad seemed to have rubbed Jack's back, and she didn't want to aggravate the area by continuing to use it, even for a short ride.

The next morning, Ronnie was standing in front of the toaster, waiting for an English muffin to pop up. When there was a rap on the door, she called, "C'mon in," without turning. "You're early," she said over her shoulder. "Want coffee?"

She turned, expecting to see her neighbor, and was horrified to find Luc standing just inside her back door. She had six huge rollers in her hair and was speechless.

"Hey—Oh!" Mindy walked in right behind Luc. "Oh, my!"

She laughed and then addressed Luc. "I'm Mindy Morrison-Myers, and you are…?" Although she knew perfectly well who he was. She didn't miss much, either.

"Let me guess. Ronnie is on Central Time, which happens to be local time, and you're on Eastern Time." She snorted when Luc's mouth dropped open. A quick glance at Ronnie's wall clock showed them that it was barely eight.

"Happens all the time," she assured him. "We're right on the line. In fact, the park itself is Eastern."

"The pad's on the porch," she told Ronnie, who, by now, had tugged the rollers out of her hair and dropped them into a drawer. Ronnie decided they might as well get started. She abandoned her breakfast and poured steaming coffee into her travel cup and into two narrow thermoses.

"Mindy, come with?" she invited. Suddenly, she didn't want to be alone with Luc.

Mindy looked from one to the other, and Ronnie knew exactly what was going through Mindy's mind at that moment. Any other time, Ronnie might have welcomed an opportunity to spend time alone with this gorgeous specimen of manhood but not here and not now.

"Sure," Mindy accepted the invitation. "It's going to be a gorgeous day! Let me just run home and tack up. I'm hooked up, so I'll see you there in a few."

Ronnie's two geldings had polished off their grain and moved on to a pile of hay in the paddock. She slipped the old leather halter off and slid a black biothane halter up over Cash's nose. She handed the lead rope to Luc and made the introductions.

"This is Cash," she told him.

"The Man in Black?" He caught on quickly.

"I would have called him 'Johnny,' but Mindy's horse is 'Johnny Walker' and she calls *him* 'Johnny.' We ride together a lot, and it's too confusing to have two horses with the same name," she explained. Luc had Cash brushed and saddled in minutes. *Well! He sure knows his way around a horse. Who knew?* They loaded both horses, and Luc walked quickly back to his vehicle for his gear. Ronnie's heart was pounding, and she took several deep breaths before she slid into the driver's seat. She felt hot and cold at the same time and was relieved Mindy had agreed to accompany them.

Mindy and Luc were dressed almost alike in tight, faded jeans and scuffed cowboy boots with roweled spurs. Both wore denim jackets, chinks, cowhide gloves, and cowboy hats. Ronnie fitted her helmet over her hair and buckled the strap. A lot of people wore western garb and looked like they had stepped right out of an ad in a magazine, but she wasn't one of them.

She wore Ariat Terrains on her feet like half the riders here, and she buckled smooth navy chaps over her own jeans. She too wore gloves, although hers were navy, and she'd knotted a burgundy bandanna around her neck.

Ronnie led the group out to the Leatherwood Overlook so Luc could enjoy the same view that had so impressed Lucinda the day before. The horses were tethered at hitching rails, and they had walked the last few hundred yards to the precipice. She was eager for her second cup of coffee but didn't want to spend a lot of time there, with the horses out of sight. It would be better to wait until they were tied up again at Coyle Branch, where they could sip their coffee, sitting in the sun, and enjoy the big blueberry muffins that were still warm from her oven. She'd used almost the last of the berries she'd frozen from the previous year's harvest.

They had introduced Luc to gaiting on the gravel roads before they began their descent to the old rail bed, and now Mindy suggested they switch horses so he could experience her McCurdy Plantation Horse, an old Alabama breed, as they prepared to move out alongside the creek. When they got back to the trailers, they were windblown, slightly sunburned, and high on the exhilaration of being outside on such an exquisite morning.

After taking the horses home and seeing to their comfort, Mindy joined the group for lunch at Andee's. By that time, although they had all protested the night before that they could never eat another bite, they were again starving. Andee set down a platter with slices of Kentucky ham and thinly-sliced rare roast beef, an assortment of cheeses, two types of lettuce, sliced tomato, and both bulkie rolls and sourdough bread. She ladled homemade vegetable soup into thick white crockery bowls and offered iced tea.

"That looks good," Chase quipped. "But what's everyone else having?"

Luc left right after lunch, allowing ample time to turn in his rental car and get through security before his late-afternoon flight.

When the four Westlakes got into their own rented vehicle a half-hour later, Lucinda had tears in her eyes.

"Luc showed me the note you gave him for Steffi," she said to Ronnie in a low voice. "That was extremely thoughtful and uncommonly kind of you. You have no idea… There will be other times to visit, many more," Lucinda promised. "We'll be in touch."

Chapter Five

Now, just a week after the successful visit from the Westlakes, Andee sat slumped on the comfortable couch in her living room. Flames flickered behind the glass doors of the woodstove tucked in a corner. It looked like a traditional enamel woodstove, but it was the propane model. She could point the remote, and, with the touch of a button, the fire would spring to life, filling the cozy room with a pleasant glow. She pulled a wool throw over her legs and reached for the half-empty bottle of beer on the coffee table. She lifted it to her mouth, then set the bottle down. The warm alcohol had gone flat. She'd been sitting there for quite a while. It was after eleven, but she couldn't sleep and hadn't gone to bed, knowing she'd just toss and turn. Just after lunch, she'd gotten a call from Dave Strickland, her childhood friend, the proverbial boy next door, now a United States senator from Tennessee, and she'd been able to think of nothing else since.

She stared up at the ceiling fan’s slow, sweeping circles and thought back through the years. She and Dave had been childhood playmates and remained friends throughout middle school and high school sharing, for the most part, the same circle of friends. They had always been each other's confidante and staunchest supporter. From the time he'd been student council president at River Valley High School in Huntsville, Dave had always had a clear goal, and that included a well-rounded education within the state of Tennessee. He'd chosen the university in Knoxville because it was a public school, enrolling in the Hansen School of Business, with a dual concentration in finance and public administration. This double major he regarded as the foundation for a career in the political arena. That was followed by three years at a private institution, Valliant University's Law School in Nashville, 'the Horvath of the South.' He had no desire to practice law and no intention of doing so, but a law degree was a serious credential, to his way of thinking, and one which would stand him in good stead as he networked his way up the ladder.

Andee, too, had attended the university in Knoxville, receiving her B.S. in landscape design and construction. She'd inherited her love of plants and the outdoors from her mother, and they had shared a passion for gardening. Andee closed her eyes, feeling her heart squeeze as she always did when she thought about her mother. Diane Webster hadn't wanted her family to worry and hadn't confided in her husband or her daughter when she'd first become aware of her symptoms. If she had, she might still be alive. Andee had been accepted into the master's program in landscape architecture at Crosby University in upstate New York but stayed on in Knoxville for their graduate program when her mother was diagnosed with metastatic ovarian cancer. Now she missed her mother terribly and was grateful for her extraordinary relationship with Rickie and Ronnie. These days, they were a large part of her support system.

The ringing phone jarred her out of her reverie, and she snatched it up.

"We have agreement on the bill to privatize Big South Fork," Dave announced without preamble. "It's enough to pass it out of committee, and we've got the votes in both the house and the senate nailed down. Almost."

Before Andee could speak, he continued, "By that I mean we're one vote short in the senate. It comes down to that new senator from Vermont. His former law practice focused on environmental issues, and he litigated a lot of cases for parks conservation and preservation groups. His name is Evan Parker, and he wants to make a fact-finding trip to Big South Fork before he'll vote for our bill."

Andee was stunned, trying to assess this new wrinkle.

"I know you're counting on privatization to attract a lot of new business to the area and I thought you'd want to be aware of it, since there could be ramifications for your development plans with those investors. It would be a major shot in the arm for real estate," he pointed out.

"I do, Dave, of course," Andee assured him quickly. "Information is power, without a doubt. I really appreciate the heads up. When will he be arriving and how many will be coming?"

"Just the senator and his top staffer and I and my staffer, so four of us will be arriving next Monday. We'll notify the National Park Service superintendent. Park people will want to escort us around."

I'll deal with this in the morning. Andee was relieved finally to have some concrete information but, while she slept, her subconscious pondered something she knew or had known or should have known but which now eluded her.

Parker—Vermont—law firm—why did that sound familiar?

The next morning, Andee leaned against the door jamb in Ronnie's office, coffee cup in hand, and asked casually, "What was your married name when you were in Vermont? Barker, Peters, Parker, Baker—something like that?"

Only three people knew Ronnie's marital status: Andee, Rickie, and Mindy. Ronnie never spoke about her marriage and her friends assumed that her divorce had been too painful. Without any particulars, they assumed she'd caught him cheating, and they assumed she wasn't eager to enter into another relationship because she'd been burned.

Ronnie suddenly had a bad feeling. This wasn't a casual question. "Parker, Evan Parker. Why?"

"Did you ever keep up with what he's been doing the last eleven years?"

"No, I shut him out of my life. I don't give a rat's ass what he did or where he went. Why? What does this have to do with anything?" Ronnie was annoyed, eager to get off this topic.

"Ronnie, your *ex* is a freshman senator in the U.S. Congress!"

"No way!" Andee had shocked her with this piece of news, but Ronnie didn't yet comprehend its immediate significance.

"Way!" Andee countered. "And we're hosting him and his staffer in three days! It seems he's the swing vote in getting the privatization bill passed."

Ronnie's gut wrenched. A senator? Evan was a senator? And he was coming *here*? She wanted nothing to do with him and his damn career, and now it was in her face. She should hide in the ladies' room until this meeting was a distant memory. Her whole body shook with anger. How dare he insert his presence into the new life she had made for herself? This simply could not be happening!

"Ronnie?"

"Andee, I can't."

"Can't what?"

"Can't be involved. It will wreck everything!"

"No, it won't." Andee was adamant, and she spoke firmly. "Don't give your ex that much credit.

Why should you be the one to shrink away? Are you going to give him all that power over you again?"

Ronnie sat motionless, unable to stand, numb with despair. Love and hate are two sides of the same coin, just as they said. Once she'd loved Evan Parker; now she hated him. She tried to force him out of her mind, but it was too late for that. She began thinking back over their four-year marriage. They met as he finished up his bachelor's degree in political science and she her doctorate in English. It was a whirlwind courtship. They both came from upper-middle-class backgrounds and seemed to have so much in common. He flew through the law school entry requirements, achieving an almost perfect score on his LSAT. The three years of classes consumed him, while she took an editor's job at the local Burlington newspaper. Journalism wouldn't have been her choice, but she loved to write as much as she loved to read, and it paid the bills.

For her husband, graduation was a mere formality, passing the bar a technicality. Evan had catapulted himself into the world of environmental law through family connections, a 501C3 non-profit called EcoGreen, LLC. He was passionate about his cases to a fault, tended to take it all much too personally, and he had a short fuse. He was greedy. He was definitely career-oriented. Did he really believe in the causes for which he fought, or was it the underlying desire to make a name for himself and garner more cases to fight while lining his own pockets? Isn't that what all lawyers wanted?

Evan had made a good living while he built a reputation as a tough litigator. He learned to work the system and had obviously established an easy path to elected office at the federal level. Ronnie had assumed he was still in Vermont and had made no attempt to look him up or any effort to follow his career.

The following morning, Andee arrived before her partners. She elbowed the office door open with her left arm and pushed it shut behind her with her heel, her right arm full of file folders.

Jackie jumped up and came around the corner of her desk, already reaching for the folders before they slid to the floor.

"Sorry I'm late," Andee told her without offering an explanation.

"I wish you'd been here five minutes ago," Jackie told her, her expression morose. "I see what you mean about being a realtor; it's a lot harder than it looks."

"Uh-oh." Andee stepped into her own office and dropped the pile of folders on her desk. "I'm listening," she assured Jackie.

"Marcia called."

"Uh-oh," Andee said a second time.

"Uh-oh is right. You won't believe what I said to her! It gets worse," Jackie added. "I hung up on her."

"Uh-oh," Andee said a third time. She leaned against the doorframe, waiting to hear the rest of the story.

"Marcia called to talk to Ronnie about the Shillen contract. She said she'd already called Ronnie on her cell, and it went to voicemail. I told her the Shillen closing would be a mail out to the seller, and I would be handling the paperwork. She told me she would only deal with a broker and to have Ronnie or Rickie call her. I told her, again, the file is on my desk, and if she wants to move the paperwork along, I would be handling it."

"She gets very defensive when she's backed into a corner," Andee agreed.

"Marcia gave me a ration of shit and talked down to me," Jackie continued. "She said the ink's not even dry on my license, and she wasn't wasting her time."

"She is a shit!" Andee exclaimed. "Hearing from her for any reason is enough to ruin your whole day."

"Well, I told her that in order for her to insult me, I would first have to value her opinion. And then I just hung up the phone."

Andee and Jackie stared at one another until Jackie grinned knowingly.

"You go, girl!" Andee chortled.

Ronnie was the next one in. She'd tossed and turned all night, looking haggard and ill in the light of day. She dreaded seeing Evan, and she felt totally violated to have him in her comfort zone, in any capacity.

Jackie handed her a cucumber and said, "Andee said to give this to you. She said you'd know what to do with it."

"Are you making something special?" she asked.

Ronnie appreciated Andee's quirky sense of humor, and she knew it was a joke. Andee was suggesting she might need to apply cucumber slices to swollen eyes in the coming day or two. Ronnie's eyes were red-rimmed and gritty this morning. She had cried, but not because she was hurt. She was long past that. Now she was upset, righteous in her growing anger over the unfairness of having Evan Parker, junior senator from the State of Vermont, arriving in Jamestown, Tennessee—in her face!

"Uh, yes," she mumbled. "I—uh—I wanted to try a new recipe, and the only ingredient I didn't have was a cucumber. Andee said she had one I could have."

"Are you okay?" Jackie asked, peering at her. "You look tired."

"I am tired," Ronnie admitted. "I didn't sleep well last night, for some reason."

When Rickie arrived a few minutes later, Andee told her quietly that they would need to have a meeting in private. Rickie immediately told Jackie that she'd like her to go and take the newest listing. Until Jackie completed the two-day orientation classes and became a member of the Knoxville

Association of Realtors, any listing she took would have to be entered under the broker's member number until she was assigned her own.

"You can write it up," Rickie told Jackie. "Get the room measurements and frame your photos with an eye to cropping them to showcase the property's best features. We can go over it later."

When Jackie left, the three met in Rickie's office. Rickie grew thoughtful.

"Jackie doesn't know it yet, but her workload is about to quadruple. I think we need to let her hire and train a new secretary, and the sooner, the better."

"We're going to have to bring her in on this," Ronnie said. "We all need to be comfortable with her running the office with minimal oversight. We're going to be up to our ass in alligators, in any case, but especially if the park is privatized."

Andee recounted Jackie's unfortunate encounter with Marcia. "Marcia is a piss-ant," Rickie snorted. "Jackie can handle her."

"I'd say she already did!" Ronnie smirked, her bad mood lifting for a moment. "But, sweet Jesus, I just can't deal with Evan!" she said, glumly. "I'm serious! This is a deal-breaker."

"You don't mean that," Rickie told her sternly. "He's the past; this is the future. His vote is the lynchpin; everything is riding on this."

"So to speak," Andee interjected. She just loved a good pun.

"I just feel sick," Ronnie said. "This is the absolute last thing I expected."

"He'll only be here for a day trip, and your contact with him will be minimal. They'll spend most of the time at the park headquarters. You won't see him until we get to The Hungry Horse. The three of us will be introduced as principals in this venture, then Rickie and I will carry it. I hate to have you miss out on the presentation, but you can just leave before lunch. You won't have to sit across from him or have him trying to catch your eye," Andee reassured her.

"In fact, we can video the presentation so you won't miss it. That will give us a chance to review and critique, and we'll also have it if we need to discuss or analyze anything with CW's group," Andee added.

As the three of them now reviewed, critiqued, and revised the points they wanted to make to the senators, Ronnie calmed down and accepted her role in the plan. She was grateful it was Friday, and she had the weekend to herself. She desperately needed some time to pull herself together. Luckily, by the time Monday rolled around, she would feel less apprehensive and far more composed.

Monday, mid-morning, Evan Parker looked on as Dave Strickland called Andrea Barton on her cell. He wanted to let her know their party had arrived and were given the red-carpet treatment by park officials. They'd been greeted by the park superintendent and then turned over to his second in command, Jonathan Wood, for a short tour of the headquarters, maintenance buildings, and the Bitter Creek Visitor's Center.

Jon had agreed to an abbreviated itinerary that would dovetail with their appointment to meet Big South Fork Pack Trips' stock trailer, with four horses tacked up and ready to go, promising to keep a careful eye on the time. The ride itself was uneventful but, even in a short hour, the visitors could appreciate the spectacular beauty offered by the gem of a national park. Dave's staffer, Derek Graham, suffered from asthma and chose to stay as far away from horses and pollen as he could get. He welcomed the chance to sit in the rental car and catch up on the morning's emails.

Neither Dave Strickland nor Evan could be called a horseman, but Evan's staffer, Molly Diaz, had taken lessons as a child and was thrilled with the excursion. They had been told the horses were used to accommodating those who had never ridden before and skillfully negotiated the trail. Evan made eye contact with Molly several times, and she understood she was expected to take mental notes now and create a written memorandum at the earliest opportunity. Evan was a stickler for detail and was very hands-on. He made the effort to come because he liked to see and hear for himself, not rely on the observations and opinions of others.

Everyone was hungry and looking forward to lunch. They were on Eastern Time so, not only was it one p.m. for them, it had been a long time since breakfast due to their post-dawn departure.

When they entered the lounge at The Hungry Horse, Dave led them toward three women who were awaiting their arrival. He introduced Andrea Barton first. "And these are Andee's colleagues," he told Evan, gesturing. "Erica Ahlers and Veronica Chandler."

Ms. Ahlers held out her hand, but Evan stood rooted to the spot, his ears buzzed, and his vision blurred. *It couldn't be!*

"Vee?" he finally managed. Molly glanced up sharply, always alert for any potential problem.

Ronnie swallowed and drew in a deep breath. She said coolly, "Hello, Evan."

She looked good, and her attitude told him she knew it. She had dressed casually, not wanting to draw attention to herself. She wore narrow navy twill jeans with a silk shirt in the same shade and a navy belt. Her navy blazer was made of buttery-soft Italian leather.

Evan took all that in, and his eyes dropped to her gray boots and traveled slowly back up, noting the understated silver jewelry, a short chain at the base of her throat, silver hoop earrings, and a wide silver cuff bracelet that he recognized. But it was her hair that shocked him. She'd gone completely gray!

No—not gray. The last time he'd seen her, her hair had been dark brown, almost black, threaded with a few strands of premature gray. Now it was a stunning silver, very dramatic, in a very edgy angled cut. Shorter in back, longer in front, elegant, expensive—his mind catalogued the details with lightning speed.

It had been how long since he'd seen her? Ten years—no, eleven. He remembered with sickening clarity the day she'd gotten the rejection letter from Daniels College. With a newly-minted Ph.D. and a paucity of publications, she knew she didn't have the depth of experience to fill a faculty position, but she'd worked hard, and it had been a deep disappointment nonetheless.

He'd told her he would take her to dinner at her favorite restaurant, and he'd meant to, but he'd gotten involved in a discovery delivered to his office that afternoon and had forgotten all about it.

It wasn't the first time he'd been too busy. That year, he'd left her birthday present on her plate at the breakfast table and gone off to put in a fourteen-hour day—that, apparently, was the straw that broke the camel's back. The next day she was gone, leaving a farewell note on his plate at the dinner table. She had vanished off the face of the earth, with no forwarding address. Her divorce lawyer, one Maryann Mahoney Esq., was a ballbuster if ever there was one. Vee hadn't asked for a penny; she wanted nothing from him except her freedom.

She had obviously used post office boxes in various towns and had unlisted phone numbers. Ms. Mahoney had created an LLC so Vee could purchase property and vehicles in a company name, never revealing her whereabouts.

Until today, when the earth's tectonic plates had shifted beneath his feet. Ronnie's unexpected presence caught Evan off totally off balance, a rare occurrence for him. He couldn't draw a deep breath and wondered for a second if he might be having a heart attack.

Only Molly perceived that Evan was wrestling with—something. She knew him better than anyone, spent most of her waking hours with him. Molly had been his invaluable assistant in almost all his lawsuits on behalf of environmental groups, and she had followed Evan to Washington to serve on his senate staff. Molly had seen him many times when he was off base in the courtroom and had to recover quickly in front of the judge.

"You two know each other?" Ms. Barton was nobody's fool. Obviously, Andee saw immediately that he had been caught totally unaware and asked her question as casually as possible.

Evan cleared his throat, trying to regain his voice and his authority. "Actually, yes, we do. More accurately, I should say *we did*, but it's been a long time, and it's a long story." At the moment, he was the center of attention. He knew he had to compartmentalize, to shove his personal feelings aside. He needed to leave that for some other time—any other time. Everyone there had some sort of agenda; in that much he was certain. Everyone was hoping to gain something, even Ronnie, apparently. She wouldn't be here otherwise. What was she—a realtor? What the hell was that all about?

Outwardly keeping his attention on the animated discussion over lunch, Evan couldn't help a quick glance every now and then toward Ronnie's end of the table. He kept his face expressionless when he watched her rise, push her chair back, and set her napkin neatly beside her plate.

"Excuse me, everyone. No, don't get up. I have a showing this afternoon and must run now, but it was nice meeting you all. Have a productive meeting. My associates will fill me in later..." She tipped her head toward Senator Parker and, with a slight nod, said, "Evan."

Jackie knew Rickie was waiting for a counter-counteroffer from the Kirchners and kept an eye on the fax machine all afternoon. Relieved that it had finally arrived, just a few hours short of the expiration date, she placed it in the center of Rickie's desk where she would see it as soon as she came in.

"Jackie," Rickie said a short while later after she'd called her sellers with the Kirchners' final offer. "I need to talk to you. Is this a good time?"

Jackie's stomach clenched when Rickie summoned her. Being a realtor was so much harder than she'd thought, and she worried constantly that she was a disappointment and not carrying her share of the workload. Rickie was probably upset about the Morans. She'd scanned the daily notebook on the title search website that morning, as she did every day, to see what real estate activity had taken place. She'd been shocked when she saw that Cara and Ryan Moran had recorded a general warranty deed.

A month earlier, Rickie told Jackie she had a commitment she couldn't reschedule and asked her to take some clients out for the afternoon. They were looking for a cabin with enough acreage for two horses and a small barn, and they were already qualified, with a lender's commitment letter to append to an offer.

Rickie was almost certain they would be making an offer if they found a property they liked. She told Jackie she'd be back by four and would catch up on some paperwork in the office, available later if Jackie needed any help with the mechanics of a purchase and sale agreement. Jackie had done a search on the Multiple Listing Service and had come up with half a dozen three-bedroom possibilities, which she'd run by Rickie. She planned to show the office's listings first, of course, but Rickie's policy was "a sale is a sale is a sale," and any suitable property should be shown, regardless of whose listing it was.

Well, regardless except for Marcia's listings, Jackie corrected herself. Marcia was borderline incompetent, and no one wanted to co-show with her nor struggle to get an offer to closing, so there was a tacit understanding among most of the agents in the area that Marcia's listings would get short shrift. That wasn't really right, Jackie knew, but Marcia hardly ever had any listings, so it almost didn't matter.

She wondered, not for the first time, why any seller would list with such a tenth-rate realtor in the first place.

But Marcia wasn't the only one who was ugly, Jackie now realized. She'd heard Rickie say there were agents she considered colleagues rather than competitors, but they were few and far between, and she was learning what that meant.

When she'd called Sandi Snyder to arrange an appointment to co-show, Sandi told her she would be out of town that day, but Jackie was welcome to run by her office and pick up a key. She said she would have it waiting for her at the front desk, and Jackie should just ask the receptionist for it. So, she did. The receptionist at Action Realty had handed her an envelope with a key in it.

Cara and Ryan Moran, Rickie's buyers, were an attractive couple in their late thirties, well informed and articulate. They had done their research, spending a day driving around and familiarizing themselves with various areas. They were childless, they'd told her, and both worked from home. Cara was an author, with an impressive number of Regency romance titles, published under the pseudonym of Catherine

Ryan. Ryan himself was a physician, but he was employed by a major drug company, manning a hotline, so he could also work from home.

The first cabin went into the reject pile because it was too close to an abutter and did not afford enough privacy. The second had possibilities, with the addition of a row of fast-growing trees as a privacy screen. The third went into the reject pile because it had two showers and no tub, a requirement Jackie was not aware of. The fourth cabin was cute, the Morans felt, but had a driveway that was too steep and there was no place to turn a horse trailer around easily. The fifth seemed poorly constructed.

The sixth was exactly what they were looking for.

"I love it!" Cara exclaimed as it came into view. "It really suits its setting! I can't wait to see the inside."

That was when Jackie discovered the key she'd been given didn't fit the lock. She tried it, Ryan tried it, Cara tried it. They walked around the cabin, but the blinds were tightly drawn, and they weren't able to get even a glimpse of the interior. When she called Action Realty, she got only voicemail. Obviously, the office was closed for the day, and she'd have to wait until morning to get the right key.

Unfortunately, the Morans were on their way to an afternoon wedding in Buckhead the following day, and they needed to get an early start the next morning. They said they'd try to come back through on the way home but couldn't promise as they planned to visit with several family members who lived near Atlanta.

Rickie's expression hardened when Jackie told her that she'd gone to the showing with the wrong key.

"You've just learned a lesson the hard way," Rickie told her grimly. "I should have warned you to look at the key before leaving her office to make sure you'd been given the right one."

"What?" Jackie gasped. "You think she gave me the wrong key on purpose?"

"That's exactly what I think. Sandi Snyder is cunning and sly. I have no doubt she did it *accidentally on purpose* if you know what I mean. She won't badmouth you, she'll make a show of being cooperative and helpful, but she'll take any opportunity to discredit you in front of your customers. Don't ever trust her and don't turn your back on her."

"Jesus!" Jackie swore, unhappily. Not being able to show the cabin was one thing, but the reality of seeing the sale consummated was a direct hit in the pocketbook, for Rickie, for her, and for the office. She checked the MLS to see who had actually consummated the sale, and it became apparent that, the second time around, the Morans had just gone straight to the listing agent and gotten the job done. She felt terrible and was sure Rickie was about to chew her out.

What Rickie actually told her was the last thing she expected to hear. It was pretty clear that Senator

Evan Parker was impressed, and Rickie had no doubt their project would get off the ground—literally—in the not-too-distant future. She would have to hold that thought and remember to tell Andee who, more than anyone, would enjoy the pun. With the groundwork laid—God, she was in rare form—it was time to get on with it.

She explained the scope of the proposed project to Jackie and showed her the proposed conceptual site plan. She said that she, Ronnie, and Andee would be so immersed in it that Jackie would be essentially running the office. Rickie told her she didn't expect her to function as a realtor and a free secretary. She wanted Jackie to interview, hire, and train someone who could take over her administrative functions since she needed to be free for listing and showing. Jackie was stunned.

A half-hour later, Jackie stuck her head into Rickie's office.

"I called the high school and asked the business ed. teacher if she had someone she could recommend, a recent graduate maybe."

"Clever!" Rickie said. "Good thinking! How'd that work out?"

"She suggested I call Geraldine Giordano. She graduated last June and has been working as the assistant manager at a local deli."

"Have you called her yet?" Rickie asked.

"I did. She's thrilled. She works a lot of evenings because they're open until nine and she's making peanuts. She said that she might be interested in getting a real estate license after a while and that, if she became a realtor, her sister, Teresa, is a junior, and she can have her job when she graduates."

"That's well thought out."

Jackie bit the inside of her lip to keep from smiling.

"She's coming tomorrow afternoon for an interview," Jackie told her. "Geri." They stared at each other for a minute and then burst out laughing.

Rickie swiped a finger under one eye, wiping tears. "You're kidding, right?"

"Oh, my God!" Jackie said. "I didn't even think of that!"

"So, Geri and—uh—Teri."

"The ideal candidate will have strong communication skills," Rickie intoned, solemnly. "Must be nonsmoker. Must have boy's name."

"Oh, it hurts!" Jackie said. "Don't make me laugh. My side hurts."

Hundreds of miles away, Liberty Airlines Flight 303 cruised at altitude, 35,000 feet above the dark Virginia countryside. Evan Parker tipped his plastic glass and swallowed the last few drops of bourbon, enjoying the burn in the back of his throat. He had not had a good day. As they were waiting in the departure lounge at Knoxville's McTaggart-Tomlin airport,

Molly had told Evan she would be leaving Washington, explaining that her father had been diagnosed with dementia. He was in the early stages, but she was needed to help her mother with the family business, as well as his care. She'd given him a month's notice.

"What do her parents do?" Dave Strickland asked, draining his own glass of bourbon.

"They own a chain of stores throughout the South that sell high-end patio furniture. It's called Patios Plus, I think—something like that. I guess they sell furniture, umbrellas, hammocks, fake plants, outdoor lighting, water features, fire pits—that sort of thing."

"What will you do about replacing Molly?" Dave asked. "She'll be a hard act to follow."

"To answer your question," Evan said slowly, "Sabrina can fill in for a while, I guess. She isn't anywhere as sharp as Molly, and the chemistry isn't there, but she's ambitious, and she'll work hard. I'll probably try to recruit a June graduate. Vermont has the top school for environmental law, did you know that?"

"That'll go over like a lead balloon," Dave cautioned. "I never paid any attention to the rumors about you and Molly, just so you know."

"I don't know what you've heard, but there's no truth to any of that. It's typical Washington gossip. Molly's almost young enough to be my daughter, and I never thought of her as anything but the best staffer I've ever had. She's smart as a whip, well-spoken, beautiful, and we're so much on the same wavelength, I never have to explain anything to her. She knows how I think, and she's usually way ahead of me. When I ask her to do something, she already has it in the works. I'll sure miss her." He sighed.

"Listen, Evan, this is none of my business either, but be careful with Sabrina. I've only seen her in passing, but she strikes me as someone who's so ambitious, she's ruthless. Don't let her set you up in any situation that could be considered compromising because I think she'd turn around and use it against you if she ends up getting passed over."

"I hear ya'." Evan nodded in agreement. "I appreciate your concern."

Being considered one of the most eligible bachelors on Capitol Hill, Evan was much in demand by Washington hostesses. He socialized constantly but made it a point never to date anyone more than three times, no matter how attracted he was to her. He worked longer hours now than ever, he knew that, so a second marriage would be a reprise of his first—and would probably end just as badly.

Truth be told, he'd never met anyone he liked as much as he'd liked Veronica Chandler. He had since dated many women who were richer, more beautiful, more well-connected, but no one had understood him better than his former wife, Vee. Seeing her in Tennessee had given him the shock of a lifetime and, if he was totally honest with himself, he realized what a fool he'd been to let her go. She hadn't mellowed with time, that was clear, and from the way she lit out after lunch, it was apparent that she didn't want to be in the same room with him.

Chapter Six

"I've been here an hour. They're forty-five minutes late! What should I do?" Jackie said, reaching Ronnie on her cell.

Ronnie remembered Jackie had a showing scheduled today with Marcia Szczypanski. Marcia was no longer afforded lockbox privileges after leaving three lights on, and two out of three exterior doors unlocked the last time she had shown one of Horse Country's listings unsupervised. Ronnie recognized it, not as carelessness, but as Marcia's typical passive-aggressive behavior, hoping to make the listing agent look bad to her seller.

She, Rickie, and Andee shared the same high standards and agreed to do things the right way, with no exceptions. One of them always swung past the listing to make sure all lights were off and doors locked after another agent had been in the house. They also changed the lockbox code after every showing, so they would know who was the last person in the building.

"You haven't heard from her?" Ronnie asked although the answer was obvious. Failing to show up for an appointment was part of Marcia's habitual display of contempt for other agents. It was well known in the real estate community that she was usually late for appointments—too often to be anything but deliberate. It seemed to please her to leave agents standing around in an opened listing, waiting for her to show up. On those rare occasions when she actually had a listing of her own, she liked to exert her erstwhile power by leaving other agents waiting on the porch or in their vehicles for her to arrive. Marcia knew that, if other agents had later appointments, it would wreak havoc with their schedules and make them appear less than competent if they couldn't get their customers in to view a property that interested them.

"No," Jackie said. Most agents had some sort of smartphone, but Marcia was too cheap to pay for one and bought minutes for a Stone-Age cell phone, so she didn't have email and text capabilities at her fingertips. She did have call waiting and used it to screen her calls and ignore those from other agents, deriving great satisfaction from knowing the frustration and inconvenience this often caused them.

"I'm not far from her so-called office," Ronnie told Jackie. "Let me just swing by and see if her car's there."

Ronnie called Jackie back a few minutes later and told her to lock up and leave. "Not only is her car there, I saw her standing in the doorway, so she's there. She's not out with buyers; she's just running you up the flagpole! I think this is payback for the time you hung up on her and because I forced a mail-out closing for the Shillen contract and denied her an opportunity to pull this shit with me."

"She knows you just got your license, and she can get away with this because you're not on to her yet," Ronnie pointed out.

"Jesus," Jackie said. "What an asshole!"

"She's just a pathetic, insecure, mean-spirited person," Ronnie agreed wholeheartedly. "Don't think you've wasted your time, though, she just helped you gain some experience."

When Ronnie got back to the office an hour later, she picked up her message slips and saw that her contract on the Crawford property had just fallen through on a contingency. She knew never to count on a commission until she had the check in her hand, but the appraisal and the building inspection had both gone well. The buyer was qualified for financing, so, with the major hurdles behind them, a closing should have been imminent.

The buyer, Owen Fleming, was a very nervous man and had barraged her with calls over the past weeks, asking for a million details and micromanaging every step. She suspected he had had a serious case of "buyer's remorse," using a loophole to get out of the contract at the last minute. When buyers had fulfilled their major obligations, and had spent several hundred dollars for a home inspection, they were usually serious.

The sellers would be devastated, and she dreaded making the call. She didn't envy Jackie, taking over the day-to-day operations of a busy real estate agency. With only a high-school education, this was the opportunity of a lifetime for her, though. She could make good money over the years if she could manage not to take most of the bullshit personally and keep her eye on the goal. For herself, while she knew there were losers in every profession, she hadn't worked hard to get an advanced degree only to find herself on a par with people like Marcia, and she was feeling increasingly frustrated and impatient. She was ready for the challenge ahead and looked forward to working with smart, sophisticated partners

She'd dressed down today, planning to spend most of the morning in the barn with the vet for the horses' annual spring farm call after spending only a short time in the office to take care of a few urgent matters she couldn't re-shuffle. Then the day got off to such a hectic start, and she'd apologetically had to re-schedule the vet. Unfortunately, she had a sinking feeling that, for the foreseeable future, this was the "new normal."

Ronnie hadn't been home long and had already gotten a thorough scolding from her cat, Purrl. Wearily, she tugged the polarfleece pullover and cotton turtleneck over her head and pulled off her faded jeans. A hot shower sure would feel good. Her neck was stiff, and she wanted to let the day's cares just swirl down the drain. Once she was dressed again, in comfortable well-worn gray sweatpants, a long-sleeved gray tee, and gray ragg socks, she padded into the kitchen and poured a glass of Merlot. She should eat something but didn't have the energy to cook. That's what frozen mac n' cheese was for! She took a box out of the freezer, peeled back a corner of the clear plastic covering, and placed it in the microwave.

She decided to ring Luc while she still had an ounce of energy left. She had promised that morning to call him back, so she would. She had felt bad when she'd had to cut his call short, recognizing he was distraught about his daughter and needed a sympathetic ear. She had almost no contact with him since the Creekside visit and was surprised when he called the office that morning.

Soon after the initial meeting, Rickie had begun receiving emails from Luc and forwarded them to her partners. Ronnie had been surprised to see that his name was spelled *L-u-c* and not *L-u-k-e*, as she'd assumed it was. She incorrectly assumed, again, that Luc was short for Lucas, and she'd asked him outright about his French surname, in the getting-to-know-each-other phase soon after CW had given them the green light to proceed.

"Yes and no," he'd told her. "It is a French name, but I'm half French-Canadian, not French French. My great-grandparents emigrated from France and settled in a village in Quebec, just outside of Sherbrooke. My great-grandfather was working as a handyman at a resort in Dixville Notch, in the Great North Woods of New Hampshire. My great-grandmother worked in the kitchen as a sort of assistant to the pastry chef. They met and married and had four sons and two daughters, and the family spread out as they all subsequently grew up, married, and moved away.

"My father and my mother, who is American, started out living in Colebrook, New Hampshire, where my mother taught school, but my father couldn't find work in an area with so few opportunities, and they later moved to southern New Hampshire. My dad is a civil engineer who works for the department of transportation, so he travels all over the state. My mother works in the bursar's office at Daniels College. I wasn't a legacy applicant like Chip, but it gave me a leg up when I applied to Daniels needing major financial aid." Ronnie was fascinated.

"My full name is Jeanluc Michel Deschaines," he told her. "Believe me; life would be a lot easier if it had been Anglicized as Luke, but my dad is proud of his heritage and proud of me, so there you have it."

Now, he answered on the second ring.

"I just got in," she told him. "What a day! The bane of our existence, the area's scraping-the-bottom-of-the-barrel agent, gave Jackie a ration of shit and had her almost in tears, and a contract that was within a whisker of closing fell through at the eleventh hour, so basically I worked my ass off, and there's no payday." She sighed. "But, I have a glass of wine, and I want to hear what you started to tell me this morning about your daughter. Do you mind if I eat while you're talking?"

"What're you having?"

"I just zapped some Stouffer's mac-n-cheese. I'm sure you're envious!"

"Actually, I am." Luc laughed. "That's one of my very own favorites. Maybe I should have had that, too. I could use some comfort food. I've had a pretty terrible day myself," he confided.

"CW and Julia learned this morning that CW has colon cancer. It's pretty advanced. Until now, they thought it was Crohn's Disease. He's insistent that he doesn't want chemo or radiation, so, needless to say, we're all just devastated."

Luc mistook Ronnie's silence and quickly added, "He's groomed Chip to take over so there'll be a seamless transition."

"Oh, no, Luc! I'm not thinking about that at all. My God! Poor Julia! My heart goes out to her," Ronnie said, her eyes filling with tears.

Luc spent the next half hour detailing his increasing concern for his daughter. Ronnie was both surprised and flattered that he'd chosen to unburden himself with her. "You'd be horrified if you saw her," he said.

"She's an emotional mess, but I'm becoming more alarmed about the health aspect. She's gained so much weight, and I'm afraid of what it's doing to her heart."

"I don't have much experience with adolescents, but here's what I'm thinking…" Ronnie said slowly, still formulating an idea.

"If you're going to be spending a lot of time in Tennessee, it's going to get worse. She's going to ramp up her efforts to get your attention. If you bring her with you, she'll resent us right from the start, and you'll have a disaster on both ends."

Luc was silent.

"Are you there?" Ronnie asked.

"Sorry," he replied. "I was nodding in agreement. She's made appalling scenes before, and, as you know, we had a meltdown on the tarmac when we were on our way there with the Westlakes. Chip and Lucinda are well aware of it, but I try not to let CW and Julia see her behavior. I'm sure it doesn't, but I feel like it diminishes my capabilities in their eyes. I mean, if I can't control my own daughter or if I'm distracted by my personal life—see what I mean?"

"Well, maybe we can get out ahead of it."

"What do you mean? I'm not following," Luc said.

"Does she ever go to Texas with you?"

Ronnie knew that The Westlake Group had spent a lot of time there and still did, having invested in a ranch that bred both cattle and horses.

"She loved it when she was young," Luc said. "She went with Kelli and me. After the divorce, I guess we were both trying to make it up to her. We each spent time with her, and when it was my turn, Steff and I often went to Texas. She loved to fly with me and was turning into a pretty good co-pilot. She also loved to ride so much that I gave her a nice Quarter Horse mare for her tenth birthday. "

Ronnie didn't comment; she just waited for Luc to continue.

"Then Kelli met her new husband, Benedict Macklin, at a dinner party, and she became consumed with nightlife in the nation's capital," he said. "Well, he founded one of those clubs people join, and he gets them invited to diplomatic bashes at various embassies, galas, masquerade balls, wine tastings, champagne cruises up the Potomac on yachts, after hours at museums, and the like.

"I think he's a charlatan with a phony name, but the results are what counts. He's rich, handsome, attentive, and life's a ball—quite literally. Kelli's existence now is a daily routine of shopping for the right gown, shoes, bag, etc. Then she does whatever else it takes to stop time by having facials, manicures, herbal body wraps, spray-on tans, collagen injections, lifts this or lipos that. It's never ending; she has a standing appointment for those botox injections that treat frown lines, crow's feet, and the lines on her forehead. The Macklins are out every evening, which is exactly the lifestyle Kelli embraces.

"I was a big disappointment to her," Luc continued. "She assumed that venture capitalists led a very glamorous life when, in reality, it's a lot of long hours and hard work."

"That's why Stephanie lives with her mother?" Ronnie asked.

"We have joint custody," Luc told her. "Obviously that doesn't work too well on either end. Steph seems intent on mortifying her mother and torturing me."

"Let me run this by you…" Ronnie started, then stopped.

"I'm open to suggestions," Luc said. "I'm desperate, I'm serious. I'll try anything."

"What if you dropped her off here for a weekend on one of your trips to Texas? I think things would go better if she spent time here on her own instead of tagging along with you and feeling like a fifth wheel. If we could get her interested in some aspect of this project, maybe we could create a role for her, and she'd start to regain some self-esteem."

"Holy shit!" Luc burst out. "It's a great idea, but why would you want to put yourself through that? It won't be any picnic. You have no idea—."

"I don't think we'll make much progress in one weekend," Ronnie assured Luc. She wasn't ready to drop the subject. "It's a lot like working with a horse that doesn't trust you," she explained. "The first weekend will just be to lay the foundation. I'll have to build a relationship one increment at a time and not move on until I've earned her trust."

She was still thinking aloud.

"If I offer too much too soon, it will spook her. She'll figure I'm your girlfriend or something, and she'll do her best to make you miserable."

"More miserable," Luc corrected.

"Give me her email address," Ronnie suggested. "And stay tuned."

Ronnie was aware, on one level, that she was playing cat-and-mouse with Luc, encouraging his confidences, discussing plans, yet keeping him at a certain distance. She could almost hear her mother's voice in her head, warning her against people who gave with one hand and took with the other. She was torn between wanting more contact with this interesting, kind man and being terrified of her own history.

With each conversation, she found herself comparing him to Evan. The past decade had been kind to her ex-husband, Ronnie had observed over lunch at The Hungry Horse. The fast pace on Capitol Hill and the whole Washington scene, social and political, obviously agreed with him. He had an authoritative air that drew people to him like moths to a porch light. He spent money on a good haircut. The cut of his clothes was expensive, conservative, and his tie understated and tasteful. She would have expected no less. He would appeal to her, she acknowledged, if she was meeting him for the first time. During the last few years of their marriage, she'd given up trying to please him. Nothing she did, wore, or cooked seemed to impress him, no matter how much time and effort she poured into it. She'd come to think of their house as 'The Dead Zone.'

The qualities about Evan that had attracted her then were the same qualities that attracted her now to Luc. If she had known that Evan would morph into a major workaholic, parsimonious with his presence and his affection, would she have married him? Hell, no! That's exactly what she was doing now, she saw that. She was testing Luc, wanting to make sure he wasn't another Evan Parker. No way was she going to let history repeat itself.

When Ronnie reached the office the next day, she found Jackie showing Geri how to crop photos and add a caption to them.

"Make the canvas larger than the image," Jackie said. "And then construct a text box just below the picture. Use the largest font that'll fit. You're limited to six hundred characters for your description on the Multiple Listing Service, but this way you can spoon-feed the piece of information you want the buyer to know about each particular picture. And don't ever rely on spell check or Andee will rip your head off. You won't believe some of the stuff that other realtors publish."

Ronnie hid a smile. Jackie was repeating, almost word for word, the instructions Rickie had given her when she was teaching her how to put photos on the MLS. Jackie had done a good job of finding Geri. She was a quick learner and was proving a good fit.

That reminded Ronnie that she wanted to email Stephanie. She kept it short and simple.

Hi, Steph,

Your dad gave me your email address. I have an idea I want to run by you. We're feeling a little overwhelmed by the scope of our project and have decided to hire someone for data entry. Since you'll probably be coming down here pretty often with him, I wondered if you'd like to be involved and make a little money.

How much? Stephanie responded rudely, a few minutes later.

Jackie, one of the realtors in the office, has a niece who would love to do it, but I thought of you. Let me know if you're interested.

Not only did Jackie not have a niece who was interested, the task was something Ronnie could easily do herself, but she wanted to let Stephanie rise to the bait and then set the hook.

"Ronnie?" Geri stood in the doorway. "I was wondering. Can you take a quick look at something? Can you still have listings when your license is expired? You can't, can you?"

"Wow!" Ronnie peered at Geri's screen in astonishment. "No, girlfriend, you sure can't."

"I was on the Tennessee Real Estate Commission's website to look at y'alls' continuing education so I could make a chart and know who's going to be due or let you know when courses are offered that you might want to get out of the way, and I saw this," Geri explained. "I thought TREC was pretty strict, but I guess not. How can he even renew his license if he hasn't done any Continuing Ed during this licensing period?" she asked, pointing to a name on her screen.

"I think you have sixty days after your license expires to get the CE done," Ronnie told her. "If you don't, you have to take the real estate exam all over again and re-apply for a license. This is interesting."

Ronnie knew exactly what needed to be done.

"Call TREC," she told Geri. "Give them his license number and ask why his status is still showing active when his license is expired. Then get on the MLS and see if he has any active listings. If he does, call the Knoxville Association of Realtors and ask why he has still has listings when his license is expired. They'll check with TREC, and I'm sure they'll shut him down. The broker will have to put the listings in his name or assign them to other agents in the office. And well he should! A monkey with a corncob up its butt can get a realtor's license. Half of them are incompetent; it's no wonder people don't respect realtors."

Ronnie stopped herself. "Jackie told me you might be interested in getting a license; I didn't mean to be a bucket of cold water. Experience is the best teacher, and you'll learn a lot working here. In most agencies, it's sink or swim, and other agents will go out of their way to steal your customers, snag your listings, make you look bad, inconvenience you. Here, we believe in mentoring, so don't hesitate to ask about anything you don't understand."

She looked around, wondering why Geri was alone in the office. "Where is Jackie?"

"She said she was going to weed eat and would be back in about an hour," Geri replied.

Ronnie nodded her approval.

"We keep a lightweight battery-powered weed eater in the sign closet so we can trim around our signs," she explained. "And we always keep them straight. That's our curb appeal. You know that old saying, 'You only have one chance to make a good first impression?' Our signs are the first thing a lot of people know about us, so Rickie is adamant about doing things the right way. And we always keep our information boxes filled. According to her, nothing's worse than an info box with no fliers."

She stepped back into her office and then stuck her head out.

"If you want to get Andee's goat sometime, tell her you 'weed ate' as the past tense of 'weed eat.' I guarantee you'll be able to hear her grind her teeth!"

"Phone for you, Ronnie," Geri called a while later. Ronnie was deep in thought. She'd been searching online for places to advertise their Emery Pond project and trying to come up with a catchy, appealing name that would communicate the spirit they intended to convey. There had been one major brainstorming session, and they came up with a tagline that they all agreed was perfect. So far, they were all on the same page. They wanted to see what ideas they could come up with together before involving ad agencies or marketing consultants or, worse, interior designers. So far, it was 'Something, something. Where Nature Is Your Neighbor.'

Ronnie reached for the phone, still absorbed.

"Ronnie Chandler," she said crisply, forcing her eyes off the screen and directing her attention to her caller.

"Hey! Lucinda Westlake here," the caller responded. "Are you free to talk for a few minutes?"

"Yes, perfect timing," Ronnie told her, giving the caller her full attention. "What's up?"

"Well, I can't stop thinking about Tennessee," Lucinda confided. "Luc and Chip have been closeted with CW and I think they're eager to start advertising for architect/engineer firms to do the Emery Pond master plan. I think we all think so much alike that I want us to bounce our ideas off each other and have a list of specific 'wants' and 'don't wants' before someone else sticks their finger in our pie, you know what I mean?"

"You read my mind. I was just sitting here getting my thoughts in order for our meeting." Ronnie pulled her pad of yellow legal in front of her and picked up her pen.

"About Emery Pond," Lucinda continued. "There are models for this kind of thing all over the place; it's not exactly an original concept. Seaview comes to mind. Have you been there?"

There was a moment of silence. Ronnie was stunned.

"Lucinda?" Ronnie choked, her voice high and strangled.

"I'm sorry; I'll have to call you back." She placed the receiver in the cradle, dazed. She felt as if all the oxygen had been sucked out of the room and her head started to pound. *Damn it!* She had thought she was over this!

Seeing Evan after so many years was a shock to her nervous system. She never thought about him and hoped never to see that bastard again. By the time she'd vacated her marriage, her self-esteem lay in shreds and it took years before she got her feet back under her. Seaview was where they had spent their honeymoon, five glorious days in paradise, stolen from a harsh, gray, bitterly-cold New England winter. Oh, yes, she'd been there. Closing her eyes, she was instantly transported to the narrow, sandy lanes and the pastel pseudo-Victorian cottages with their wide front porches, picket fences, the sweep of gulf coast sand, so white and fine, and the warm emerald-green water. It had been an idyllic interlude, a time out of time.

When she opened her eyes, she found Rickie standing in front of her desk, studying her worriedly.

"You okay?"

Only Ronnie's partners and Mindy knew of her history with Evan. Slowly she shook her head, still feeling dazed and disoriented.

"I haven't been okay since Andee told me Evan Parker was coming to Tennessee. I feel so off-balance, lightheaded, like there isn't enough oxygen."

"I just hung up on Lucinda, she must think I'm barking mad," she told Rickie, feeling queasy and swallowing hard. "All she did was mention Seaview—you know, that town in the Florida panhandle—was an earlier model of a planned community like we're going to be doing…" She trailed off, tears welling up against her will. She angrily swiped at her eyes.

"It's where Evan and I spent our honeymoon. God, I hate him!"

Rickie moved behind Ronnie's chair, putting her hands on Ronnie's shoulders. "You *are* upset; the muscles in your neck are like iron." She squeezed, digging her thumbs deep into the trapezius.

"Send Lucinda a text," she directed. "Tell her something came up at the office and you'll call her tomorrow. You know, we can't put the toothpaste back in the tube. He did come and his vote is crucial to our success. Jesus, what are the odds?"

"I've been talking to Luc a lot." Ronnie met Rickie's eyes and continued. "But mainly about his daughter. If I'm totally honest with myself—and with you—I'd have to admit I'm really attracted to him on a lot of levels. I don't think it's appropriate to get romantically involved at this point when our relationships with CW and Julia and Lucinda and Chip are still so new and so fragile, that might be really unfair. I thought I was totally over having a man in my life, that I could be healthy and whole having friendships with girlfriends but, when I have a bad day, I want to put my head on someone's shoulder and feel his arms around me."

"Why don't you call it a day?" Rickie suggested. "Go home and pull the covers over your head. You'll feel better tomorrow," she soothed.

Ronnie accepted her advice gratefully. A good night's sleep was exactly what she needed. She nodded in agreement, plucking her jacket from the back of her chair and shrugging into it. She dug into her shoulder bag and scrabbled for her car keys.

Once she was home, she pulled her vehicle into the carport and went straight to feed the two horses, dumping hay over their stall doors, something she only did during inclement weather. Usually she towed it out into the paddock in a plastic toboggan but today she simply couldn't summon the energy. She glanced at Purrl's bowl as soon as she entered the kitchen to make sure it didn't need to be refilled and dropped her jacket and her bag on a kitchen chair. She wasn't hungry and was too tired even for her customary glass of wine after work. Stripping off her clothes, she washed off her makeup and fell into bed.

She dreaded the idea of lying awake all night, tossing and turning, thinking about Evan and what might have been, but she was emotionally drained and fell into a deep slumber almost immediately.

Chapter Seven

"Ronnie? Hey, it's Rickie. I just wanted to give you a heads up in case you weren't planning to come straight to the office."

"I was just on my way out the door. What's up? Is there a problem?"

There was a moment of silence, and then Rickie said slowly, "Yes and no. No, not really. I don't know." She halted again and Ronnie waited.

"You know Jamie Thiel?" Rickie asked. It was almost a rhetorical question because everybody in the eastern half of Tennessee knew who Jamie Thiel was, on-air reporter for the television station in Knoxville. Jamie was uncommonly attractive with smooth black hair. He had a low pleasant voice that commanded his viewers' attention. And he was smart. The station's motto was 'From our heart to yours.'

More like 'In the heart,' Rickie thought the minute she heard he was coming to Jamestown. He wanted to do an investigative segment on bears in the national park and interview a local realtor to ask if there'd been any hesitation on the part of would-be buyers, any trend. Jamie was a skilled facilitator, and, with some expert editing, Rickie could just imagine the upcoming sound bites on the evening news.

Ronnie saw the van with the station's logo emblazoned on the side as she pulled in and wondered if the interviewer had come alone or if he'd brought a cameraman, but there were only two people in the office when she entered the room. Ronnie said nothing, just quietly took a seat out of view. Rickie sat waiting patiently as Jamie set up a tripod for his video recorder, then clipped a mike to her collar and did a quick soundcheck.

"I'm here in Jamestown at the office of Horse Country Real Estate with the managing broker, Erica Ahlers," he began. He didn't waste any time.

"Are you aware that the bear population in Big South Fork is multiplying exponentially as favorable conditions allow bears to thrive, with sows delivering multiple cubs each year instead of the normal one or two every other year? Aren't there pamphlets with information about being in *bear country* stacked on the desk at the visitor's center? What about the plaques affixed to picnic tables, warning people to secure their food and not to leave greasy grills behind?"

Rickie parried his questions methodically. She suspected that overwhelming their subjects with a barrage of questions was a technique journalists often used to unnerve their sources. Startled, perhaps the source would reveal a piece of information, violate a confidence, or let something slip that would unwittingly create a masterful piece.

"Look at that bear at Pickett State Park a couple of years ago that crawled into a camper's tent," Jamie pointed out. "What would have happened if the camper had been in there, eating a peanut butter sandwich?"

Rickie remembered that incident. They trapped that bad boy in a bear cage and euthanized him because he had 'crossed a line.'

But, now, Rickie had a few pointed questions of her own for Jamie Thiel.

"This is a national park," she reminded him calmly, "and bears are a natural element in the wilderness ecology here just as they are in the Smokies. How does being in grizzly bear country affect real estate in Montana or Wyoming?"

She continued, "Or how about living someplace like Louisiana or Mississippi or Florida where people have to worry about alligators and water moccasins? Nothing is perfect, but I think this is about as close as you can get."

This was a topic she felt passionately about, and her enthusiasm was apparent. She made a few more remarks about the low cost of living, the four distinct seasons, the low property taxes as plusses that more than offset what some people might consider a minus. She bet he would probably edit all that information out and slant the piece the way he intended before she ever opened her mouth. She'd done the best she could, and what happened in the editing booth was beyond her control.

Rickie's immediate concern was that she felt this was a subject they should get out in the open, so to speak, and bring it to The Westlake Group's attention before they saw some kind of adverse publicity about Big South Fork on TV or some form of social media. CW had a well-deserved reputation as a straight shooter, and she wanted to be sure there was no subterfuge and no secrets among them, certainly not on her end. An opened pizza box and a six-pack of diet soda sat on the coffee table at lunchtime, largely untouched. Rickie, Ronnie, and Andee sat at Rickie's desk, their chairs crowded together so all three were visible when the video chat session began. CW was too ill to participate in a video conference, but Chip, Luc, Lucinda, and Julia appeared before them.

Rickie explained about the interview that had taken place that morning.

"I'm not sure what the ramifications might be for our project, but I thought we should discuss it openly. There have been bears sighted on horse trails here in the park, and, while there hasn't been an actual bear encounter, negative publicity won't do our project any good. A lot depends on who else is interviewed and what they have to say."

She continued to clarify. "We weren't sure if any adverse publicity about the area would scare off our investors."

Lucinda had immediately grasped the significance of Senator Parker's swing vote on the upcoming legislation when it was originally explained. There was no doubt in Rickie's mind she was a key player, albeit behind the scenes. It was something Rickie suspected and just confirmed. She respected Lucinda's acumen and had decided she would prove an asset. She especially admired the relationship the woman enjoyed with her husband and sons and looked forward to spending more time together with them, building a friendship. Now she hoped it wasn't all going to vaporize in the space of a few hours.

Lucinda reassured her, "You don't know CW! He takes on commitments for the long haul, and he's experienced enough to know that you can't control something like this. They don't call Chip 'Chip off the Old Block' for nothing. His father taught him well, and they are absolutely on the same page. Now, more than ever, Chip will want to do things as he knows CW would if he were able. If there's a media frenzy, it will play itself out. This will be yesterday's news—literally."

Chip picked up, ""In the meantime, we intend to move ahead with the Emery Pond project as a stand-alone, irrespective of the privatization aspect. As soon as the sale of the land closes, we'll complete the site plan and start the surveying. Andee and I will be in close communication from now on, and we'll be looking for an architect because we'll need elevations sooner rather than later."

Julia had been silent until now, listening intently. "Have you ever seen a bear yourself when you were out riding?" she asked.

"I have, but only once and only from a distance, nothing more than a glimpse," Andee said.

"Do you carry a gun when you ride?" Chip wanted to know.

Although the question had been directed at Andee, it was Rickie who replied.

"You know, I'm hearing more and more riders say that they do carry or intend to carry a gun in their saddlebag because they've become increasingly fearful of encountering a bear. I have a concealed carry permit and a handgun, but I don't carry it on horseback, nor do I intend to."

Before she could continue, Chip interrupted, "Because…?"

Rickie chose her words carefully, but this was a subject that had been discussed among area riders many times, and her position on it was clear.

"My feelings are that all riders in a group would have to be made aware that a member has a weapon. The riders' horses would have to be desensitized to the sound of gunfire, for fear of startling a horse and throwing a rider or riders, if that person were to shoot suddenly. Each member of the group should feel reasonably certain that the person wielding the weapon is competent to use it and would not simply compound the problem," she explained.

"Why would the weapon be concealed?" Chip asked. "Why not carry it where you can get to it?"

"Well…" Rickie said again, trying to formulate a thoughtful response.

"I don't think it matters where the gun is," Ronnie said. "Any weapon small enough and light enough to carry either on your belt, in a holster or in a saddlebag wouldn't prove effective against a bear. You might just as well throw the gun at the bear and hope it scares him off."

"Never mind the fact it's a crime to kill a bear," Andee told them. "You would lose your gun, find yourself charged with a felony, pay a whopping fine, or even end up doing some jail time."

"To tell you the truth," Andee added, facetiously, "I might actually be in greater danger from a gun in the hands of some of those women than I would be if I encountered a bear."

Lucinda stifled a laugh.

"We need to see what the fallout is from this thing if there even is any," Chip said.

"People want to know that they're making a sound investment when they buy property. They want to believe their families are safe. No place is perfect, so I don't see the project being affected to any great extent. However, we always need to be well informed and able to counter any concerns that might arise, just as you counter concerns about ozone and air quality or any one of a hundred things that get thrown at you when you develop land," Luc summed it up.

The conversation had flowed smoothly with questions asked and answered. None of the seven saw this for what it actually was, a harbinger of things yet to come. They couldn't have predicted, anticipated, or guessed, nor could they have been prepared any more than they already were. They talked for about two hours, agreeing that they might have to do some damage control at some point but that it should not affect the project in any significant way, solidifying the scope of work, and laying out a time table. It had been time well spent.

Rickie brought the Virginia partners up to speed on the day-to-day aspects as well.

"We've hired a new secretary for the office," she'd reported. "Jackie has gotten her license, and we've been giving her a crash course so she can handle the routine listings and showings. Ronnie and I have had our plates full identifying the parcels of land, approaching landowners, and getting those purchases underway."

Lucinda had an effervescent personality, and her enthusiasm was contagious. "Maybe we can plan to meet in about a month and review our progress, even if it's just an overnight. We had such a good time when we stayed at Creekside, and Chip and I have fallen in love with your part of the world. We're looking forward to many more visits!"

Later that evening, Luc called Ronnie at home. "I'm still thinking about the conversation we had earlier." When Ronnie didn't reply, he clarified. "About the bears. Have you ever seen a bear when you were out riding?"

"Yes. I have, and I hated it. One day, a cub ran across the trail a couple of hundred yards ahead of me, and all I could think was, 'Oh, shit! Where's Momma?' It's a really easy trail, and everybody rides there all the time."

"What would you do if Momma came out of the woods?" Luc persisted.

"I don't know what I'd do," Ronnie said slowly. "Every situation is different. Ricky told you she doesn't carry a gun, and neither do I. A lot of people do, but I think firing from horseback would just make a bad situation worse. I'm sure I'd get dumped, or somebody would. I never ride alone. I have a canister of bear spray, but I don't think that's the answer either. It tells you right on the packaging to know which direction the wind is coming from and avoid getting it in your eyes. How am I supposed to think about which way the wind is blowing when my horse is whirling in circles?" Both Ronnie and Luc understood that was a rhetorical question.

"What's your honest opinion? Do you think there's a problem?" Luc was serious but more for personal than professional reasons. He was starting to care for Ronnie, and he didn't like the idea of her in harm's way.

"Are you uncomfortable riding in Big South Fork?"

"No, not really," Ronnie replied. "There are no trails in urban areas so, if you want to ride, you have to go where the trails are. And where the trails are, that's where the wild things live. I just try to be aware at all times and to take precautions to avoid or minimize encounters. That includes snakes, ticks, chiggers etc. With regard to bears, people here know enough to keep their trashcans secured, to keep their grills wiped down and not to hang bird feeders. Sometimes, new property owners from suburban areas get quite a surprise, finding a bear on their porch and learning the hard way not to hang hummingbird feeders. I've read that bears have an extraordinarily well-developed sense of smell, and they can recognize scent from five miles away," she clarified. "That sugar water is an engraved invitation."

The conversation moved on to other topics and Ronnie asked about Stephanie. She was convinced that the stress in Luc's home life would be ameliorated by involving Stephanie in the project.

"What do you have in mind?" he wanted to know.

"Well, no time like the present," Ronnie said. "What does your schedule look like? What about some weekend soon?"

"I can find a reason to spend a weekend in Texas and figure out when I might get away to do that," Luc told her.

They agreed on a plan where Luc would drop his daughter off in Tennessee for a weekend visit while he continued on to Texas. He was looking forward to spending some time at the ranch, however brief, and hoped both visits would prove equally productive—although he had his doubts about Tennessee.

"So," Stephanie said flatly four days later, minutes into the visit. "Looks like you're my father's latest squeeze."

Ronnie had a feeling Stephanie knew exactly what buttons to push, and she expected Stephanie to try and put her on the defensive. She didn't miss the sarcasm dripping from Stephanie's words, but if the girl expected her to flounder and protest or try to explain, she was going to be disappointed.

Ronnie kept her eyes on the road ahead. She wasn't going to give this punk the satisfaction of getting a rise out of her, knowing that's exactly what the girl was hoping for.

"I'm glad you aren't planning to major in journalism at Colburne," she said matter-of-factly.

"How do you know I'm not?" Stephanie asked angrily.

"Journalists need to be fair and impartial in their reporting," Ronnie replied. "They gain credibility and acclaim through accuracy. You don't have fact one, and you're already jumping to conclusions."

Taking note of Stephanie's sullen silence, Ronnie asked, "Are you hungry?" She was careful to keep an edge out of her voice and to remain upbeat.

"There's a little café up ahead. It's a tourist trap but the food is good, and it's actually one of my favorite places. You might like it."

"I could eat," Stephanie said, flatly. A few minutes later, Ronnie pulled up in front of the Plateau General Store and cut the engine.

"This is a restaurant?" Stephanie's lips curled. "What a dump!"

"It's actually pretty clever marketing," Ronnie countered, her tone determinedly cheerful. "You think it's a hole in the wall, but take a look at the prices. There are just enough actual antiques mixed in with all the repro to make it interesting. They do a great business, and you can't argue with a healthy bottom line."

Ronnie walked to the rear of the store and into The Rusty Rooster Roadside Café. She was sure Stephanie would find the red-and-white tiled floor, the ice-cream-parlor-style wire chairs and the old-fashioned soda counter cute, but Steph trailed behind, her mask of total boredom carefully in place.

Ronnie led the way to the counter and ordered a cheeseburger, fries, and a diet soda. "That's the five-dollar lunch special," she explained. Ignoring her, Stephanie ordered a double bacon cheeseburger, a double order of fries, and a large soda.

"I'll bring it to you," the pert blonde waitress said with a smile.

Stephanie's expression was sullen, but her eyes were wary, and Ronnie guessed that there was, more often than not, a comment about the quantity of food she ordered. Still feeling her way, Ronnie said only, "We'll swing through Jamestown on the way home so you can see the town. JJ's Diner N' Dairy has an ice cream window, so save room for a cone."

"This place sucks! You're stuck in East Bumfuck USA!" was Stephanie's only comment about Jamestown, as they drove slowly down the main street. A sullen sneer pulled the corners of her mouth into a grimace, but she showed slightly more enthusiasm for double-scoop butter pecan a few minutes later, grabbing the cone from Ronnie's hand and starting to lick it without a word of thanks.

Poor Luc! He had a tough row to hoe with this one.

After Ronnie stopped the car in the driveway, she retrieved Stephanie's bag from the rear seat and was dismayed when her guest made no attempt to get out of the vehicle. Refusing to enable the behavior which she was sure was intended to provoke her, she went up the walk, set Stephanie's bag down and unlocked the door.

Stephanie followed grudgingly and, snatching up her overnight bag, she clumped into the cabin and dropped it at her feet.

"What's with the décor?" she asked meanly, looking around. "It looks like a friggin' operating room."

"That's a first impression," Ronnie agreed. "If you look, though, you'll see that everything is a different shade of off-white. Some have yellow tones, some blue, some green, some reddish. To me, it looks clean and open, and I can accessorize with different curtains or pillows or throws to pick up the different tones."

Ronnie picked up Stephanie's bag and led her up the stairs and into a room large enough to accommodate a queen bed. The walls and all of the furniture were in various shades of off white.

"I don't know what your favorite color is yet, but I guessed maybe blue."

The bedspread was a simple coarsely-woven natural-colored cotton. Pillows of all sizes and shapes in myriad shades of blue were artfully arranged against the off-white wooden headboard. A chenille throw in shades of blue and tan was draped across the end of the bed.

Even the pine floor was painted off white, with a sisal rug in a pale neutral tan. The overall effect was very soothing.

A Jack-and-Jill bath served this guest room and a second smaller room just beyond that contained a chair-and-a-half that could open into a twin bed. With its oversized ottoman, it made a comfortable reading chair. Both pieces were slipcovered with faded blue denim. A creamy white wooden chair was pulled up to a matching desk that held a keyboard and a good-sized flat-screen monitor. Bath towels were a rich navy and there was a fat cake of blue soap in a white ironstone dish on the vanity.

Stephanie's lips no longer curled with disdain, but the expression in her eyes was cold and unyielding. The purpose of the weekend was to gain her trust, and Ronnie hoped she was pleased with the accommodations. If she was, Ronnie suspected it would probably be a cold day in Hell before she'd admit it to anyone but herself. She felt a headache developing and resisted the urge to massage her forehead.

"You'll probably want to freshen up or even take a nap," Ronnie suggested. "I thought we'd eat around seven. Is it okay if I throw a couple of steaks on the grill? I'm making just a simple supper—potato salad, corn on the cob, blueberry pie for dessert. I thought we could have a drink on the porch first. I usually feed the horses around five on weekends, if you want to come along and meet them."

When five o'clock rolled around, and Stephanie hadn't reappeared, Ronnie set out for the barn. She saw one of the curtains move in the upstairs window and guessed that Stephanie was watching. At quarter to six, Ronnie called up the stairs.

"Steph? How about a drink on the porch?" She carried an off-white tray with a glass of Merlot for herself, and a matching stemmed glass with cranberry juice for her guest. A small blue plate held toasted bagel rounds and a wedge of Brie.

Ronnie hadn't thought about where Stephanie would sit. Two off-white Adirondack chairs faced a porch swing, but she'd never fit into a chair. Ronnie wondered how much the girl actually weighed. It must be somewhere around three hundred pounds, all of it unhealthy pasty rolls. Her legs had no discernible shape; they were like tree trunks. *Her thighs are thicker than my waist.* She'd noticed the way Stephanie's ankles puffed over the tops of men's running shoes and surmised that women's shoes probably weren't wide enough. The poor girl was only fourteen. Luc was right; she was killing herself.

A screech snapped Ronnie out of her reverie and she looked up to see Purrl leap off the swing and fly into the house in a blur.

"What the fuck?" Stephanie snarled. "Even your damn cat's white! How the hell was I supposed to see her on that white cushion?"

Ignoring her ugly outburst, Ronnie said mildly, "She was asleep, so you probably didn't notice that her eyes are two different colors. One's blue, and one's yellow. She's actually purebred; the breed is called Odd-Eyed White. My partner, Andee, loves puns, so I thought her name P-u-r-r-l would be a good play on the words purr and pearl."

Stephanie rudely rolled her eyes.

"You'll meet Andee tomorrow," Ronnie promised. "And Rickie, my other partner. You'll meet her, too, if we can catch up with her."

"What's the deal with all the boys' names?" Stephanie demanded. "Is that another of your stupid word games?"

"Nope." Ronnie took a sip of her drink. She set the glass down, spread some Brie on a bagel, and held it out to Steph, who was clearly torn between wanting to refuse anything Ronnie offered and eating.

Stephanie snatched it, stuffing the whole thing in her mouth, chewing twice and swallowing.

"Andee is a nickname for Andrea," Ronnie explained, making small talk to fill the awkward silence. "Rickie is short for Erica, and my name is Veronica, which I've never liked. Ronnie suits me so much better, don't you think?" Her question was rhetorical since she didn't expect to hold a conversation. It was pretty clear that she'd be doing all the heavy lifting. She made a mental note to tell Andee about that double entendre. It was going to be a *long* weekend, at this rate.

"I love the weather here in Tennessee," she offered. "There are such long springs and falls that you can eat outside most of the time. I wrapped corn in foil and put it on the grill a while ago, so it should be just about done. I made the potato salad this morning, now all I have to do is grill the steaks. Medium rare good for you?"

Dinner was delicious, and they both did justice to it. Stephanie reached out and helped herself to a second huge piece of blueberry pie without asking. After she'd gulped it down, she stood abruptly, threw her napkin on the table, and retreated up the stairs without offering to help clean up.

An hour later, Ronnie was curled in a corner of the couch, wine glass in hand, and Purrl pressed companionably against her side. She felt her phone vibrate in her pocket and drew it out, then read Luc's text.

—You doing ok? —

—Still standing— she texted back.

The rest of the weekend passed in the same vein. Stephanie continued to be as disagreeable as possible, and Ronnie did her best to maintain her equanimity. She made no mention of Stephanie's appalling bulk or her dreadful mud-colored size thirty-four polyester pants and the muu-muu-like top, her fingernails bitten to the point of bleeding, her gray skin tone, or her lank, thin hair.

On Sunday morning, she made pancakes with the very last of the blueberries she'd frozen the previous year.

"Anyone who thinks berry picking is romantic has never been berry picking," she said, conversationally. "It's always too hot and too buggy when the berries are ripe."

"Worth it, though!" She sighed. "I have to resort to store-bought berries until mine are ripe."

Stephanie scowled at her plate. Ronnie didn't rag on her though, persisting in treating the girl with what Stephanie understood on some level, but was too young yet to recognize, as respect.

This trip was just to set the hook, to give Stephanie a look at the way things could be and let her process it, and perhaps to engage her interest in the project. Luc would be spending quite a bit of time in Tennessee in the next couple of years, and it would certainly lessen the stress if his daughter was on board.

Her plan was to ask Rickie to be at work for a short while on Sunday morning so Steph could see their office and meet them all. Then she and Steph would meet Andee in Emery Pond for a tour of the property. The girl was too big and heavy to ride on an ATV, but Andee had a full-size king-cab 4WD pickup, which Ronnie had borrowed for the weekend. She herself drove a silver mid-size SUV, but Luc had warned her that Stephanie was too large for the passenger seat. She thought he surely was exaggerating, but she and Andee had traded vehicles on Friday afternoon, just in case.

"You sit up front, Steph, so you'll get a good view," she offered after their office visit. She hopped into the back with a cooler containing a picnic lunch for the three of them and a sheaf of papers with the property's boundary map and preliminary sketches of the proposed site plan.

Luc had arrived back in Crossville ahead of schedule, his flight time and fuel consumption aided by a strong tailwind. His plane was chocked when they had pulled in, but he was nowhere to be seen. He must have gone into the terminal to use the men's room, Ronnie figured.

She set Steph's bag down and turned to her.

"I guess this is so long, for now. I hope you'll come back for a visit again soon." She meant it sincerely. This weekend was a challenge unlike any other, but Luc had the best chance of getting through to the girl here in neutral territory.

"Don't get your hopes up," Stephanie snarled. They waited for several uncomfortable minutes.

Stephanie stood stiffly on the tarmac, keeping her back to Ronnie and making it abundantly clear that any further attempts at polite chitchat were unwelcome.

Ronnie realized that Stephanie was too ungainly to clamber into the aircraft unassisted, although she noted that the fuselage had double aft doors for passenger convenience and comfort. She assumed that steps would unfold once Luc returned and unlocked it. A few weeks earlier, he mentioned a one-sixth share in a leased six-seat twin-engine. A few days ago, he told her that Steph could no longer sit in the co-pilot's right seat and, in fact, couldn't sit in the comfortable club seating mid-cabin. The two rear seats were removable so the craft could be reconfigured to accommodate extra baggage and, when Luc used the plane accompanied by his daughter, a bench seat could be slid in temporarily on the rails. Unfortunately, while Luc flew, Stephanie sprawled there, immersing herself in her own activities and feigning disinterest in flight operations.

"Hey, Steph. Hey, Ronnie," Luc greeted them with a jaunty wave as he approached the pair. "You know, I found out there's a very nice little county airport in Oneida, with a 5500-foot runway that can take small jets. I thought we'd land there next time we come."

"The next time *you* come," Stephanie challenged. Ronnie's heart sank, and she resisted a glance at Luc. *I've made such an effort to win Stephanie's approval, and it hasn't made much of a difference.*

"I'm glad you're going to be helping out with the Emery Pond project," Luc addressed Stephanie as if he hadn't heard her snide remark. "Ronnie can start sending you the data, and I'll help you set up a spreadsheet to keep track of the land purchases."

Stephanie was horrified when she'd first heard about her father's plans to dump her in Tennessee. She figured he had a girlfriend in Texas and didn't want her tagging along. When she received Ronnie's invitation, she saw at once that the weekend had potential; it might be a lot more fun than staying home and baiting her mother. Stephanie craved her father's approval and had no intention of sharing him, not if she could help it. Although there were no overt indications, it was clear that Ronnie was now someone special in his life. *This could be trouble.*

It was a gift to escape her mother's disappointment and disinterest, but it was only for two days, and now Stephanie was on her way back. It was obvious that she didn't fit in anywhere, not in Virginia, not in Texas and, now, not in Tennessee. She wanted to lash out at them all, the smart, thin, attractive people who made her feel so repulsive and unwanted.

Luc was attuned to Stephanie's moods and had warned Ronnie before their arrival what to expect. His daughter was utterly miserable, and she tried to conceal her despair with obnoxious behavior. Ronnie was right; the best way to win her over was to get her involved, and the carrot he was holding out was time spent with him.

"Call you later," he mouthed to Ronnie, rolling his eyes, as Stephanie stomped toward the plane without acknowledging Ronnie or thanking her for her hospitality.

Then, a few minutes later, they were gone.

Chapter Eight

The next month passed quickly and uneventfully. One sunny Saturday morning, Mindy's houseguest, Caroline Jamieson, pulled on her sweatpants and an old flannel shirt and shoved her feet into muck shoes, thinking she'd feed the horses and then surprise her hostess with a big breakfast. She'd brushed her teeth but hadn't combed her hair, pulling it up into a messy topknot, knowing she wouldn't encounter anyone but a barn cat or two.

She had gotten in late the night before from North Carolina and, tired as she was, she found herself unable to sleep. She'd fallen into an uneasy slumber but awoke again as soon as the sun was over the horizon. The grass was soaked with dew and tickled her bare ankles when she stepped off the porch steps and started for the barn; she should have thought to pull on a pair of socks. *This is some getup*, she laughed to herself. *But when was the last time a horse had said, Jeez, you look so awful I've lost my appetite!*

Morning feeds were neatly stacked in four small buckets inside the feed box. Mindy didn't stall her horses, and the two McCurdys knew the routine. They each hurried into their own stall and waited expectantly. Caroline's two Walkers were outside in the guest paddocks, browsing desultorily through clumps of grass along the lower edge of the fence while they awaited more serious sustenance.

"Hey, you guys," Caroline called softly. They didn't waste any time, rushing into the two empty stalls. She turned toward them and nearly dropped the buckets when she saw a shadowy figure under the stairs that led up to the hayloft.

"What the hell?" she swore. She wasn't actually frightened—yet—but this unexpected development was certainly startling. Instinctively, she reached for a long-handled shovel and gripped the shaft. It wasn't much of a weapon, but it was all she had if she needed it. There was a man, slumped on a bale of straw stowed under the stairs. Without taking her eyes off the figure, she stepped slowly backward until she reached the big sliding doors and, with her foot, pushed them farther apart. When the sunlight penetrated the gloom at the back of the barn, she saw that it was not a man but—what? A very large woman, she thought, dressed in such drab, shapeless clothes it was hard to tell if the figure was a man or a woman.

She approached the person, still gripping the shovel and discovered, when she was a few feet away, that it was female but not a woman. It was a girl, an overly obese teenaged girl, her tear-streaked face a mask of misery.

"Are you hurt?" Caroline asked softly. "Do you need help?"

Deep, visceral sobs racked the girl's body, and she buried her face in her hands. Caroline swiftly dumped grain into the waiting horses' feeders and then sat on the straw bale next to her. Although she was clearly an unwelcome intruder, instinct developed from long experience with distraught animals told her that the visitor needed human comfort. Caroline took one of the girl's hands in both of hers and asked gently, "What's your name?"

The girl shook her head violently from side to side, her face still covered.

"Do you live around here?" Caroline stroked her hand and waited while she continued to sob. When the sobs finally subsided to sniffles, she put her arm around the girl's massive shoulders and stroked her arm with a repetitive circular motion, just as she would attempt to calm a distressed dog, cat, or horse.

"My name is Caroline," she offered. "I live in North Carolina, but I'm visiting my friend, Mindy. Two of the horses are hers, and those two are mine."

The girl raised her head and looked at Caroline through reddened eyes that were almost swollen shut.

"Can you tell me your name?" Caroline asked again. She waited.

"Stuvanuh."

She'd gotten an answer, but Caroline had no idea what the girl had just said. She tried again. "Do you live nearby?"

"In Vuginya." The girl's nasal passages were so swollen Caroline could hardly make out the words, but then she put it together.

This was Stephanie, Ronnie's houseguest, the problem daughter of the investor from Virginia. She'd heard bits and pieces from Mindy over the past couple of months. Ronnie was one of the kindest, most sensitive, most considerate people Caroline knew. She couldn't imagine what had happened to send her guest fleeing while it was still dark and taking refuge in a neighboring barn.

"I'd like to hear what has you so upset, but you must be hungry. I know I am. Why don't we go into the house and fix ourselves some breakfast?"

A moment later, she pointed out the half bath just off the kitchen and suggested that Stephanie might like to splash some water on her face to freshen up. Thankfully, Mindy had an on-demand coffeemaker sitting on the counter, and within seconds she had a cup of scalding coffee in her hand. She inhaled gratefully, then sipped. She could hear the water running in the bathroom and found Ronnie's cell phone listed with the frequently-called numbers taped to the inside of a cabinet door. She quickly sent a text, telling her that Stephanie was at Mindy's and not to worry.

"I love to cook," she told Stephanie when the girl emerged. "I brought a recipe for pumpkin pancakes that I wanted to make for Mindy. I made the batter last night."

She knew her way around Mindy's kitchen, pulling an electric griddle out of the pantry and plugging it in. She opened a box of breakfast sausage, arranged the links on a paper plate, and got those going in the microwave. She placed a mug of cocoa on a pretty placemat in front of Stephanie and was pleased to see her wrap her hands around it, drawing comfort from the warmth.

Caroline dropped a big handful of grated cheddar into the frying pan and expertly scrambled it with some eggs. Within minutes, she'd placed a generous scoop of cheese eggs on a plate with two links of sausage and three silver-dollar sized pancakes. She poured warmed syrup into a small pitcher and set it within Stephanie's reach.

"My cousin lives in Vermont and keeps me supplied with real maple syrup. I visit Mindy a lot, so I always bring her some. Least I can do." They ate in silence for a few minutes, and then Caroline asked, "Are you mad at Ronnie?"

Stephanie's face crumpled momentarily, but then her head snapped up, and she glared at Caroline. "I fucking hate her!"

Caroline was speechless.

The kitchen was silent until she heard the shower start running upstairs. Mindy was up. She didn't have a lot of time. In a moment of inspiration, she said slowly, "You don't hate Ronnie. You hate yourself. Am I right?" Her eyes were glued to Stephanie's face, trying to gauge her reaction.

Their eyes locked, and Caroline continued, "You used to be happy when you were a family before the divorce. Then the bottom fell out of your world, and it got a whole lot worse when your mother remarried and got involved in a whole new life that didn't include you.

"Right so far?" She was gentle but persistent.

"Your father tried to make it up to you, but you were angry and thought he'd let it happen, so you decided to punish him," she guessed. "If they were a problem for you, you decided to be a bigger problem for both of your parents."

Stephanie's eyes filled, and Caroline saw her lower lip start to quiver.

"You controlled the one thing you had control over—your body. When you gained all that weight, you got their attention. How am I doing?"

The tears running down Stephanie's face told her she'd hit the nail on the head. Mindy had heard the whole story from Ronnie, and Caroline had heard it from Mindy. She flicked her eyes toward the doorway and saw Mindy standing there, just out of Stephanie's line of sight.

"But now you're totally miserable, and you don't know how to get out of it." She reached across the table and took Stephanie's hand again. "Will you let me help you?" she asked.

"Well, who's this?" Mindy asked, crossing the kitchen and pouring a cup of coffee for herself. Caroline made the introduction.

"Stephanie, this is my friend, Melinda Morrison-Myers."

"Steph's visiting Ronnie, but things aren't going all that well, so she took a little break and came over here to see the horses," she explained, ostensibly for Mindy's benefit.

"Does Ronnie know where you are?"

When Stephanie's expression hardened, Caroline realized immediately that Mindy had said exactly the wrong thing.

She quickly changed tack. "Was Ronnie mean to you?"

"N…n…n…*no*," Stephanie wailed.

Bingo!

"I had a surprise visitor the other morning," Mindy told her friend, Sara, a few days later as they gaited companionably, side by side, riding down Tar Kiln, a five-mile stretch of level woods road. Reaching the end, they'd turn left on the O&W and would tie up at one of their favorite lunch stops, a huge boulder jutting out into the North White Oak Creek. A tree had fallen conveniently across the rock and served very well as a lunch log.

"Yeah?" Sara turned to face Mindy, her eyebrows raised with interest.

"You know the investors from Virginia I told you about? One of them has a teenage daughter who is so heavy it's unhealthy. He's divorced, with joint custody, so he's a single parent part of the time. The mother doesn't give the kid the time of day, and Ronnie has taken it upon herself to befriend the girl. She hasn't admitted it to herself yet, I don't think, but I get the feeling she's fallen hard for him—Luc—and she knows Stephanie's an important part of his life."

"How's that going, the investor thing?" Sara waited for an update.

"So, anyway," Mindy continued, "Ronnie thought she could make some headway with this girl—I think she's fourteen or fifteen. She's been inviting her to come and stay with her for the weekend. Last weekend was the second visit, and it blew up in Ronnie's face. The kid ran away and ended up hiding in my barn. Caroline was here from North Carolina and found her when she went out early to feed the horses. Hiding under the stairs, the kid scared the crap out of her."

"She didn't get far," Sara observed. "You're only—what?—a couple of hundred yards through the woods?"

"I don't think she wanted to get far," Mindy told her. "It's the old cry for help, know what I mean?"

"So, what happened?" Sara asked, fascinated.

"Caro brought her in and fixed her some breakfast. She broke down and poured out her tale of woe. You have to feel sorry for her. I think she stuffs herself to punish her parents."

"Ronnie's probably wishing she'd never opened that can of worms." Sara obviously didn't envy Ronnie's rocky relationship with Stephanie Deschaines.

"I'm not so sure about that. She's pretty buttoned up, so she hasn't said anything but—stay tuned." Mindy laughed. "I think she's fallen hard for Luc!"

Sara felt sorry for Stephanie Deschaines. She knew what it was like to be the proverbial round peg in a square hole. She'd grown up in this small, rural town. She loved her family with their country ways, their caring neighbors and friends—the gentle people she knew who were first outraged, then saddened, then submissive as they were dispossessed when the new national park was created. They knew there was no way to 'fight city hall.' Unlike many of her peers who had no more than a high-school education and never traveled far from Fentress County, Sara had been a devoted student and the first in her family to attend the university on a full scholarship. Four years in Knoxville provided a wealth of new experiences and friendships. By the time she graduated, she was more polished and far more sophisticated than she would have been otherwise. Now, she felt like she had dual citizenship, still a 'local' but readily accepted by the influx of 'horse people' who were, for the most part, well-educated and often wealthy.

She'd been Sarah Bethany Blevans when she'd arrived at college, named after both of her grandmothers. "Sarah Beth, why don't you spell it S-a-r-a," her roommate suggested during her sophomore year, "and lose the 'Beth' altogether." Sarah valued tradition but loved the idea of a more contemporary name, and Megan had assured her this was a good compromise.

Like most graduating seniors, Sarah had attended several job fairs. After several grueling interviews, she was pleased to be hired as an administrative assistant in a large media group. She was ready to spread her wings and see the world.

After the novelty wore off, she found that Chicago terrified her and left her lonely and overwhelmed. She stuck it out for two long years and then, when her father's emphysema became debilitating, she gave up her fledgling career and returned to Tennessee to help care for him until his death eight months later.

She knew she'd never return to Chicago, or live in any large city for that matter, and the decision made itself to stay in her beloved home place.

Sara was computer savvy and had pitched an online position as a contributing editor for the group's lucrative horse magazines. Telecommuting, with a laptop balanced on her knees while her father slept, allowed her to work from home and support herself.

She and her sister spelled each other in the sickroom, and she used her free time to explore the network of trails in the park.

"How could you?" her mother demanded when she heard Sara hanging her jacket in the mudroom one afternoon. Her voice was shaking, her face was ashen and her lips tight. Sara saw that her mother was clutching a magazine, her hand trembling.

"What is it?" Wordlessly, her mother handed it to her, and Sara recognized the familiar logo of *Ride! Magazine*. Splashed across the cover were the words 'Tennessee Trailriding Adventure: Exploring Big South Fork.'

Tears rolled down her mother's face. "This will kill your daddy; we cain't let him see this! I've never been so ashamed of you!" she hissed.

Sara was stricken. "Ma..." Her voice broke, and tears filled her eyes. "I thought you understood. This is my job!"

Sara had parlayed her experiences into a number of articles that appeared in issue after issue. She was thrilled to see her name in print and thrilled with the raise she'd received after the six-month mark, but she felt like a traitor in many ways. She rationalized that, in this case, the park was a good thing because it allowed her to live at home at a time when she was needed and still make a decent living. It also led to something else special.

She remembered the first time she'd met Jon, her lover. He'd been overseeing a group of volunteers.

She'd planned to write an article on trail maintenance, and, while she felt guilty committing most of a day, she needed to get some good pictures to go with it.

The day hadn't gotten off to a good start and went downhill as she moved backward to widen her angle and stepped into a hole, twisting her ankle. Great, she thought, as a tall man in uniform approached. *Here comes Ricky Ranger. Wouldn't ya' just know it?*

He held out his hand to steady her as she attempted to put weight on the injured ankle. "I don't think it's broken," he said. It's probably a mild sprain."

"No shit, Sherlock!" she snapped. "What was your first clue?"

Ignoring the outburst, he simply said, "Jonathan Wood."

She looked up into his weathered face and the kindest brown eyes she'd ever seen and promptly burst into tears.

It hadn't taken long for her and Jon to fall in love. They were kindred spirits and soul mates, and the physical attraction was still almost unquenchable. Over the next two years, their relationship grew and deepened. Both knew—Sara, especially—that their association would be viewed poorly both by her family and friends, most of who were dead set on never having anything to do with the park. Park ranger was the only job Jon had ever held. He'd double majored in wildlife biology and resource conservation at the university in Missoula.

Growing up in Montana, he'd spent his life outdoors and wanted nothing more. He'd come to Tennessee soon after the Big South Fork National River and Recreation Area was turned over to the National Park Service. He thought it would be exciting to be part of the first team of park rangers to manage such spectacular resources and knew the number of visitors would be sparse until the park gained some visibility. He had intended to stay for only a few years, adding to his résumé and watching for openings in larger parks, always intending to go back to the part of the country he loved best. His goal was a coveted posting to Yellowstone. Then he'd met Sara, and everything had changed.

Fending off her mother was an ongoing battle, more so as birthdays passed and Sara turned twenty-five, then twenty-six, then twenty-seven, with the dreaded *Big 3-0* as her mother's looming point of no return.

"Ma!" Sara scolded, "No one's considered an old maid anymore! I'm fine!"

It was a lot easier to deflect her mother's interest in her social life when she stopped living at home. She'd discovered that she could keep expenses to a minimum by becoming a professional house sitter and with the constant moving around it was that much easier to escape her mother's scrutiny.

The equestrian communities provided a pool of clients, booking her time months in advance as the residents in Split Rock and Seven Oaks traveled frequently. Her love of animals served her well, and she thoroughly enjoyed the various cats, dogs, birds, horses, and mules entrusted to her care. More importantly, as a knowledgeable horse owner herself, she was well equipped to assess her charges for illness or injury.

She discovered a wealth of material for articles and had become a prolific contributor to several equine publications, keeping her laptop close at hand and working wherever and whenever she chose. That's how she'd met Mindy, as a matter of fact.

Several years ago, she had been riding part of the White Oak trail, and just decided to do a feature on what trail riders carried in their saddlebags—and what they should carry. There was no one at the hitching rails when she arrived at the White Oak Overlook. After tying up her mount with the sturdy nylon lead rope that had been knotted around his neck, she unclipped the bit hangers and removed the bit from his halter/bridle. She stripped off her gloves and pulled out her lunch sack. Just then, a woman on a sturdy bay horse came into view.

"Hey," she greeted Sara. "Nice day!"

"It sure is," Sara agreed. "I'm Sara Blevans. I'm a writer and thinking about doing an article about what riders carry in their saddlebags. I was just noticing yours."

"Mindy Morrison-Myers. They're new. Mine are only a couple months old as I don't really need them, but when I saw them at the local tack shop, I had to have them. Look, the bags come off, and this piece is backed with neoprene so you can hose the sweat off it instead of having the backside of your bags get grungier and grungier."

"Are you going to eat lunch?" Sara asked. "Any chance you could bring them and let me have a look at what all is inside?"

"Sure, but you carry them," Mindy agreed with a straight face but then winked. "Just kidding!"

The two women climbed the steep wooden stairs to the overlook, sat on a flat rock in the shade, and unwrapped their sandwiches. Between bites, Mindy pulled items out of her bags.

"Medical kit for horses and humans. A syringe of antispasmodic/painkiller in case you have a colic or a horse ties up while you're on the backside of beyond. If you can't inject it intravenously, pull the needle off, and plunge it into his mouth; the mucus membranes will absorb it pretty quickly."

Sara nodded, and Mindy continued, "Electrolyte paste. Coagulant. Aspirin. Antacids. Benedryl. Visine. Tweezers. I've got everything in here but a CT scanner!" She held up an object, and Sara laughed.

"Now that I recognize—biodegradable campers' toilet paper!"

"Tie wraps," Mindy continued, laying one object after another on the flat rock. "Nylon line, double-ended snaps for tack repair, compass, signal mirror, double-chambered survival whistle, waterproof matches, and magnesium fire starter. Space blanket. Light sticks. All items I hope never to need. Bear spray."

"Why would you carry bear spray?" Sara was startled. "Have you ever seen a bear?"

"Oh, I didn't mean me, personally," Mindy said. "I don't carry bear spray, but I thought your readership was national, and riders in western states like Montana, Wyoming, and Idaho are advised to carry it because that's Grizzly country."

"Right." Sara bit her lip, deep in thought. She had the article half-written in her head.

"You should probably make a list." Mindy scrabbled in one of the saddlebags and produced a small plastic bag containing a pen and several strips of surveyor's tape. She explained, "In case you get separated or need to leave a message for other riders, write on a strip of fluorescent tape and tie it to a branch."

"Never mind," she ordered. "Here, give me your email address." She told Sara she'd make a list of all the items as soon as she got home and would email it to her.

"Now you can relax and enjoy your ride. Which way are you headed?" The two women exchanged phone numbers, each agreeing they'd like to ride together again.

That was four years ago, and they had become fast friends, despite the differences in their backgrounds and more than a few years between their ages. Mindy was invited to many meals in Sara's mother's kitchen and had gotten to know her family well. She had asked Sara several times over the years why she didn't date, wasn't in a relationship, had never married.

"Don't you ever want kids?" Mindy had asked once.

Sara had become adept at compartmentalizing and kept her relationship with Jon from everyone, including her mother, her sisters, and her friends. She was, literally, 'sleeping with the enemy.' House sitting turned out to be a perfect cover because when Jon visited, no one knew whether he was seeing Sara or had stopped by for the homeowner.

For his part, Jon was considered one of the area's most eligible bachelors, and his family and friends occasionally still tried to introduce him to suitable prospects. For a time, his co-workers had wondered if he was gay, but there had been no evidence to support it, and he made a point of being seen every now and then with a companion who went along with the ruse.

With his twenty years in, Sara and Jon talked endlessly about the day when they would finally marry, and she would no longer have to straddle the stream, with one foot on either side. Now, at forty-one, Jon was largely off the hook. He would suffer a huge financial hit by taking early voluntary retirement, but it was eminently clear that Sara's family would never accept him as long as he was associated with the park, and he had no qualms about supporting a wife and family with his carpentry skills. It would be a relief to retire, marry Sara and settle down in a little cabin tucked into the woods, one he'd built himself, with a couple of horses, a couple of cats, a dog or two, and a vegetable garden.

During the time she'd lived at home, Sara and her mother had an unspoken truce. Her mother was sensible enough to see that Sara had essentially taken lemons and made lemonade. When Sara's articles appeared in various magazines, her mother put them in her room and never said another word.

Sometimes she felt like she was in a parallel universe and wondered if Rickie felt the same, pulled in two directions. Rickie was two years ahead of her in school, so they didn't travel in the same circles, but they'd known each other, essentially, all their lives. Their situations were so similar; both were small-town girls from local families. The same guidance counselor had touched both their lives, encouraging both of them and several other students who showed promise during her thirty-year career, to leave home and pursue higher education.

Sara had spent four years on the university's main campus in Knoxville. Only an hour and forty-five minutes from home but a world away, she was exposed to people, ideas, and opportunities that would have been totally beyond her reach if she'd remained in Jamestown. The time she'd spent in Chicago working in a high-profile and high-powered agency had provided a sophistication that only life in a big city could produce.

Rickie had been only two hours away in Nashville. She was the first in her family to contemplate earning more than a high school diploma and, overwhelmed, she had lobbied for a smaller school in Cookeville, a town she was familiar with and one much closer to home.

"The whole point, my dear, is to leave the known and embrace the unknown; you must learn to spread your wings," Mrs. Tolliver told her, quietly and firmly.

Once they'd accepted the idea, Rickie's parents insisted on a Christian college, so the guidance counselor wisely recommended Bartlett University and recruited scholarship funds. Rickie's roommate, a young woman from Dyersburg, in the western part of the state, was adventurous and fun-loving. The two were soon inseparable, studying hard and playing hard. Nashville was a veritable feast, and they didn't miss many meals.

It was at Vortex that Rickie met Gregory Ahlers, a second-year medical student at Valliant University. It was purely coincidence that they were in the same place at the same time. Greg rarely had time to socialize but had been persuaded to attend a friend's surprise birthday party.

"An hour, man, one lousy hour," his lab partner had persisted.

When he arrived, Greg's attention was riveted by the girl standing at the railing of the rooftop restaurant, laughing, a glass of ginger ale in her hand, backlit by the setting sun against the city skyline.

When Rickie eventually met Greg's mother, she was totally overwhelmed. Pamela Ahlers was unfailingly kind, but, in her presence, Rickie felt like the proverbial 'little nobody.' When Greg's relationship with Rickie seemed to be getting serious, Pamela said she had two choices; she could fight it and hope he would eventually lose interest or she could accept it and do her best to mold Erica Hull into the wife Greg would need and the daughter-in-law she would want.

When Greg graduated from medical school, Rickie had one year of college remaining. He rented an apartment in a complex which, while price-y, was convenient to both Valliant and Bartlett and Rickie moved in with him for her senior year. She continued her work-study program as an administrative assistant in Bartlett's admissions office to defray the cost of on-campus housing, which her parents insisted on. She was assigned to a suite with three roommates she barely knew who were thrilled to have one less body in residence. Greg took a one-year internship at Valliant, earning a pittance. It was his mother who covered the couple's rent, eager to smooth the path for her son and recognizing that he intended to marry Rickie as soon as she graduated.

Although Pamela Ahlers longed for the large New York wedding she'd dreamed of for him, she astutely saw it was important to Rickie's family for the ceremony to be held in Jamestown and to be a simple celebration that they could afford. What would come after was more important to her when Greg began a surgical residency in New York, and he and his bride moved to Manhattan.

Now, years later, Sara and Rickie were back where they had come from, but there was no vestige of a resemblance to the shy, naïve teenagers who had left home for the first time. In Rickie's case, the veneer she'd acquired during her years in Manhattan stood her in good stead in the profession that suited her like a hand in a glove, selling horse properties to horse people *from away.*

For the past several years, Rickie had been sustained by a platonic relationship with a real estate appraiser she'd met when the national realtors association held their annual convention in Atlanta. The convention rotated between Atlanta in the east and Denver in the west, and Rickie attended each year, wherever it was held. Chris Wilson didn't have the luxury of travel. His wife had been diagnosed early in their marriage with Multiple Sclerosis and was now confined to a wheelchair.

He wasn't a cheater, wasn't looking for an affair when he took the last empty seat next to Rickie, hurrying into the crowded auditorium just as the doors were closing. And Rickie, a widow since she was twenty-seven, was sure she could never love again and didn't plan to. But they had much in common, enjoyed each other's company briefly whenever she happened to be in Atlanta.

Rickie's standards were high, and she would never do anything she had to be ashamed of. It was a relief to her that they both understood there would never be more than that, and Chris never pressured her for more. He was a thoroughly honorable man, a trait she valued and admired in him. Although she felt lonely from time to time, she had yet to meet someone who touched her heart the way Greg had.

Rickie knew Chris would not, could not, leave his wife, and she didn't want him to. After that first meeting, Rickie and Chris always sat together during seminars and would duck out at lunchtime to eat together. The first year, Chris mischievously swapped place cards at the large round tables so they could sit together at dinner but, after that, both felt they didn't want to spend time making small talk with strangers and near-strangers, so they always found a little out-of-the-way place and caught each other up on what had occurred in their respective lives. They enjoyed what little time they could have together, and each derived an inexplicable measure of comfort from the other.

But, at the end of the evening, when Chris walked to her hotel room before returning home, he always said, "It's so good to see you, Rickie," and stepped away.

Rickie didn't communicate with Chris between visits—didn't call or email, didn't text or send him pictures. Chris never made any attempt to contact her either, but the light in his eyes told her how glad he always was to see her. If circumstances had been different, would she have pursued a relationship? Probably not. He was just one of her favorite people.

Chapter Nine

Another few weeks flew by following Stephanie's disastrous second visit. Most of the parcels needed to put the Emery Pond project together had been identified, and quiet sales consummated. Luc was traveling extensively while Chip spent more and more time taking over for his father.

"Have you seen this?" Geri asked that morning, hearing Rickie at the door. Looking up, she saw Rickie juggling an armful of file folders. She jumped up and rushed over to grab them before the whole stack slid to the floor, and each of them disgorged its contents.

“Thanks!" Rickie said. "Just put them on my desk. Have I gotten any packages?"

"Yep," Geri said. "A big flat box was delivered this morning. I put it outside in my car because you said you didn't want anyone to see it."

"Oh, good! Thanks. It's Ronnie's birthday present," Rickie confided. "When I placed the order, I was having it delivered to my house, but it's been back-ordered for weeks, so I changed the shipping address. Talk about getting here in the nick of time. I was afraid I'd have to put a picture in the box and wrap that. I've got the wrapping paper and ribbon under the seat in my car. I'll go get it. You can stand guard while I do it." A few minutes later, she was back.

"What did you get her?" Geri asked. Rickie slit the top of the box and drew out the gift, a cashmere bathrobe in a classic wrap style. Geri had never seen a robe as elegant. "Oh, it's great," she exclaimed. "The color is fabulous!"

"Yeah, I thought so," Rickie agreed. "It's such a deep burgundy, you'd call it Merlot. Once I saw it, there was no going back, but it was so expensive, we all had to chip in. Forty is a big birthday, and it deserves a big gift!"

"She got flowers already this morning," Geri told her. "The florist guy and the delivery guy came at the same time. I put them in her office."

Rickie's eyebrows rose, peeking into Ronnie's office. "Oh! Beautiful! I wonder who they're from." She more than wondered, Geri could tell that she was dying of curiosity. "They're probably from Luc," Rickie guessed.

"They better not be from that rat bastard," she muttered.

"What rat bastard?" Geri was agog.

"Here, put your finger on this," Rickie ordered, ignoring her question. She re-folded the robe and laid it in a nest of tissue paper almost the same color. She carefully wrapped the box in shiny foil paper the same deep Merlot and tied it with a wide ribbon the exact same shade. She bent the wire-reinforced ribbon and fluffed it until it was full and lush.

"Can you hide this in your car again?" she asked. "You can drop it off at the house when you pick up the cake."

A surprise party had been in the works for the past month. Jackie would lure Ronnie to one of her listings, on the pretext of needing her to take a look at something and get her take as to how to market the property. The cabin was vacant but fully stocked so+ there were plenty of dishes, glasses, and silverware. Andee and Jackie had already decorated with streamers and balloons and set up a music player with a careful selection of songs. The owners were friends of Andee's and had readily agreed when she told them she needed a venue for a surprise party.

Andee came in just then and laid the mail on Geri's desk.

"Holy crap! What's this?" She stared at the computer screen and then burst out laughing. "Oh, God! You can't fix stupid!"

"That's what I was trying to tell you about when you came in," Geri told Rickie. "Marcia listed Rennell and this is her lead photo. Our directional sign is clearly visible in her picture; can you imagine not cropping it out? Oh, too funny!"

"She's pathetic!" Rickie agreed.

"Why would anyone list with her?" Jackie demanded, but they all knew it was yet-another rhetorical question where Marcia was concerned. "I just don't get it."

Suddenly, Andee pointed to the floral arrangement in Ronnie's office.

"Who are those from?" Without waiting for an answer, she rushed past Rickie, plucked the card out of the plastic holder, and opened the envelope. "What? It's not sealed!"

"I didn't say anything," Rickie protested.

"You didn't have to, I saw the look on your face, but I can't stand it!"

"CW and Julia," Andee announced, nodding in approval.

"Geri, can you take these with you? They'll make a gorgeous centerpiece, and it will be fun to watch Ronnie getting more and more morose when it looks like no one but us remembered her birthday." She grinned wickedly.

They had made plans to take Ronnie to dinner at Vermillion, her favorite local restaurant, but each had made a phony excuse at the last minute, leaving Ronnie at loose ends and having no reason not to accompany Jackie.

Ronnie was silent during the fifteen-minute drive to Split Rock, staring out the window.

"You okay?" Jackie ventured. "Today's your birthday, right?" Ronnie nodded but didn't respond.

"You get any presents?" Jackie persisted.

"The usual. My mother always sends me a card with a check. That came a couple of days ago."

"Do you have any brothers or sisters?"

"Yeah." Ronnie sighed. "I have a sister. She sent me a gift card to her favorite store. I guess I'll get some ragg socks; mine are on their last legs." She giggled in spite of herself. "So to speak. Andee and Rickie and I always have dinner together on our birthdays and exchange gifts, but today got all screwed up. We were going to Vermillion, but they both had to cancel. I love that place, just walking up to that red door always makes me feel good. Oh, well. I'm a big girl, I won't starve, and it doesn't matter whether I get presents today or tomorrow." She sighed again.

"Where does your sister live? If you don't mind me being nosy?" Jackie asked. "Growing up in such a small town, other peoples' life stories have always intrigued me."

"Seattle," Ronnie said, flatly. "Her husband is a doctor at the medical center affiliated with the university. He's a urologist. Actually, he's a surgeon with a specialty in urology. It's a teaching hospital, so he puts in long hours, but he brings in big bucks. Naturally, they live in the nicest house in the best neighborhood and have the cutest kids."

"Does your mother live in Seattle, too?" Jackie asked.

"Yes," Ronnie replied. "Well, Seattle area, more accurately. She lives in Port Orchard, about thirteen miles from the city, on the coast."

"What about your father? Is he still alive?"

"He and my mother have been—well, not separated exactly. I guess you'd call it still married but living apart. He lives on Bainbridge Island in Puget Sound. It's not far; you just have to take the ferry from Seattle. It's about a forty-five-minute ride."

"Wow." Jackie had a large, very close family all in the local area.

"They've always had a weekend place on the island," Ronnie continued. "My dad retired in 2001 when his corporate headquarters moved to Chicago. My mother thought he'd finally have some time to spend with her, but he never wanted to go off-island. He got into hydroponic gardening and sells his organic produce to the farmer's market. He fertilizes with fish waste if you can imagine that."

She was silent for a moment and then volunteered, "My mother is very social. She endured the years of being on the backburner when he had a demanding high-level career, but after he retired that was too much to bear. Port Orchard is a very social place. She has an adorable little house and can walk to the center of town in just a few minutes. She works part-time in a cookware store and teaches a few cooking classes. She has a lot of women friends and seems pretty content. I know exactly how it feels to be married to someone who has no time for you," she muttered.

"I didn't know you'd been married!" Jackie gasped. Ronnie hadn't realized she'd spoken aloud.

Luckily, Jackie pulled into the driveway, and Ronnie wasted no time getting out of the car and striding onto the porch, the subject abandoned. The cabin was dark as Jackie fit the key into the front door lock but was unable to open it. "Here, you try it."

Ronnie wiggled the key and pushed on the door. It opened easily, the lights blazed on, and everyone yelled, "Surprise!"

Food was eaten, toasts were drunk, and then it was time for the pile of presents. Tears blurred her vision when she opened the big box containing the luxurious cashmere robe.

"You did good!" Andee whispered to Rickie.

There was a beautiful paisley wrap in a thin wool challis from Lucinda and Chip, a book on perennial gardening from Andee's dad, an assortment of handpicked artisanal teas from Mindy, who was a connoisseur, and a myriad of small gifts from other friends.

Jackie's gift was a pair of huge scuffs that you could slide your muck shoes into so you wouldn't have to take them off at the door if you needed to run into the house quickly. Several people asked where she'd found them. Geri had bought a package of envelopes and created a selection of cards for various occasions with her computer so Ronnie wouldn't have to try to buy a thank-you card or a sympathy card when she needed one. Geri was very clever, with an artistic flair, and Ronnie was touched by such a thoughtful gift.

The last package was a small flat box, wrapped in silver paper, embellished with a silver tassel at the end of a thick silver cord. It was obvious that it had come from an upscale shop somewhere else. Ronnie unwrapped it, and her breath hitched when she lifted the lid to reveal a deep blue sapphire set in a silver choker. It would look incredible in the open neck of a silk shirt.

"Wow! Who's that from?" Andee asked. "Do you have a secret admirer?"

Ronnie knew Andee was teasing and guessed her friend must've caught the flash of anger that flickered across her face before she replied smoothly, "No such luck. It's from my godmother. She always sends me jewelry." Ronnie was lying through her teeth, allowing Andee and everyone within earshot to think Luc had overstepped himself, giving a gift that was too personal and too expensive, making her uncomfortable.

Ronnie was shocked and dismayed, recognizing the handwriting on the envelope and realizing instantly that the necklace was from her ex-husband, the infamous rat bastard, Senator Evan Parker.

She hadn't heard from Luc all day. She thought he might have sent flowers and, when she walked into the party, thought maybe he'd planned a surprise visit. She was puzzled and, truth be told, more than a little hurt. She was really making an all-out effort to win Stephanie over, even the slightest improvement in her attitude was calculated in miniscule increments, but Ronnie was happy to see any progress and gratified to know that she had played a part in it. She and Luc talked on the phone almost every evening, sharing news of their respective days, discussing Steph, batting ideas back and forth for the Emery Pond development, and keeping each side up to date on the national park issue.

Ronnie had half-expected to find a package on her doorstep when she arrived home, but there was nothing on her porch. *Could something have happened? Could there have been an accident? Was Luc hurt? Or Stephanie?* She thought for a moment that perhaps CW had taken a turn for the worse, but he and Julia had sent a beautiful floral arrangement, which she brought home from the party and planned to take to the office tomorrow for everyone to enjoy.

Flipping on the lights, she eyed the bottle of Merlot sitting on the counter. *No, absolutely not.* She'd drunk her quota at the party and would surely feel like shit on a shingle tomorrow if she drank any more tonight.

She smiled. Turning forty sucked but it had been a great party, and she'd gotten some great presents. She was overwhelmed by the cashmere robe, but her smile faded, thinking about the card that had lain in the silver box, under the silver choker. She'd have to deal with that—but not tonight.

Right now, Purrl reminded her, none too subtly, it was time to get her dish filled with cat crunchies.

Ronnie's horses were undoubtedly wondering where their grain was, too. She didn't like to call in too many favors and ask friends and neighbors to feed her boys too often. Her schedule was erratic on the best of days but, rather than feed the horses on a strict schedule and risk colic, if their routine was disrupted, they got fed when she fed them, for the most part.

"Give me a break," she greeted them now. "Don't give me that look. When was the last time you went to bed hungry?"

Back inside, she ran hot water almost to the top of her jacuzzi and turned on the jets, lit a couple of candles, and poured in a generous amount of the bath salts she'd just gotten from Suzanne Gallagher, a realtor she regarded as a colleague. They had several closings together the previous fall, but she hadn't had much contact with her since Jackie had taken over the day-to-day real estate. She'd been pleased to see Suzanne at the party earlier in the evening.

She laid her head back, closed her eyes, and let the soothing bath work its magic. She pulled on her favorite, most well-worn pair of pajamas and folded down the duvet, relaxed, and ready for sleep. Purrl jumped up on the bed, glad to see Ronnie and more than ready to settle in for the evening. Suddenly, the cat stiffened, and a ridge of hair stood up on her spine.

There, hidden under the covers, was something that made no sense in her world—and she hissed in outrage. It made perfect sense to Ronnie. She guessed immediately that here was Luc's present, and she guessed, correctly, that he'd enlisted Mindy's assistance in placing it there, knowing Mindy had a key to her house. She scooped Purrl up, slung her over her shoulder, and stroked her back.

"It's okay, baby. It's more than okay. Let's see what's in this big box!"

She lifted out a long nightgown and matching robe of the thinnest silk. Was this some kind of hint? Her friends certainly must think she needed new nightwear. It was a shimmery silver with a dramatic design of spider mums up one side and over the shoulder and down one arm of the robe. The flowers looked like the design you'd see on a Japanese kimono, in gray, slate blue, midnight blue, and every shade in between. It was exquisite and must have cost a fortune.

At the bottom of the box was a letter, folded in thirds.

Dearest Ronnie,

Happy Birthday! This is a private moment I didn't want to share with anyone but you. I enlisted Mindy's help, as I'm sure you've guessed, in leaving the box for you to open when you would be alone. I expected our relationship to be strictly business, and, as recently as a month ago, I would have insisted that's what I wanted. Your kindness to my daughter has touched my heart, and what I want now, in all honesty, is for us to work on a relationship that is personal as well as professional. I want us to go away for an intimate weekend, without children, without partners, without daily pressures. I want you to put this nightgown on so I can take it off because I'm falling in love with you.

Luc

Stunned, Ronnie sank onto the bed with Purrl on her lap.

During the following week, Ronnie personally thanked those she had seen at the birthday party and sent thank-you notes to those she hadn't, but she hugged the contents of Luc's letter to herself, mulling it over, not ready yet to share it with even her closest friends. They noted there had been no mention of a gift from Luc but didn't pry. In light of the fact that Ronnie had invited his daughter to visit twice, a small gift from Stephanie was also conspicuously absent, and Ronnie's partners were convinced that *the kid has problems*. All three had been walking on eggshells. After the glow of pulling off such a successful surprise party dissipated, an overriding concern for CW pervaded the office.

Ronnie had blushed beet red when she finally showed them Luc's gift and told them about the weekend away.

"Hey." Andee frowned. "Wait a minute. Wasn't that necklace from Luc?"

"No." Ronnie sighed deeply and exhaled a long breath. "That was from my ex-husband, Evan Parker." The room was silent, as her friends gaped at her.

"I sent it back the next day!" she protested hotly.

"Wait. You sent the gift back and kept the wrapping? That's what that is, isn't it?" Andee eyed the long silver cord with the silver tassel that Ronnie had been wearing as a pendant and started to laugh. "Oh, my God! Too funny!" She laughed harder, and tears of mirth ran down her cheeks.

"I like it!" Ronnie defended herself. "It goes with everything. It suits me."

"Oh! Oh my God," Andee howled. The others couldn't help themselves, and soon all three had collapsed into the nearest seats, holding their sides and wiping at their streaming eyes.

"It's a metaphor for your relationship," Rickie contributed. "The packaging was better than the product."

Evan had signed for the return when it was delivered to his office, and there had been no communication from him since, which is just how Ronnie wanted it

After her friends left the room, Ronnie pulled the silver cord over her head and dropped it into the wastebasket.

Chapter Ten

The following Monday morning, Andee was first into the office. She and Rickie had a lunch meeting in Nashville with the first of three architects. He was flying in from Tulsa, and they would be picking him up at the airport in a few hours. They'd been considering architectural firms for the past month and had narrowed it down. Three were on the short list with another two as possibilities. Many architects design equestrian facilities, including stables, arenas and out buildings, but this wasn't a barn and a couple of arenas, essentially this was a small village. Andee leaned toward the eco-friendly Quality Equine Architects. Considered by many the authority on equine design, the Oklahoma firm was a pioneer in sustainable energy-efficient systems and strategies and had a significant international presence. With her expertise in a sister field, they decided to start there.

During her own years in an architecture firm, Andee was often on-site. Most of her work clothes consisted of tank tops, t-shirts, and long-sleeved tees, depending on the season, as well as cargo pants or cargo shorts with a plethora of pockets, socks, and hiking boots. For client meetings, she dressed simply, wanting only to create a favorable impression. When her mother passed away, her dad had told her to take whatever she wanted from her mother's closet before he donated her clothes to the church he attended. At first, she'd hesitated, fearful that seeing his dead wife's things would prolong his grief.

It was the ever-practical Rickie who offered to go with her to sort through her mother's wardrobe and had seen instantly that the clothes were classic and timeless as well as well-made.

"Just try it on," Rickie suggested, holding out a tweed skirt. Wordlessly, Andee shook her head.

"No skirts!" Andee croaked. Although she immediately tried to stifle a laugh, Rickie couldn't hold it in. Rickie's laugh was infectious, and Andee found herself laughing too.

"Oh," Rickie gasped, finally comprehending Andee's refusal. "You're willing to try on a few things, but you don't wear skirts, is that it?"

She persuaded Andee to try on a few jackets, then sweaters, and soon the pile of keepers far outgrew those that would be given away. Over the years, her father told her seeing his late wife's favorite clothes on the daughter who so closely resembled her pleased Eugene Webster immensely and kept his beloved late wife's memory alive.

Today, Andee wore narrow black gabardine pants with her black Ariat trail boots, a simple black shirt, and a black linen jacket. Her hair, worn long all her life and still such a dark brown it was almost black, was braided as usual, but today the braid was coiled into a figure eight at the back of her head. The only spot of color was the red leather Levenger portfolio she carried. It had been a Christmas present from her husband a few years earlier, and she carried it everywhere. Today, her notepad contained several pages of questions distilled from countless hours of discussion with her partners.

When Aaron Marks stepped through the wide glass doors in arrivals, both Rickie and Andee recognized him immediately from the photograph on his firm's website. Sandy hair fell over his forehead, and his eyes, behind trendy tortoiseshell glasses, were a striking clear green. He wore olive chinos with an ecru-colored oxford shirt, and his olive linen jacket had a faint windowpane check in tobacco brown. No tie, Andee noted approvingly. His watch had a leather band the same color as his trendy tan brogues, and, in the crook of his arm, he held the tan counterpart to Andee's leather portfolio.

"Andrea Barton." Andee stepped forward and introduced herself. "My partner, Erica Ahlers."

"I'm so glad you could come," Rickie greeted him warmly. "Please, call me Rickie."

"I see that we share the same taste in leather," Andee said, turning to Aaron and gesturing at his portfolio.

"Thanks. It was a birthday present from my wife."

"Mine was a Christmas present from my husband," Andee replied. "Who indulges in that for themselves?"

"We're in short-term parking," Rickie said. "Do we need to go to baggage claim first?" She wasn't sure if Aaron would be flying back that evening or staying over in Nashville.

"I checked a bag when I boarded in Tulsa." Aaron made a wry face. "I'm continuing on to Atlanta, so it's checked through, where I hope to be reunited with it." Andee wondered if that was a pun on the airline he was flying on and then decided that it probably wasn't.

As they entered the parking garage and waited for an elevator, Rickie told him, "We'll be having lunch Nadine's downtown, where I've reserved the private dining room so we can spread out. Andee has quite a bit to go over with you, and you'll want to take those materials with you."

Andee grinned wickedly. "Tell him the real reason you chose Nadine's."

Before Rickie could respond, Andee continued, "Complimentary valet parking. Rickie didn't want to waste two hours driving around the block a few hundred times or finally finding a parking space twelve blocks away."

"Our senior investment partner, Charles Westlake, wanted to arrange for a member to sign us in to Cityscape because he thought you'd enjoy a view of the city skyline from that height." Rickie said. "But the food is fabulous at Nadine's, and I know we'll be comfortable there. It's one of my favorite places. My parents and I first went there when I graduated from Bartlett University."

Three hours later, Andee stood and began gathering her exhibits into a tidy package. Aaron's jacket hung over the back of the chair next to him, and his shirtsleeves were rolled.

"The concept is very well thought out," he told them. "I'm confident this is a project my firm would do justice to." He added, "I'm sorry your colleague, Veronica, was unable to be here today. I would have liked to have met her."

"She's sorry, too, but she cracked a tooth and is probably in the middle of a root canal, as we speak," Rickie said.

"Ouch!" he commiserated.

"You'll meet her when you come back for a site visit," Andee assured him. "We want you to understand, in all honesty, that we intend to interview representatives from two additional firms before making a commitment, as I said earlier. Part of our decision will be based on the rapport we feel, part on your grasp of our concept, your schedule, and, of course, your bid.

"Once you tour the site," she continued, "we'll plan a visit to your offices in Tulsa. Our investor, The Westlake Group, is headquartered in Arlington, Virginia. Charles Westlake, his son, Chip, and their partner, Luc Deschaines, will pick us up in Tennessee in the corporate plane, and the six of us will meet with your proposed team."

A short time later, they pulled up to departures at the Nashville airport and said quick goodbyes. Rickie merged into traffic, and it was several minutes before she spoke.

"What did you think?"

"I like him a lot," Andee replied. "I think we're on the same page, and I feel very comfortable with him. He's going to be a hard act to follow. Too bad Ronnie couldn't come. I think she would really like him.

"*Like him*, like him," she clarified. "If he wasn't married, of course, he would so be her type."

Rickie shook her head. "I don't know about that," she equivocated. "She'll like him but maybe not *like him*, like him. There is something cooking between her and Luc, what with him giving her lingerie and suggesting a dirty weekend."

"Well, she hasn't gone, has she?" Andee countered. "She's too smart to get involved with one of our investors, don't you think?"

"She's too lonely not to, is what I think," Rickie responded. "Sometimes when the chemistry is there, it takes on a life of its own and you can't stop it, no matter how much you tell yourself you're just friends, or it's just business."

Rickie signaled for a turn and pulled swiftly into the left lane before speaking again.

"I'd say Luc's made it pretty clear what he wants, and he doesn't seem concerned about mixing pleasure with business."

"Well, we'll see." Andee paused while Rickie passed a white Subaru before settling back into the stream of cars engaged in the daily exodus from the city. "I don't think either of them would do anything stupid to jeopardize this project."

Two days later, Ronnie was introduced to Aaron Marks in a short video chat, and she, too, was very impressed.

"What'd you think?" Andee asked her later.

"His firm's portfolio certainly speaks for itself," Ronnie replied. "And I see why you like him so much; he seems to understand perfectly what we have in mind. I'd say we're on the same page."

"It's Charles Westlake who has to like them, and I'm sure he will. It almost makes you not want to waste time talking to anyone else," Andee agreed.

They had planned to give each of the three prospects a level playing field and to repeat the second and third interviews in the same venue to minimize any variables. That Friday, they were again on the way to Nashville with Ronnie at the wheel. Unfortunately, there was an accident on the interstate, leaving them caught in a bumper-to-bumper one-lane buildup that delayed them by twenty minutes. Several men stood under the portico in front of arrivals, and they weren't sure which was Lewis Wagner until one stepped forward, recognizing the distinctive shape of Ronnie's Lexus. Andee had texted to let him know they had been delayed en route and described their vehicle after he said he'd meet them in front of the terminal.

Andee muttered under her breath.

"Uh-oh, a tie. And tassel loafers."

She'd already made an unfair value judgment and hoped that she hadn't spoken loud enough for the other two to hear. She knew Rickie intended to move into the back seat with her so Lewis could sit in front, but he quickly opened the rear door and sat next to her, placing his briefcase on his lap.

After they had settled into the restaurant and placed their orders, they made perfunctory small talk while they waited to be served. Rickie asked about the unusually harsh winter in Chicago that was just winding down.

"Naperville, actually," he corrected. "It's thirty-three miles west of the city."

He's done, Andee thought, *before we've even started. She asked about the weather, not the geography! We can't work with a quibbler.*

"I'd like to see each stall with its own turnout paddock." Rickie passed one of Andee's sketches to him. "Do you think that can be accomplished without wasting a lot of interior space, Lew?"

"It's Lewis," he responded immediately.

Andee saw Rickie's mouth tighten almost imperceptibly. The list of prospects had just gotten shorter by a majority vote. Rickie had obviously arrived at the same conclusion but not for the same reason. The firm's reputation was impeccable, and their portfolio included a sufficient number of similar projects, which made them a strong contender but it quickly became clear that Lewis was a nuts-and-bolts guy, concerned with the scope of work and budget development. That would appeal to Charles Westlake, but this was a project that would all but consume the realtors for the next two years. It was of paramount importance to all three of them that they spend that time engaged with someone who was not just competent but compatible. This person needed to share their passion, have a sense of humor, and an upbeat, positive outlook.

To her credit, Rickie kept her expression blank and her voice level. "Lewis, you haven't answered my question."

He then explained that, while his firm did not have any start-to-finish equestrian projects in their portfolio, they had in the past used the services of a North Carolina-based design group which often worked as a consultant with other architects and contractors as part of the design team, contributing equine expertise to the process. When he told them that project expenses, like consulting and printing and travel, are billed in addition to the hourly fees, they were certain that he and his firm were firmly out of the running. It was a relief to drop him off at departures for his return flight.

"Looks like Charles won't waste jet fuel flying to Chicago," Ronnie said once they were headed east on I-40, making the veto unanimous. "Looks like it's going to be either Tulsa or Houston."

Monday's trip to Nashville provided a surprise. Lily Montgomery had traveled in business class from Houston and was among the first to deplane. Again, the partners recognized the woman immediately from the photo on her firm's website. She was a stunning, svelte six-footer with a deeply-tanned olive complexion and platinum hair so blonde it was almost white. When she smiled, her teeth were dazzling.

"Holy moly!" Andee muttered under her breath.

It was apparent within the first five seconds that Lily was as smart as she was beautiful and as nice as she was smart and beautiful. All three realtors liked her instantly.

Lily had been an architect for almost ten years. She must be in her mid-thirties, although she looked younger. It took longer to become an architect than to become a vet or a doctor, Andee thought, something like five years. Or was it seven? She was trying to work out the math.

"Where did you get your degree?" she asked, both as a way of putting Lily at ease, encouraging her to respond to simple queries, and also a means of eliciting information.

"I'm originally from Greenwich, Connecticut," Lily told them. Her father was an investment banker with one of the big Wall Street firms. She had skipped two grades and was a legacy student on both sides at St. Philip's Academy.

"Isn't St. Philip's considered a feeder school for Horvath?" Rickie asked.

"Pretty much, although, St. Philip's graduates have an exceptionally high rate of acceptance at Horvath, Yates, and Pemberton. I went to Crosby," Lily replied.

"It was Ivy League which mollified my father somewhat, and it had one of the highest-ranked undergraduate architecture programs in the country which was important to me," she continued to explain. She'd chosen Ithaca because her boyfriend had been accepted into vet school there. "He was two years older than I, but you don't have to have a baccalaureate to apply. Derrick Ramsey had completed his junior year with a pre-vet major at St Albans's, dean's list every semester, so he and I began our respective first years at Crosby together."

Andee stiffened for just a split second, and Rickie squeezed Andee's hand under the table. Clearly, her friend understood she was thinking of her acceptance to Crosby too.

"Your program was longer than his," Andee pointed out, recovering her composure. "Wouldn't he have graduated in four years to your five?"

"Yes, that's true," Lily affirmed. "The integrated path didn't exist when I was a student. Now you can complete the requirements for architectural licensure at the time of graduation, including the mandatory internship and taking each of the seven divisions of the Architect Registration Examination. But, as it turned out, it was a lot easier to plan our dream of becoming a vet and an architect than it was actually doing it. By the time Rick was a fourth-year student, academic demands and conflicting schedules had put a serious strain on our relationship. My mother had been diagnosed with stage II breast cancer, and I was going home to Connecticut as often as I could. Without telling me, Rick applied for a fellowship at Texas S&A. He didn't think he'd get it, so he didn't say anything—but then he did get it."

"You broke up?" Ronnie asked.

"Not right away," Lily admitted. "I was devastated, especially that last year. Luckily, I was so busy I didn't have time to be depressed. Then I graduated and moved back to Greenwich to be as helpful to my mom as I could in what ultimately proved to be a successful battle against the cancer, after a seemingly endless struggle with chemo and radiation. I was working as an intern for a very upscale firm in Newtown, learning a lot, making a lot of great contacts, traveling some, dating some."

"I met two people in particular who were very influential," Lily continued. "One was Meredith Rawlings; you may have heard of her?"

Andee felt as perplexed as Rickie looked, but Ronnie exclaimed, "Yes! The Eventer?"

"Medalist in Three-Day Eventing, yes, and former model. I kept my pony at the hunt club in Darien and did the whole pony club thing, showing in hunter-jumper. St. Philip's doesn't have an equestrian team. My father absolutely gagged at the idea of the prep school I chose, which is known for its riding program but not for its academics, so the compromise was that I took my horse with me to school and kept him at a nearby boarding barn in Concord. I was already a pretty good jumper, and, with some dressage lessons, I started doing some low-level eventing. I met Meredith when I signed up for a clinic she was giving one weekend in Vermont."

"Did you take your horse with you to Crosby?" Andee wanted to know.

"I was planning to. Crosby has an equestrian program, and I could probably have made arrangements to lease him for lessons to help defray the cost of keeping him there. But he colic'd the winter of my senior year at St. Philip's, and we rushed him to the big equine hospital in Portsmouth. They tried to save him with surgery, but he already had a torsion. Once they opened him up and saw how much of his intestine was compromised due to lack of blood supply, there wasn't much they could do. I was heartbroken, but, in the long run, it was probably just as well because I wouldn't have had time for a horse.

My coursework was pretty intense, and my schedule was insane.

"Anyway, years later, when I was interning, I bumped into Meredith in New York, and she remembered me. She said she was astounded by my grown-up good looks and asked if I wanted her to introduce me to some of her contacts from her days in fashion and fragrance. I wasn't making much, so I took her up on her offer."

"Wow," Rickie exclaimed, and then asked, "Who was the other?"

"An interior designer from Boston. Her name is Alix Hamilton, and I met her through work. She's extremely selective about accepting jobs, but she was doing one on a huge waterfront home in Fairfield for our firm. I was just the junior 'water carrier' that day, but she and I really hit it off, and we've kept in touch all this time. In fact, I just got back from Jackson Hole. She was doing a job on one of those monster lodges."

"Were you the architect?" Andee rotated her wrist under the table to sneak a peek at her watch and was shocked to see how much time had gone by. They'd all been mesmerized by Lily's bio, but now Andee needed to get this meeting on track or all they'd still be sitting there when the dinner crowd started appearing. She nodded in her partner’s direction, discreetly pointing at her watch.

"Me?" Lily queried. "No. Alix was there with architects from Denver. I'd taken a few days of vacation because Rick had a conference in Jackson Hole and, if I went along, it was an opportunity to do a little skiing and see Alix."

Andee didn't miss much, and she didn't miss this. "Rick?" she asked. "Rick from Crosby?"

"Oh! Yes, Rick from Crosby," Lily clarified. "He loved living near Houston and had dated extensively for a couple of years. In fact, he was actually engaged, but he broke it off. He said I was the only one he wanted, and we got back together. By that time, he was an assistant professor in the vet school, and I was just finishing my internship requirement and had passed all seven sections of the Architect Registration Exam. I was toying with the idea of applying to Yates for their advanced Master of Architecture program, but I was at a crossroads, and, with a license, I could go anywhere. So, I went to Texas, and the rest is history."

Lily consulted her schedule, and they agreed on a tentative date for her site visit to Emery Pond in a few weeks, before dropping her off at the departures terminal.

This time Rickie, Ronnie, and Andee were all stunned into silence as they began the drive to Jamestown. No one said anything for quite a while and then Andee broke the silence.

"Holy crap! That's some résumé! I thought Aaron Marks had a lock on it, but he's got some mighty stiff competition. You asked her your question about the turnout paddocks, Rickie, and she didn't even hesitate. I guess she knows her way around a barn."

"She obviously does from a lifetime's experience with horses. Her husband teaches equine sciences and they both ride." Rickie was thoughtful, then added, "That gives her a leg up."

Andee snorted. "But Aaron does too, because his firm has done so many equestrian projects, and he worked on those two huge equestrian complexes in Abu Dhabi."

"Well, girls, we have a problem. In a good way," Ronnie summed it up. "Let's see how it goes when they both come for a site visit. It's still early days."

Chapter Eleven

"Andee? Aaron Marks on line one," Geri called.

Rickie had tactfully notified Lewis Webster that his firm was not being considered for their project, citing lack of experience with equestrian facilities. "It's a world-class firm, but he's a world-class asshole," Andee summed it up. "No, thanks!"

In the ensuing weeks, both Aaron Marks and Lily Montgomery were immersed in other commitments, unable to clear their respective calendars to plan a site visit to Emery Pond. Andee hoped that Aaron was calling to tell her he'd soon be on his way to Tennessee because, although she always built in plenty of slack, they had a timeline and needed to stay pretty much within its parameters.

"Good news," he told her, "I'm ahead of schedule on a senior living complex in Sedona, and I can get away for a day or two. I'll fly into Nashville and rent a car. Can you recommend a place to stay on your end?"

Rickie, Ronnie, and Andee had discussed this. They agreed it would be inappropriate for a single woman to host Aaron, but he could stay with Andee and her husband overnight, and either Rickie or Ronnie would host Lily when it was her turn.

When Aaron pulled into a parking space at Horse Country Real Estate shortly after noon a week later, his ruby-red convertible, its metallic paint glinting in the midday sun, earned an admiring look from the mail carrier who was just approaching.

"Aaron, you made such good time!" Andee greeted him warmly. "I want to spend the afternoon showing you the area, including several of the equestrian subdivisions that are here. Tomorrow, you can follow me to Emery Pond and leave from there because I'll be towing a trailer with our new UTV. My husband just traded one of our ATVs for a side-by-side so—don't laugh—the dog can ride in comfort."

Aaron had told her he'd be on an early flight and would grab something to eat along the way.

She liked his look. Today he wore pressed jeans with hiking boots, an open-neck shirt in pale olive, a navy linen sport coat, and Ray-ban aviator sunglasses. "I rented a convertible, let's take it. You know where you're going, so you drive," he told her as they walked outside. He handed her the key and laid his jacket on the back seat, folded neatly with the lining side out.

After several hours, they retrieved Andee's truck, and Aaron followed her home.

"Frank's not here yet, but he should be any minute," she said, seeing that his truck wasn't in its usual spot. She led the way into the house and showed him to the guest room, with its adjoining bath. "I'm going to start feeding the animals."

She unlocked and opened the back door, letting a large German Shepherd into the kitchen.

"Ready for a beer?" Andee asked as Aaron joined her. The dog hadn't taken her eyes off Andee, but now she looked inquiringly at the visitor.

"This is Luna; she's Frank's baby."

"Hey, girl." Aaron held out his hand for her to sniff, but she immediately offered her own paw. "Where does she stay during the day?"

Andee re-opened the door to show him a large porch that served as a kennel, with access to a fenced, covered area in the backyard. As an architect, Aaron should admire both the design and the construction.

"Frank has a nice workshop; he loves projects. We both wanted Luna to be safe and comfortable so we don't feel too bad when she's left at home."

It was apparent a few minutes later that Frank had arrived when Luna bolted for the side door to welcome her master.

"Hey, princess!"

Andee gave Aaron a wry smile. "See what I mean? He's not talking to me."

An hour later, the three sat on the patio, drinks in hand. Aaron had accompanied Andee to the barn to feed the horses while Frank showered. It was the first thing he did after a long day outside in the sun, wind, dust, rain, or snow.

"What do you do for work, Frank?" Aaron asked. “No, let me guess— construction, given the quality craftsmanship I saw in the kennel, and your windburned, sunburned face and roughened hands.”

"Surveyor."

"I just got a drone," Frank explained, his eyes alight. "I'm still learning how to use it. I always look at where I'm going to be working with a mapping program. Sometimes though, I'm in such deep woods, it's hard to see the 'big picture' without an aerial view. But this thing, wow, it's a whole new world!"

After Aaron asked several knowledgeable questions, it was apparent that he was seriously interested in drone technology.

"You want to see it work?" Frank asked.

Dinner was an easy, casual affair. Andee had put the ingredients into a slow cooker that morning, so all she had to do was to make a salad and set the table. She'd made an apple cobbler for dessert the day before with her aunt's tried-and-true recipe that only had four ingredients plus the fruit.

"Hey, hon," Frank said, over coffee. "I don't need the drone tomorrow, and Aaron is a quick study; he can fly it. Why don't you take it to Emery Pond?"

Andee bit her lip, thoughtful.

"That's a great idea and it would probably be very useful as well as fun but my concern is in giving

Aaron an advantage that Lily Montgomery won't have." She turned to Aaron and met his eyes.

"It's not just me making decisions," she said. "I have partners and investors who are part of this, too, and I have to look out for everyone's best interests. At this point, I'm trying to be impartial and fair."

"I understand," Aaron quickly reassured her. "It seems a shame not to use such a wonderful tool if it's available. What if I shared the film with any and all competitors so you won't have to worry about a level playing field?"

"That's a good idea and a generous offer," she said slowly, "but I'm still afraid you'd have an advantage since you'd be the one doing the flying and will have a frame of reference that others might not have."

"Can you fly it?" Aaron offered an alternative.

Frank groaned teasingly and grimaced, baring his teeth. Luna was dozing nearby, but her head snapped up, and she scanned Frank's face, searching for clues as to whether he might actually be in distress. He shook his head from side to side almost imperceptibly, and she relaxed once again.

"How about this?" Frank said, thinking aloud. "My crew can start without me. What if I went to Emery Pond with you for an hour or so and did the flying myself?" He turned to Andee.

"You can give the film to anyone you want, and you can stay at arm's length. So to speak."

Her lip curved in a slight smile as she acknowledged the play on words.

The following morning, Andee packed a cooler with lunch and drinks for herself and Aaron, as well as a smaller one for Frank. The day was sunny and mild, with a light breeze. All three wore sweatshirts, which they would shed by mid-morning. Aaron also wore a tactical vest with about eighteen pockets. Andee gave him a thumbs-up when she saw it.

"I have one almost like that," she told him. "I wore it almost every day when I worked as a landscape architect, and now I wear it when I go to take a listing, so I don't have to keep running out to the truck for stuff. That way, I have everything I might need—tape measure, flashlight, whiteout—it's an old habit."

The UTV was the perfect vehicle for covering the terrain and allowed Andee to point out various features to Aaron without having the wind snatch the words out of her mouth as she spoke over her shoulder, the way she had to do with a passenger behind her on an ATV.

"I'll write up my notes on the flight back to Tulsa, and I'll have some time, too, at the Nashville airport. I want to get my impressions down while it's fresh in my mind," he told her at the end of the day.

"Don't hesitate to call, email, or text if you need any information or want to clarify anything. It's so exciting for us to see this project start to take shape.

I'm sure we'll be talking to you in the meantime, but we'll be in touch to firm up a date to come to Tulsa. You can present your bid to Charles Westlake then."

"C'mon in!" Ronnie heard Geri greet someone the following Thursday. "I'm Geri. Ronnie is expecting you. That's her office, just go in. You don't have to knock."

"What a crappy day," she commiserated when Lily came in. "How does a cup of hot tea sound?"

"I'm sorry it's so late," Lily apologized. "The TSA line in Houston was horrific. I wouldn't have made my flight at all if it hadn't been delayed. Then I had a rental car screw-up once I landed, and I actually had to pull over in Mt. Juliet and wait until a particularly nasty 'red cell' passed because visibility was zero for about twenty minutes. I thought the plan was to see the area today and the site tomorrow, but that's pretty much out the window at this hour."

"Well, how flexible is your schedule?" Ronnie asked. "Here's what I'm thinking. If you can stay over an extra day, it's supposed to clear off after midnight so we could see the area tomorrow and maybe do a short ride later in the afternoon and then see Emery Pond on Saturday."

"That's such an inconvenience, I'd feel terrible," Lily said.

"Not at all!" Ronnie assured her. Lily accepted the cup of tea that Geri brought in and sipped appreciatively.

"I'm the only one here who drinks tea," Ronnie said. Lily pulled out her cell phone.

"Well, let me call Rick first and clear a change of plans with him. Shouldn't be a problem. And the airline, let me see if I can change my ticket. Can I take you out tonight so you won't have to be responsible for two dinners instead of one?"

"Don't worry about that; it's not a problem. I was planning on having you stay tonight, so today's dinner is all set. Actually, I invited my next-door neighbor, Mindy, because you have a mutual acquaintance, and I thought you'd enjoy meeting her." Lily looked perplexed, and Ronnie clarified. "You mentioned that you'd been out in Wyoming to see your decorator friend, Alix Hamilton. Well, Mindy's very good friend from North Carolina designs wallpaper that she licenses to Alix, and they often collaborate on projects."

"Are you talking about Caroline? I can't remember her last name, but I met her in Wyoming. She was working on wallpaper for all the rooms in that big lodge with Alix," Lily exclaimed. "How cool is that? What a coincidence!" Then she warned, only half in jest, "If you ever meet Alix, don't let her catch you calling her a *decorator*. She is a trained, licensed interior designer, whereas anyone who thinks they have a flair can call themselves an interior decorator, without any real credentials."

By the time the two women were ready to leave the office, the rain had tapered to a drizzle, and, by the time they got to Ronnie's, it had stopped altogether. Already, there were patches of sky visible through scudding clouds, promising better weather the next day.

Lily hadn't taken two steps inside Ronnie's house when she stopped and looked around, nodding in approval.

"I love the way you've used all these shades of white, off white, and cream. What a great house!"

One side of Ronnie's mouth quirked, and she said sarcastically, "Really? My last houseguest said it looked like 'a friggin operating room.' Her words."

"Well, her taste is all in her mouth, as we used to say in third grade." Lily laughed.

After Ronnie showed her upstairs, Lily immediately made herself at home in the guest suite. The pillows arranged along the headboard were now covered in a variety of natural fibers in several tans and olive tones from light to dark. Ronnie had swapped the blue denim on the chair-and-a-half with a slipcover in olive linen. The blue towels and blue soap had also been replaced with olive.

Lily picked up the bar of soap and sniffed.

"Oh, it's vervain!" she exclaimed in surprise. "My favorite. I love the citrus-y scent. I was expecting avocado."

She was equally complimentary about Ronnie's barn arrangement, her practiced eye taking in the simplicity and functionality of the layout.

"Have you ever ridden gaited?" Ronnie asked. Jack nickered impatiently. A moment later, he lashed out with a front hoof, striking his stall door. It would be far better if Ronnie kept her mind on the task of bringing his supper and not standing around making chitchat with some woman he'd never seen before.

"Whoa! Someone wants his supper, and he wants it now!" Lily said, clearly amused.

Ronnie unlatched his feed door and slipped the small bucket through.

"This is Black Jack." She moved to the second stall. "And this is Cash. You'll ride him tomorrow."

"We have Quarter Horses in Texas," Lily said. "I did a lot of equitation and hunter-jumper when I was a kid, as I told you, so I've only ever had the opportunity to ride trotting horses."

"You're in for a treat," Ronnie told her. "I love introducing people to gaited horses."

Ronnie had assembled dinner rather than actually preparing it. She had a box of wild-caught salmon, perfectly seasoned with garlic, and put it on the grill with three foil packs of potatoes that would be done and ready to serve simultaneously. Already-husked corn on the cob went into the microwave. She sprinkled shredded parmesan cheese on ovals of ciabatta bread, and those went into the toaster oven. She'd put wide-mouthed salad plates into the fridge that morning so they would be chilled, and she'd washed and shredded romaine for a Caesar salad before leaving for the office. With no elaborate preparations, dinner was a breeze, and the three women enjoyed a relaxing evening. The house sat atop a small rise overlooking the pasture, giving them a view of the horses as they grazed.

"Have you met Alix?" Lily asked Mindy while they ate, after explaining that she'd met Caroline only the once, through Alix.

Mindy dropped her napkin and bent to retrieve it, giving herself a moment to compose a careful answer. She kept her voice level, and her expression bland as she responded.

"Actually, Alix, Caroline, and I go back years because we were at school together in Connecticut."

Lily seemed fascinated to learn she and Mindy had not one but two mutual acquaintances. Ronnie knew the conversation would surely take this tack, but she was confident she could count on Mindy's good sense and discretion. This wasn't a gabfest among girlfriends, after all. Lily was here on business. Ronnie knew she'd see Lily again in Houston but had no way of guessing if her firm would be the one chosen for the Emery Pond project.

There was an awkward silence, then Lily asked, "Where did you go to school?"

Ronnie realized that saying too little would create more questions than it would answer and was relieved when Mindy responded simply, "Marshfield Academy, in Simsbury, Connecticut. We were roommates."

Lily looked astonished. "Really? You and Caroline and Alix were roommates?"

"Yes and no."

When Ronnie invited Mindy to join her and Lily for dinner, she was thinking only that their mutual acquaintance would be a bond that might put Lily more at ease. She hoped Mindy could ease herself out of this fraught conversation and change the subject—*soon.*

"Alix and I were suitemates with two other girls the first year."

Ronnie heaved a silent sigh of relief when Mindy neglected to say that one of those girls was none other than Alix's identical twin, Asha.

"Caroline was a year younger. She moved in during my second year when Alix moved out and freed up her room."

Ronnie held her breath, releasing it only when Mindy also neglected to say that Caroline was Alix and Asha's first cousin and that they'd lived next door to each other all their lives.

"Alix was an art major and wanted to be alone to draw and paint at all hours, without all the distractions of ordinary dorm life, so she requested a single."

There, good; sweet and simple. Ronnie stood and asked, "Ready for dessert?"

"Do you still keep in touch?" Lily persisted, to Ronnie's dismay. At the kitchen door, she turned and caught Mindy's attention over Lily's head.

"Decaf okay with everyone?" she asked.

"I see Caroline quite often," Mindy explained. "We both love to ride, and she comes to Big South Fork often. I want Ronnie to find her a cute little place once I persuade her to move here from North Carolina. Alix doesn't ride, and we've essentially lost touch."

Mindy had told Ronnie the whole sordid story involving her high school roommates soon after they met, talking about their backgrounds when they were getting to know one another. Ronnie knew Mindy had lost touch with Alix not because she didn't ride but because she was a Grade-A shit. She was sure it made Mindy's blood pressure rise just thinking about her now.

"I'm going to spend most of the day giving Lily a tour of the area," Ronnie skillfully steered the conversation into safer channels. "We're hoping to get a short ride in at about three. She's never ridden gaited. You want to go?"

"Sure!" Mindy agreed. "Where are you going?"

"Well, we won't have more than a couple of hours. Too bad, I'd love for her to see Lost Springs Lodge."

"Let me think about this," Mindy said. "It could work if we rode one way from Bitter Creek. We could pre-position trailers at the Powerlines Trailhead."

"How would we do that?" Ronnie asked.

Mindy grinned. "Easy peasy, I'll take care of it while you're busy. Sara can help me."

"Need a little more info there, hon." Ronnie grinned.

"Okay," Mindy said after a minute, "you take your two-horse trailer to Bitter Creek, and I take my two-horse. That gets three riders and three horses there."

Ronnie liked the idea, but the logistics still needed some work.

"I'm way ahead of you," Mindy teased, forestalling Ronnie's next question. "I'll follow Sara to the Powerlines Trailhead tomorrow morning, and she can leave her three-horse there, then I'll run her home. She's doing something later with Jon so she'll be free first thing in the morning, and she won't be using her trailer tomorrow. Then, when you, Lily and I ride up the hill from Lost Springs, we can just load up and leave."

"Sounds like a plan!" Ronnie turned to Lily. "I love it when you can have your cake and eat it too!"

"What a wonderful evening," Lily said, as she picked up her sweater and headed for the stairs, preparing to retire. "You're lucky to have such a great neighbor."

The next morning, Ronnie was up an hour earlier than usual. She'd made a breakfast casserole ahead of time and heated it up in the oven while she went out to feed the horses. Lily came downstairs just as she walked back into the kitchen.

"How'd you sleep?" Ronnie asked her guest.

Both women were dressed casually in jeans and tees, not expecting to do more today than drive around and ride horses later. Ronnie eyed Lily's boots and belt, suspecting she had some of the best leather goods Texas had to offer in her closet at home.

The day passed quickly. Lily carried a tablet and camera to make notes and take pictures as they went. Ronnie brought her map so Lily could orient herself, but Lily wanted to purchase one that she could take back to Houston with her.

"They sell maps at the park's visitor center but you'll see Bitter Creek when we trailer over there later," she told Lily. "No point in spending time on that now. There is also a huge campground, stables, and a pool, as well as both a hiking trailhead and an equestrian trailhead."

Instead, Ronnie pulled into the Circle T Horse Campground near the park's west entrance so they could run into the mercantile where maps were sold. Lily was very taken with the western facade and thought it must provide a wonderful photo op for campers and their horses.

"There's a feeder trail leading into the park just over there," Ronnie pointed out. "You can literally ride for hours, days, or weeks. Big South Fork straddles the Tennessee/Kentucky line. There are also trails, trailheads, and horse campgrounds in both states."

A rider herself, Lily obviously understood the powerful draw of this special place.

"They call this The Trail Riding Capital of the Southeast," Ronnie said. "You won't even scratch the surface in the short time you're here, but you can understand why it's such a destination. That's what we intend to capitalize on." Lily laughed.

"In both senses of the word!"

Chapter Twelve

"Oh, my God!" Lily exclaimed, as Mindy expertly pulled Sara's rig out of the Powerlines Trailhead late that afternoon. The days were lengthening, but shadows lay across Fork Ridge Road as they made their way down five miles of narrow gravel road.

"What happens if you meet another trailer?" she asked.

"You know, that rarely happens," Mindy replied. "Usually, everyone's going in at about the same time and coming out at about the same time. With the hiking trailhead co-located, hikers' cars and trucks come and go all day because they may only be out for an hour or two, but horse trailers rule. Everybody is considerate, and the smaller vehicle can usually pull over without a problem."

"I can't tell you how much I enjoyed this ride," Lily enthused. "I can see why you love riding here so much. Lost Springs Lodge took my breath away, and I loved the little wooden footbridge; it's so picturesque."

Lily had instinctively understood gaiting, and the three horses had flown down Duncan Hollow Road in a fast running walk.

"I spent years and countless sums of money learning to ride English correctly, elbows in, heels down and all that, and now all that is out the window," Lily said, wryly. "I never in a million years thought I'd willingly ride western or ride a Quarter Horse, for that matter, but all that changed when I got to Texas. Now that I usually ride with a long stirrup and a long rein, there's not much transition to riding a gaited horse. I must say, I loved going that fast and not having to post or stand up in the stirrups." Both Ronnie and Mindy were nodding in agreement.

"I'd love for Rick to try this," Lily added.

It was on Ronnie's lips to reply, *well, hold that thought!* but she stopped herself before she spoke. She and Mindy and Lily had had such an easy, companionable time together that she'd momentarily forgotten that Lily was not a friend and not even a business associate.

It was growing dark by the time they'd taken the horses home and gotten them settled in. They dropped Johnny off at Mindy's first and, with a group effort, got him hosed off and the tack stowed. Mindy quickly gave her two horses their grain and turned them out with piles of hay. They repeated the process at Ronnie's, and then Lily drove them to Bitter Creek to retrieve their trailers.

With that accomplished, Ronnie said, "We still have to get Sara's trailer back to her."

"Well, what are you doing for dinner? Maybe we could drop her trailer off and stop at Vermillion," Mindy suggested.

Ronnie nodded enthusiastically. "That would work! Here, let me just call her."

"Y'all are going to Vermillion?" Sara asked. “How about this? We just got home, and I don't have anything in mind for supper, why don't we meet you? If you bring my rig, I can just take it home from there." Ronnie could hear Jon speaking in the background. "Jon wants to know if we'd have trouble finding a place to park it while we're inside. I don't think that'll be a problem, do you?"

Ronnie was actually relieved to have Sara and Jon joining them. Conversation would be much more general and the evening would go quickly. Tomorrow would be all business for her and Lily. She could see, tonight, that Lily was processing what she'd seen and experienced and wanted to forestall the myriad questions she knew were surely forming in Lily's mind. When the opportunity presented itself, she had a quiet word with Mindy, explaining that it would be totally unfair to Aaron Marks for Lily to have an inside track on the Emery Pond bid and asking if she could surreptitiously speak with Sara and Jon.

Lily raved about how she found Vermillion's rustic ambiance charming, and Jon explained that the building was actually an old schoolhouse. She asked about the falling-to-ruins structure at the intersection on the main road where they'd turned onto the side road where Vermillion was located. Jon explained that it looked like a derelict garage because of its concrete block construction but had actually once been a small grocery store. Between him and Sara, they provided a wealth of information about the establishment of the national park in the '80s and '90s.

In previous years, the park service had placed a premium on the value of interpretive rangers, and Jon told her the history of some of the hamlets and settlements such as Christian and No Business while Sara told her about the intertwined history of local families. Lily was astonished to hear about Lost Springs's tenure as a hunting lodge for boar hunters. Jon told her it was known as the hog farm years ago.

They had talked at length about places they'd lived, about regional and cultural differences, food, weather, and a variety of other interesting but inconsequential topics. Ronnie was surprised when she realized that the servers had set up for the next day, and they were the only patrons remaining.

"I guess we need to clear out!" she commented.

Once outside, Lily said her goodbyes to Sara and Jon, thanked them for an entertaining evening, and Sara for the use of her trailer.

"Talk to you soon," Ronnie told Mindy as she dropped her off. Ronnie's tone told Mindy, in that special shorthand they'd developed, that she needed a porch session where they'd open a bottle of Merlot, put their feet up on the porch railing, and Ronnie could use Mindy as a sounding board. Ronnie obviously had something. It sounded like it could be several somethings.

By the time Mindy hurried through her errands in Crossville the next day, blasting through the liquor store, the grocery store, and several other places, she was ready to flop down in a rocker.

"How'd it go today?" she asked as she set a bottle of wine and two glasses on the table an hour later.

"Here, try this. It's a Zinfandel. It's new, and it was on special at the liquor store. They said it was really smooth. I only got a couple of small bottles because I didn't want to get stuck with a case of big bottles if it isn't good. I just can't get my mind around living in a dry county; what a pain in the ass."

"Pretty crazy that Fentress would choose to remain a dry county and forego the tax revenue," Ronnie agreed. "I'm not sure the day will come when liquor sales pass a referendum. They've tried in the past, but it always dies on the vine."

"You've been hanging around with Andee too long," Mindy teased her. "Now, you're starting to speak in puns."

Ronnie was a private person, and things had to really build up before she would unburden herself so Mindy didn't probe, just waited, because it usually wasn't until Ronnie had refilled her glass that she was willing to open up.

"I'm tired, I guess," Ronnie said. "I went with Jackie this morning to look at a listing. The seller wants her to take it. But she doesn't want to get stuck with a no hoper and asked me to take a look at it to see if we could come up with a marketing plan." She stopped but didn't say anymore, seemingly lost in thought.

"And?" Mindy prompted.

Ronnie shuddered. "It's awful! The house is okay, I guess, if you like brick trying to be pretentious and a lot of people do. I personally don't like that gray brick that's all different shades. I'm a Yankee, through and through; just give me good old classic red brick any day. Or brick with a good coat of gloss white paint and some black shutters."

"And ivy?" Mindy was pulling Ronnie's leg. "Don't leave that out!"

"It's not on trails or even near trails," Ronnie continued. "The fencing is falling-down barbed wire and there isn't a blade of grass in the pasture. It's all buttercups, ragweed, and chokecherry ten feet high. Horses ate the grass a long time ago and left everything that's unpalatable or toxic."

"They do that," Mindy commiserated. "And thank God they do."

"I told her not to take the listing, no how, no way." Ronnie shook her head back and forth for emphasis, then slashed her hand across her throat.

"It'll be a hard sell. She'll have to show it and service the paperwork without a paycheck in sight.

The trick is getting out of taking the listing without hurting the seller's feelings."

"How do you do that?" Mindy asked.

"This has worked for me, and it'll work for Jackie. She can tell the seller that since our focus is on horse properties and theirs isn't on or near trails, we would be doing the seller a disservice to take the listing, and he or she would be better to list with a realtor in Crossville who has a much broader customer base."

"That makes sense," Mindy agreed.

"The thing is, we have to be good businesswomen, both for ourselves and for the seller. It's a disservice to both parties to take a listing that you don't think you can close within a reasonable period of time. Nothing is worse than a listing that lingers on the market, getting more and more stale." She warmed to her topic.

"Nothing is a bigger red flag for a buyer than several price reductions. You know, Marcia shows the customer the listing sheet and says, 'This has only been listed for seventy days, it won't last long at that price!' " She tsk'd in disgust. "She doesn't realize when the buyer finds out that the house has actually been on the market for four years and it's only been seventy days during the current listing period, they will distrust her. Sometimes, it's after the fact, but they always find out, and then they tell someone who tells someone. We always print out the whole history, with the number of times the property has been re-listed and all the price reductions so the buyer can make an informed assessment."

"Jackie is doing very well, isn't she?" Mindy observed. "She really took to real estate."

"We need Jackie to be strong, so we can concentrate on other things at this point," Ronnie said. "Horse Country Real Estate has a very good reputation that makes sellers want to list with us. Jackie is slowly but surely benefitting from our mentoring, something she wouldn't get anywhere else. We've taught her to be selective and only list the cream of the crop, not to waste her time and energy taking every listing that comes along. And we taught her to be truthful because if you're anything less, it will bite you in the ass sooner or later.

"I can think of two listings—not ours—where the house was on one side of a ravine, and the barn was on the other. The agent put pictures of both on the MLS, and the buyer assumed you could walk from one to the other when, in reality, you couldn't. An agent will include a picture of the plot of land, but the customer who's researching online doesn't always realize they're not looking at a topographical map. They have quite an unpleasant surprise when the listing in their pile of must-sees doesn't meet expectations down the road."

"So to speak." Mindy smirked.

"Anyway, to answer your question, I'm tired because I haven't been sleeping well," Ronnie said.

Here it comes. Mindy nodded.

"I'm so angry that fucking Evan actually came here," Ronnie said vehemently. "It's so unfair! I haven't thought about him in years, literally years, and now it's like the scab has been ripped off. I hate him! I never wanted to see him again!"

Ronnie's eyes filled up with tears, and she made no attempt to swipe them away.

"C'mere," Mindy said, pulling Ronnie up out of the rocker and into a hug. She rubbed her hand up and down her friend's back, comforting her.

"You have every right to be upset." She smoothed Ronnie's hair back and looked into her face. "Is that the only reason you're upset?"

Both women sank back down into the rockers. Ronnie set hers in motion. She leaned back, silent for a few moments.

"No, but that's most of it. Sometimes I feel overwhelmed by the Emery Pond thing. It's exciting, and we wanted it, but the responsibility is terrifying. What if we're wrong and it's a big, fat flop?"

"Well…" Mindy pondered this. "Don't investors do some sort of risk/benefit analysis? They don't want to lose their shirt, so they must weigh the risks pretty carefully before getting involved. The responsibility isn't all on your shoulders."

"I know that," Ronnie acknowledged. "That's part of it. The waiting is killing me, the *waiting for the other shoe to drop* thing. I just want to get on with it, if we're going to." Her face darkened, and she said again, "I hate having Evan involved, however peripherally. I wish he'd just get his damn vote over with and go on his merry way!"

"How much say does he have in this?" Mindy inquired. "If he votes against privatization, does that mean that your project is scrapped?"

"No. CW has already assured us it won't. But it will sure be a leg up—stop it!" she said when she caught Mindy's bemused expression. "It will be a leg up, literally, if the park is privatized and more businesses are attracted to the area. More businesses attract more visitors, and more visitors will attract more sales. It's not a deal-breaker, but it's pretty important."

"But you don't actually have to see him again, right?"

"I don't intend to," Ronnie was adamant. "God, let's not talk about him! I just need to put him out of my mind. It is what it is, and whatever's going to happen is going to happen without me worrying about it. He came, he saw, and he went away, end of story."

"Is that all that's bothering you?" Mindy asked, gently.

Ronnie shook her head slowly.

"Luc," she said simply. "I can't stop thinking about him."

"Is that a good thing or a bad thing?"

"I wish I knew," Ronnie admitted. "I really don't want to get involved with one of our investors. Think how awful it would be for everyone if I did, and it went south while we're in the middle of the project. It would be horribly awkward and uncomfortable for everyone. I just can't do that!"

"Who are you trying to convince, me, or yourself?" Mindy probed. Ronnie laughed.

"Girlfriend, that's exactly why I'm not sleeping well! I keep turning it over and over in my mind, trying to look at it from this angle and that angle, asking myself what happens if I encourage him and it doesn't work out—what then? Or if it does work out, what then?"

"That's kind of a good problem to have," Mindy pointed out. "He's pretty terrific. If you want my opinion, I don't think you should let him get away."

"I'm really starting to have feelings for him. We talk on the phone almost every day," Ronnie said. "He's asked me to go away for a weekend. I don't know what to say, so I haven't said anything."

"You're going to have to give him an answer. Pretty soon, I would imagine."

"I know. Plus, his daughter hates me. I can't imagine that getting any better if I accept."

"She sure is a mess. He definitely has his hands full," Mindy agreed. "I'm sure she'd be jealous of you. I think she already senses something in the wind. I don't envy him that."

"How about this," Mindy suggested. "If you, Rickie, and Andee are going to Tulsa and Houston with Charles and Chip and Luc, why don't you put off a decision until after you spend some more time together? You can get a better sense of what might be appropriate, don't you think?"

"That's a good idea, Mindy," Ronnie said, gratefully. "Julia and Lucinda will be going as well. I could probably sound them out at some point. Most wives going along on a business trip go off together to shop and have lunch, but Charles and Chip value their input, so they're pretty involved in most of the projects The Westlake Group takes on. I like them, very much."

"Well, then, that's a plan," Lucinda agreed. "How'd it go in Emery Pond with Lily?"

"Good!" Ronnie said, "She's wonderful. Very organized, very professional but very easy to be with, and a lot of fun. I wasn't there, but Andee said the site visit went very well. Lily met Andee in town on Saturday morning and followed her to the site and then left from there, just as Aaron Marks did."

"Who do you think will get it? The contract?" Mindy asked.

"Boy, I don't know. They're both wonderful, and I'd be happy with either one. I guess it will boil down to how the Westlakes feel and which firm turns in a better bid."

"I know this is premature," Mindy said, "but the thought crossed my mind—if Lily's firm gets the contract and she is the lead architect, do you think she might want to collaborate with Alix Hamilton since they've worked together? Wouldn't it be great if

Caroline somehow had a hand in the project? She'd have more reason to be here."

"Wow! I hadn't thought of that. I guess it might be a possibility. I don't think anyone's gotten that far. Lucinda mentioned getting our own ideas together before getting a professional designer involved. I'm leery of that too-put-together look that screams *decorator,* and I'm also a little leery of Alix. From what I know of her, she sounds arrogant and autocratic."

"She's all of that and then some!" Mindy hooted. "I'd know; better than most. But, she is good, and you can't take that away from her. I wouldn't worry about it. It may never come to pass."

"You're the one who brought it up," Ronnie protested. "You're not supposed to be putting things in my head that will give me nightmares. I'm having enough trouble sleeping, remember?"

"When do you go to Tulsa and Houston?" Mindy inquired.

"I'm not sure. Soon, I think, maybe a couple of weeks. I'm looking forward to it. I've never been to either city. I really don't know much about the whole middle of the country."

"Um, hmm." Mindy nodded and winked. "Yes, I'm sure a trip to Tulsa is very enticing," she teased.

"What about you?" Ronnie asked, chagrined. "All we've talked about is what's going on in my life. What have you been up to?"

"Spending a lot of time with Sara, talking to her on the phone, or texting," Mindy said. "She and Jon are ready to set a date, but she has to tell her family first. It's going to be hard to explain how she's serious enough to marry him when they're just hearing about him for the first time. They've been seeing each other for about three years."

"Whew," Ronnie commiserated. "Her mother will be baffled and hurt, her brother will be baffled and angry, and her sister will be baffled and envious. Poor Sara!"

"Jon put in his application with human resources to retire," Mindy told her. "That will start the ball rolling. Once he's got his pension squared away and an actual retirement date, they don't want to wait. Sara says that, once her mother meets Jon and gets over the shock, she'll want to have the wedding at her house, and she'll want to prepare all the food. Sara wants to have it at some sort of venue—other than in a church—with caterers so her mother won't have to lift a finger and can just enjoy the day."

"What kind of venue?" Ronnie asked.

"I don't know. She'll ask her sister, Ruth, to be her maid of honor, and her brother can give her away. She wants something simple so her family won't feel out of place. They've had enough of that for a lifetime."

"She should talk to Rickie. She was in the same boat when she married Greg. His mother wanted a big, fancy wedding in New York at one of the luxury hotels, and she wanted something simple in Jamestown. She might have some good ideas."

"One thing's for sure, Sara doesn't want groomsmen in those god-awful rented tuxes like it's some high school prom. We're thinking maybe just khakis and a good white shirt, with a bow tie—you know, clothes they already own and that fit. Well, except for the bow tie; that might take a little convincing. Jon would like to have a cabin built that they can move into after the wedding, so they're thinking spring of next year. Valentine's Day would be pushing it, but it might be do-able. We can see red velvet bow ties for the groomsmen and fitted red velvet jackets for the bridesmaids and a fitted winter-white velvet jacket for Sara."

"That's it?" Ronnie teased. "They'd have to wear more than bow ties or jackets, wouldn't they?"

The two friends shared a chuckle, then Ronnie said seriously, "Thanks so much for listening. It really helps to talk it through. I feel a lot better about a lot of things."

Chapter Thirteen

The next few weeks went by almost in a blur, as each of the three realtors committed to long-standing plans or planned to wrap up long-standing commitments. "I'm not crazy about California," Andee had said one evening as she and Frank sat on the patio before supper. "But I'd like to get away from here for more than a few days. The Emery Pond project is so overwhelming that I need some distance and a fresh perspective. Tahoe is appealing, but your reunion is always a three-ring circus. I love seeing your family and wouldn't miss a minute, but it's not exactly relaxing."

"What do you have in mind?" Frank asked.

Originally from the Midwest, he had received his B.S. in civil engineering from the state university in Ohio, with a minor in mapping and surveying. Andee's husband always had a fascination with the west and, after graduation, pursued a job with a surveying firm based in Durango, Colorado. He loved that part of the country and had no intention of ever again living east of the Mississippi. That changed when he met Andee at a GPS workshop both were attending as part of their continuing education.

Andee already had something in mind, before broaching the idea. They batted the subject back and forth with Frank suggesting the southwest, which he loved.

"Too far," Andee told him. "That's a trip all by itself, and it would be hard to combine with Tahoe. I'd love to spend some time in the Pacific Northwest, but even that's too far." Frank sipped his beer, waiting for her to continue.

"What about a leisurely drive through the Napa and Sonoma Valleys, ending with a few days back in San Francisco?" she suggested. He nodded. They weren't wine drinkers, but they'd have to turn the rental car in and fly out of the San Francisco airport, so it made the most sense, and the scenery would be spectacular in its own special way.

"Do you want to plan a route and make reservations?" he asked." She shook her head and wrinkled her nose. "Just wander?" he confirmed. This time she nodded.

"No schedule! Just do whatever we want when we want then," he agreed.

It was almost a hiatus, waiting for Aaron Marks and Lily Montgomery to put their bids together. Ronnie continued to work on the jigsaw puzzle that was the land purchases needed to put the entire Emery Pond tract together. When Andee had gone over the map with both Aaron and Lily, she'd shown them the parcels colored in green had been purchased, and the ones colored in pink were under contract while the parcels colored in blue were still in negotiation. They'd been careful to ensure that the twelve hundred acres central to their plan were solidly locked in. The smaller pieces on the periphery would almost double the acreage, but locals were not eager to sell to developers, and overtures had to be made diplomatically.

As the disposition of each parcel was determined, Ronnie sent the information to Stephanie. She herself kept accurate and detailed records, so it was a duplication of effort. Luc had grasped how important it would be in the long run to enlist the girl's cooperation and not have to contend with her hostility, so he quickly made arrangements with his partners to fund her services from his own pocket. "That's only fair," he insisted. He was unrelenting, and all agreed.

"How's she doing?" Ronnie asked in one of their daily phone calls.

"So much better, thanks to you!" Luc assured her. "You have no idea how much it means to me for you to have taken an interest in her and given her this project to make her feel included."

He hesitated, and Ronnie held her breath, not ready for the swept-under-the-rug subject of a weekend away together. Then he abruptly changed the subject, telling her about the problems they were having on a huge project in Pittsburgh.

"That's one place I've never been," Ronnie said. "Never wanted to and still don't."

"I thought that once, myself, but you wouldn't believe how it's changed. You'd have to have seen it before in order to appreciate the renaissance that city has had. It used to be just a dingy steel town. Chip and I were horrified when Charles made arrangements to bury us there for a whole summer."

"Before when?" Ronnie asked.

"Now it's called 'The Paris of Appalachia.' You didn't know that?" Luc teased.

"Before when?" Ronnie persisted. "When were you there before?"

"Oh, right. It was between our junior and senior years at Daniels. Charles got Chip and me internships with corporations in Pittsburgh, both Fortune 500 companies, of course. We loved working right downtown." Luc warmed to his topic, describing some of the preeminent office buildings in detail.

"One of the older buildings was commissioned in the 20s, and it's distinctive for its Art Deco architecture and style. And one of the newer ones is a neo-Gothic tower, complete with spires, made of reflective glass that's considered the jewel of the city skyline. It's awesome, seriously.

"Anyway," he continued, "there was a huge steel mill on the south side, the other side of the Monongahela River, that was an ethnic enclave. Most of the population was Lithuanian, and most of them were blue-collar steelworkers. That's all been gentrified now, of course. The mill buildings stood empty for years, just deteriorating, and then were actually dismantled—four miles of them on the flats with river frontage. Now it's the usual mix of high-end eateries, galleries, and national-brand stores. Go figure!"

Ronnie listened closely as Luc continued. "Both of the companies we interned with are involved in the construction business in some form or another, and Charles wanted us both to have the opportunity to start making contacts and, of course, he knew someone who knew someone..."

"How long were you there?" she asked.

"Just for the summer. We sublet an apartment in Shadyside from a grad student. It was a very cool area, and we had a blast."

"And you're going there now because...? For how long?"

"I don't really know. A week, maybe ten days. One of our major projects is in trouble, so Charles wants me and Chip to spend some time trying to figure out what's wrong and what has to be done to turn it around. It's bleeding red ink at only a third done and way behind schedule. It's a hot mess!"

Ronnie waited for him to continue.

"I'd like to see you, Ronnie," Luc said quietly, his tone more intimate. "I guess we'll see each other in Tulsa. The original plan was that we'd come from

Virginia and pick up Rickie, Andee, and you in Nashville en route, but now it looks as if Charles, Julia, and Lucinda might have to make that leg by themselves. Chip and I will fly commercial and meet you there if it comes to that. We'll be going to Pittsburgh Monday morning and, if it looks like we'll have to be there over a weekend, the company plane can bring Steph up late Friday to spend the weekend with me and take Chip back home and then the reverse late Sunday afternoon. We've done that before when his kids were little. He'd go there to be with them, and Kelli and Steph would have some time with me. Chip and I would probably just have worked straight through, but Charles was insistent because he knew what a toll prolonged absences took on marriages and families." Then he added, "Not that it mattered, in my case."

Ronnie heard both regret and bitterness in his tone, in equal measures.

Whoa! Is that a red flag? That was something she'd run by Mindy in one of their girl talks; no way would she get involved with someone who wasn't over his first wife. After another five minutes or so, they agreed to talk again the following evening and reluctantly hung up.

Ronnie spent the rest of the day holed up in her home office, absorbed in looking through the collection of pictures she'd taken on various trail rides, and identifying those most appealing for the brochure she'd started to rough out. But she couldn't concentrate on Emery Pond when Luc's comment kept niggling. At about four, she called Mindy.

The phone rang several times, and she was about to hang up when the call connected. She winced as there was a loud crash, and she heard Mindy say, "Shit!"

She guessed, correctly, that Mindy was in the middle of something and had dropped the receiver.

"Ronnie? Can I call you back in a few minutes? Sara's here, and we're blanching peaches." *Blanching peaches? Where did that come from?* Mindy didn't cook much and didn't usually seem too interested in domestic pursuits.

Mindy called Ronnie back a half-hour later.

"You have peaches?" Ronnie asked.

"I do!" Mindy was enthusiastic.

"Where did you get peaches at this time of year?"

"You know I planted two trees a couple of years ago?" Without waiting for a response, Mindy continued, "I don't actually have any yet, but this year will be my first harvest. I can't wait; they'll be so sweet and so juicy! These are store peaches, but Sara got them at a health food place in Knoxville that specializes in organic produce, so they're the next best thing. She's staying here for a few days. We're practicing preparing peaches for all the cobblers I'll be making. Sara is showing me how to make one right now."

"What's happening with Sara?" Ronnie demanded. "Did she and Jon have a fight? The wedding's not off, is it?"

"No! No, that's not it," Mindy reassured her quickly. "No, Jon's great. It's her sister, Ruth. She went nuts when Sara told her family about Jon. Her mother didn't say a word, not one word, but Ruth said enough for both of them. She said some really hurtful, really terrible things that she meant and can't take back. Sara is devastated!"

"Did Sara tell Ruth she's planning to get married? I'm sure she's jealous, and half of what she said is pure spite."

"Yeah," Mindy agreed. "Anyway, Sara is pretty upset. She doesn't have a house-sitting gig at the moment, so I told her to stay here for a few days while they get used to the idea."

"Did she tell Jon?'" Ronnie asked.

"She did, and he was great. He's so calm, he's the best thing that ever happened to Sara, and she's crazy about him. That's all that matters. Her mother will be fine once she meets him and gets to know him. Ruth will be jealous of Sara's fiancée, then Sara's wedding, then Sara's house, then Sara's baby—it will just be more of the same."

"I guess today's your day to be sob sister," Ronnie said. "I wanted to run something by you myself."

"This is amazing," Mindy blurted, still on a roll. "Sara said I was losing half the fruit when she saw me start peeling the peaches with a paring knife. She showed me how to blanch to get the skin off. I cut an x on the pointy end and put them in boiling water for thirty seconds and then dropped them into an ice bath for ten seconds. The skins peeled right off in the four sections that the x made. It was amazing! It also took her mind off her problems for a while. Now, Jon's coming over to pick her up and take her somewhere for dinner. He'll talk her through this."

"Do you want to come over here for dinner?" Ronnie asked. "I have some of that garlic salmon, Spanish rice, and some fresh corn. I could make a Caesar salad. You know me; I can assemble dinner." She laughed.

"Sounds great," Mindy agreed eagerly.

"I'll bring some cobbler," she added triumphantly.

Ronnie was about to hang up when she realized Mindy was still talking.

"Here's another thing I learned today. You know how when you make a pie crust, you add two tablespoons of cold water to the flour? That's what forms gluten. Well, if you add too much water or work the dough too much, the crust gets tough, from the gluten. You knew that, right?"

What a strange conversation this is. Mindy's not much of a cook, so what's with all these culinary secrets?

"Well, Sara told me that if you add vodka instead of water, gluten can't form. The alcohol burns off, and you have a light, flaky, tender crust!"

"Um, wow! Who knew?" Ronnie agreed. "I didn't think Sara drank hard liquor at all. What's she doing with vodka? Is that something she read somewhere? She sure didn't pick up that little tip in her mother's kitchen."

"No, that's for sure!" Mindy laughed. "Jon's mother told her after Sara complimented her pie when they went to visit last month. Remember? She told her family she was on assignment, researching a story, but she and Jon went to visit his folks so they could meet Sara. They loved her, of course, so that's one thing she doesn't have to worry about."

"So, you're going to give this miraculous crust a try?" Ronnie teased.

"Hell, no! You know I don't like to cook! I'm going to tell Caroline; she'll bring a pie sure as shit next time she comes, and you can see for yourself."

Later that evening, after the dishes had been put in the dishwasher, the two women sat companionably on Ronnie's porch, dessert forks laid across plates that were scraped clean. After polishing off the cobbler, Ronnie told Mindy about her conversation with Luc earlier that day.

"I just heard something in his tone I didn't like," Ronnie confided. "I've been feeling raw from Evan popping up out of nowhere and having to see him. I thought I'd worked through all those feelings and put all that anger behind me. I thought I was completely healed with a new life—a new job, new house, new friends—and there was no scab to rip off anymore, but I was wrong. All those awful feelings are still there. I don't ever want to feel that way again, and I don't want to get involved with someone who isn't ready or able to give me one hundred percent."

Mindy didn't say anything and, while the silence stretched, it wasn't uncomfortable.

"This is how I see it," she said at last. "I don't think it's a bad thing if he is regretful or bitter. I hate it when there are children involved. It's so much uglier, and parents feel so much guiltier because kids are usually messed up. If he feels bitter, he's probably mad at himself for getting into a bad marriage in the first place, and he's probably entitled to those feelings. From what I've heard, his ex-wife sounds like a bitch on wheels. He's probably wondering how he let himself become involved with someone who would disappoint him so badly and not hold up her end of the bargain to provide a safe, secure, nurturing environment for their child."

It was Ronnie's turn to be silent for a moment.

"I didn't think of it that way, but I think you're right." Relief and hope filled her at what the future could still hold.

"And," Mindy added, "why shouldn't he be regretful for what should have been but isn't? You'd think less of him if he wasn't."

"Are you talking about Luc, or about Evan and me?" Ronnie asked perspicaciously.

"All of the above," Mindy replied, thoughtfully. "Myself included." Ronnie was startled because Mindy never talked about her ex or the upscale life she'd left behind in New England.

Mindy's ex-husband was a maxillofacial surgeon, specializing in reconstruction. The two had parted amicably, and with her two children, a boy and a girl, living out of the country, Mindy had shed her old life like a snake shedding its old skin and had, in what seemed to be the natural course of things, simply grown a new one. Her daughter, surprisingly, had chosen Penn State, spending four years on their main campus, and had been snapped up by an international hotel chain during a job fair in the spring of her senior year. She was now midway through an eighteen-month training program in Queensland, New Zealand, and loving every minute. Her son, too, intended a career that would include a lifetime of living abroad. He was always an exceptional student, much more serious than his gregarious and fun-loving sister. At Beacon University, he'd had a double major in German and in math/economics and was posted to Prague as the first rung in his career ladder with large and a well-known banking institution.

"You know, Mac and I were friends before we got married, we were friends while we were married, and we're friends now," Mindy said. "I'm certainly not bitter, nor do I feel guilty, but I am sometimes regretful that we drifted apart because, once the kids were off to college, we realized that we had no common interests and nothing much to say to each other. I remember how happy I was on my wedding day. I thought we'd be Dr. and Mrs. Malcolm Morrison-Myers until the day one of us died. I never imagined our marriage dying a slow death. I still love him, but I was suffocating."

"How does he feel?" Ronnie was curious.

"About the same," Mindy said. "Although it's much more inconvenient for him not to have a wife on his arm for all the ongoing dinners and parties and functions he attends. There's a tennis partner I'm hearing more and more about when I talk to Mitch or Jana so I wouldn't be surprised one of these days to get the phone call, telling me he's going to re-marry."

"You'd be okay with that?" Ronnie asked. Before Mindy could reply, Ronnie asked, "What about you? Do you think you'll ever re-marry?"

"To answer the first question, he needs someone, and if he finds the right person, I'll be happy for him," Mindy replied. "To answer the second, I wouldn't rule it out entirely, if I myself met the right person, but I'm not looking and will say it's extremely unlikely. I'm certainly not going to get on one of those internet dating sites if that's where you're headed!"

Both women gave a mock shudder.

Chapter Fourteen

Ronnie was expecting that they'd make the short trip to Tulsa and Houston in about two weeks, as she'd told Mindy. The plan was to fly from Washington to Tulsa, with a quick stop in Nashville only to take on passengers. It was to their advantage to gain an hour traveling west so they would be arriving in the late morning, local time. They'd have a brief tour of the host's facility, enjoy lunch there, and had allocated three hours for Aaron Marks to pitch his proposal, go over his drawings, and field questions. With bid in hand, they would continue on to Houston in the early evening and eat while they were airborne.

"How's Charles feeling?" Ronnie had asked Luc some days earlier. "Is he up to making this trip?"

"His plane has a very adequate galley, and Julia made sure Chip specified meal service to be included in the flight planning. We'll have to get a very early start so it will be a long day, but she'll keep a close eye on him. We all will."

Ronnie was in her home office that morning, still toying with ideas for the development's brochure. She wanted to have something roughed out for the upcoming trip. When her cell rang, she saw Horse Country Real Estate come up on Caller ID and pressed accept.

"Hi, Ronnie," Geri said, "Rickie just got a call from Chip Westlake, but he can't reach her, and neither can I."

"You probably won't be able to for a while. I'm sure she doesn't have coverage. I'll call him back. Thanks."

"Hey, Ronnie," Chip greeted her cheerfully a few minutes later. "Thanks for calling me back so quickly. I tried to reach Rickie earlier and then called the office when I couldn't."

"She and Andee are in Emery Pond this morning, trying to lock in another landowner. You know, that's something to put on our list. Our buyers aren't going to be happy with poor cell service; we'll have to address net extenders at some point. So, what's up? Everything okay?"

"Yes, but it looks like there is going to be an unexpected change of plans. Charles's doctor wants him to have some tests, and he's scheduled them for the end of the week. We were wondering if we could expedite the trip to see the architects. I've spoken with them both, one has a completed package for us, and the other is done except for the finishing touches. They both can clear their schedules. So, the question now is, can you three be able to go with such short notice?"

"How short?" Ronnie asked.

"Pretty short," Chip told her. "Tomorrow."

"Oh!" she yelped. She almost said, *Holy crap!* but bit her tongue just in time. Her mind was racing.

"Wow! Well, I'll get right on it, but it might be a few hours before I can get back to you."

"Our pilot is going to do his flight planning this afternoon so he can file it first thing in the morning, assuming we're all on board, so to speak," Chip said. It was apparent he expected they would be leaving in the morning.

"I'll do my best and will let you know as soon as I can," Ronnie reiterated, before concluding the call.

Still unable to reach Rickie or Andee, Ronnie sent texts to both of her partners, alerting them that she needed to speak with them ASAP. She called Geri to apprise her that all three would probably be out of the office for two full days. Then she called Jackie to tell her, as well, so she could cover any real estate activity during that time.

Mindy was next, to confirm that she could look after Purrl, and Ronnie's two horses. When she'd done all she could, she went upstairs and took her small overnighter out of the closet and began laying clothes on the bed.

Her first choice was the same thing she'd worn to The Hungry Horse the day she'd seen Evan. The navy twill jeans and navy leather blazer were simple, elegant, and understated, would travel well, and could be relied on to present a polished professional appearance once they reached their destination. She frowned, not wanting any reminders of an event she'd tried to put out of her mind. *No. Fuck him! I'll wear any damn thing I want!*

She decided to wear a thin navy cashmere turtleneck on the first day of the two-day trip, thinking it might be cool in Oklahoma in early October. She laid her silver choker, silver cuff bracelet, and silver stud earrings on the top of her dresser, then she frowned. She would pack a small travel iron and could wear the same jeans the following day with her navy silk shirt that would be better suited to Houston's heat. The choker was perfect with the shirt but too short to wear with the sweater. *Oh, well, the world will still keep turning.* The navy belt had a silver buckle that would have to suffice.

Thankfully, Rickie called back while she was packing and said what Ronnie hadn't; *"Holy crap!"* Ronnie told her she'd notified both Geri and Jackie all three would most likely be out of the office for two days, so that aspect was squared away. Rickie and Andee just needed to pack and make arrangements for their own animal care. Since she'd had more time to prepare, she offered to drive to the Nashville airport the following morning.

It was dark when Ronnie awoke, and still dark at this time of year when she pulled out of her driveway shortly after five-thirty. She, Rickie, and Andee were familiar with arrivals and departures at the international airport in Nashville, but none had had occasion to fly from the general aviation side.

"You know where you're going?" Andee had asked as soon as she'd settled herself in the passenger seat.

"Well, I've never been to the Gilbert P. Blair Airport, if that's what you're asking, but I've built in plenty of time and have GPS," Ronnie replied testily.

"Sorry, sorry, I was just teasing. Sounds like you need more caffeine. I'm glad you brought your travel cup." It was common knowledge that Ronnie needed her first mug of coffee before engaging in conversation, and Andee wisely didn't speak again until Rickie was in the car.

The Washington contingent had departed at seven a.m. eastern. Charles explained that the jet's cruising speed of four-hundred-thirty knots reduced the distance of five-hundred-sixty-six air miles to a flight time of just about an hour and a half, which put them in Nashville just before eight, local time.

They were airborne again a few minutes later. The girls helped themselves to coffee, croissants with a selection of jams and jellies, and fresh fruit once they'd leveled off at altitude.

"You don't need to refuel?" Andee asked Charles. He shook his head.

"We have a range of almost two thousand miles with forty-five minutes of reserve fuel, so there's no need. The pilot will take care of that once we're in

Houston. This morning, he'll radio ahead when we're about twenty minutes out, and your Mr. Marks will meet us when we land. It's about five hundred fourteen miles or so from Nashville to Tulsa, so we should be landing right around nine-thirty. It's central time as well, and so is Houston."

Ronnie would have had to use a calculator, but Andee was already doing some calculations in her head. "I thought it took about nine hours to drive from Nashville to Tulsa, wouldn't that be six hundred and some-odd miles?"

Charles smiled. "We're both right! You're thinking of road miles, and I'm talking air miles, which is a straight line from Point A to Point B."

Aaron Marks was waiting for them, and introductions were made.

"This is my associate, Dean Yost," he said. "My SUV won't hold all of you, so I recruited him to help ferry you to the office and back to the airport again later this afternoon. He has four children, so his vehicle has a third row of seats and can accommodate quite a few passengers. He's actually the draftsman who produced the drawings for my presentation. If ours is the bid you accept, he'll be working closely with us on this project, so he'd be with us today, in any case."

Ronnie knew from Luc that a new venture always energized Charles, and he was certainly the lynchpin in this one.

"I sure hope this goes well," Andee whispered to her as the group stood outside the vehicles for a few moments. Charles was conversing animatedly with both men, favorably impressed if his expression and body language was any indicator. She breathed a sigh of relief as she and her partners had made the recommendations for the three architectural firms. Charles would have taken a visceral dislike to Lewis Wagner in spite of his excellent résumé and references, of that she had no doubt.

"Why don't you three ride with Aaron?" Charles suggested to Andee, "And we five will ride with Dean."

They were pleased to find Quality's offices in a venerable country house, hidden from view by high hedges in a leafy suburb, rather than in one of the oil-boom skyscrapers that distinguished the city skyline.

Aaron had given them an overview with a concise visual presentation which corresponded to the folders that had been placed on the table at each seat. When he finished, they spent about an hour engaged in a lively discussion about the general concept. Ronnie had made a quick call to Quality's office the afternoon before, leaving a message for Aaron, so he'd be aware that both Julia and Lucinda would be attending the meeting. Both wives not only participated but were as interested and knowledgeable as the principals. Chip's wife, Lucinda, in particular, raised several questions and made several suggestions that had them all nodding thoughtfully. Aaron always recorded his client meetings; he'd probably go back over this portion of the meeting more than once.

When Julia signaled to Ronnie that Charles was beginning to flag, she discreetly caught Aaron's eye. He adroitly suggested they break for a midday meal a few minutes later.

"I want to give you a little time to digest figuratively and, now, literally. After lunch, we can get into specifics of timeframes, scheduling, subcontractors, costs, and the rest of the not-so-glamorous nuts and bolts. You'll have more questions than I'll have answers for, at this point, but we need to ensure we're on the same page and define what our expectations are."

Rickie, Ronnie, and Andee sat side by side in the conference room with Ronnie in the middle, but now, at a large circular table in the dining room, Lucinda was on her right and Luc on her left. Although they were immediately drawn to each other, both Ronnie and Luc were especially careful not to engage in any way, verbally and non-verbally, that would be anything other than cordial and professional. Now, with the pale blue tablecloth reaching almost to their knees, he quietly hooked her ankle with his and pulled her leg to rest against his, hidden from view.

On the one-hour flight to Texas early that evening, the shortest segment of the trip, drinks were served once they were again at cruising altitude, and each placed a dinner order immediately from the choice of two entrees. Both Lucinda and Julia held a glass of white wine, Andee had a beer at her elbow, Ronnie and Rickie sipped a cabernet, and whiskey had been poured in cut-crystal glasses for each of the three men. When Charles finished only half of his drink and dozed off with his dinner untouched, Chip motioned for his mother to join him at the front of the cabin

"Is Dad okay? Should I be concerned?" he asked in a low tone.

"Today has tired him; this little nap will do him good," Julia reassured her son. "Once we're settled at the hotel, I'll order him something from room service. We'll have an early night."

In contrast to the Quality offices, Lily Montgomery's firm occupied three floors of pricey office space in downtown Houston's tallest skyscraper.

"Our firm has actually been in existence for almost fifty years," she explained as she showed them around, "But we were one of the first tenants when this building was completed in 1982. It was designed by I.M. Pei. His innovative style is evident in the hexagonal floor plate. This allows windows on five sides, so the light is unparalleled."

"As is the view! As well-traveled and cosmopolitan as I am, even I'm awed," Chip enthused.

Lily, too, began with a visual presentation. She had folders laid along the conference table for each participant but apologized at the outset that her proposal wasn't as polished as she would have liked, given the time constraint. As it was, she had worked through most of the night. Chip, Luc, and Charles would have approved of her work ethic had they known, but she didn't allow her appearance to betray her lack of sleep.

She dressed to minimize the first impression her stunning beauty invariably created, wearing a tailored linen pantsuit the color of heavy cream with a simple long off-white V-neck over blouse. Her jewelry was eighteen-carat, small gold hoops at her ears, a thin gold bangle on one wrist, and an elegant watch set into a wide faux-tortoise bracelet on the other, along with a narrow gold wedding band.

When the group moved into a nearby room filled with drafting tables, Julia touched Lily's arm and held her back.

"Ms. Montgomery, I hate to do this to you because you're already at a disadvantage, but I'd like to ask if you can cut your presentation short. Charles' color this morning is concerning, and I'm afraid he's feeling less well than he's willing to let on. He has several medical appointments scheduled for later this week, but I'll feel much better when he's home and close to his own doctors."

"Call me Lily, please. Of course, whatever you need. Your husband's health is the most important thing. You've checked out of your hotel? Where's your luggage?"

"We've checked out, and the hotel is holding our bags at the front desk," Julia told her. "It's only a few minutes from here, and we plan to pick them up on our way to the airport this afternoon."

"Let me give this fifteen-minute presentation so as not to raise any alarms, and then we can have a quick lunch in the dining room. In the meantime, I'll have my assistant cab over to your hotel to get your luggage and run it out to the airport so it will already be on board when you're ready to leave. Mr. Westlake will be better off with lunch than without, would you agree?"

Tears filled Julia's eyes, and she blinked them back. "Thank you so much. You're extremely thoughtful and very kind."

When she rejoined the group, Lily took up a long pointer, bending over a drafting table.

"I've taken liberties with your original concept," she informed them. "I had a residential complex, including stabling in mind, but it was serendipitous that I was able to go trail riding in Big South Fork while I was in Jamestown for a site visit. In all likelihood, that gave me a perspective my competitor was not afforded because I viewed the site the following day envisioning how to lay out a trail."

Rickie, Ronnie, and Andee were all nodding. Lily felt relatively sure she had just nailed it.

"Here..." She ran the pointer along the bluff line. "You can set the trail back far enough that the terrain will be fairly level and riders won't feel imperiled but can still enjoy the magnificent views of the gorges and ravines below."

"She's just described the trails at High Point without ever having seen them!" Andee burst out, turning to the investors. "That's exactly what we want for our development!"

Lily moved the pointer to the far end.

"I was also thinking that you might want to consider a small barn to house horses that could be rented for a short period of time by part-time residents who weren't bringing their own horses or who didn't want to own any, for one reason or another, or who need extra horses for guests."

"Airpark Acres!" Rickie and Andee exclaimed in unison.

Lily looked quizzically at them, making a mental note to pursue that comment at a later time, mindful that she needed to shorten up her presentation and not get a lengthy explanation started.

"Also, there should be a small apartment attached for a live-in barn manager and some extra stalls with turnout where resident horses could be boarded whenever their owners travel."

She was astonished when Andee and Rickie high fived, exclaiming, "Trail's End!"

She turned to Ronnie, eyebrows raised, who told her, "Without even realizing it, you've just incorporated the best features of each of the equestrian developments in our area."

Feeling more confident, Lily said smoothly, "All of this is detailed in the portfolio I've prepared for you to take with you. Since this is just an overview, I suggest we adjourn for a light lunch in our dining room. We can't send you away without having some of the Black Angus Texas is so famous for." She motioned for the group to follow her into a room paneled with weathered wood.

The western-motif décor was so artfully juxtaposed with the sleek efficiency of the office space that it was as if they'd been instantaneously teleported onto a cattle ranch. A black-clad waiter efficiently poured glasses of iced tea, then placed a romaine salad with homemade blue cheese dressing and oversized homemade croutons in front of each. He returned with a woven basket, reaching into it with tongs and putting two steaming cheddar biscuits onto everyone's bread plates. A few minutes later, he was back with a large tray, holding heated plates with paper-thin slices of beautifully-seasoned sirloin. Lily had phoned Rickie well in advance to describe the menu and make sure it would suit. Although it had clearly been catered, everyone assured Lily it was one of the best lunches they'd ever had, and they all thoroughly enjoyed the Texan hospitality.

Chip told Lily, upon leaving, they would know which firm they had decided on by the end of the week, and she could expect a call from him, one way or the other, by close of business on Friday.

Each person was lost in his own thoughts during the time it took for the return flight from Houston to Nashville, the second-shortest leg of the trip. Julia thumbed through a magazine, Lucinda and Chip were discussing their son, Charlie's, abrupt change of majors at Pemberton and wondering what had brought that about. Charles was dozing in his seat, head back and eyes closed. Everyone was tired, and it was tacitly understood that the forthcoming discussion of their fact-finding trip would be tabled until they'd had adequate time to read and study the materials they'd been given.

Rickie and Ronnie sat side by side, with Ronnie on the aisle and Rickie staring out the window, her expression woebegone.

"What are you thinking about?" Ronnie asked.

Rickie's voice was so low, Ronnie had to lean in to hear her whispered words.

"I don't expect ever to have again what I had with Greg, but I can't keep shortchanging myself. When I look at Charles and Julia, I know that's the real deal. That's what I want, truth be told. I envy couples like Andee and Frank, and Chip and Lucinda," Rickie said.

At that moment, Andee twisted around in her seat and addressed Rickie.

"Do you still have that little knife you carry? The one with all the tiny tools? It has a tweezer, doesn't it? I picked up a splinter somewhere today, and it's starting to throb. Can you take a look at it?"

"Go get a little of that whiskey in a glass," Rickie ordered. "We'll sterilize the wound and the instrument, and I'll perform battlefield surgery."

Ronnie slid out of her seat so Andee could sit next to Rickie.

Luc was sitting by himself at the back of the plane, flipping through an aviation magazine. When Ronnie approached, he stood and nodded toward the window seat, indicating she should join him.

"Just a second. I need to give this glass to Andee."

"Here you go, ladies," she said, handing the whiskey to Rickie. "I'll be back. Luc wants to talk to me."

When she returned and sat next Luc, he took her by surprise when he reached for her hand. At his touch, and in that instant, she decided that she did want to get to know this wonderful man better, and she didn't want to waste any more time. Rickie's remark a few minutes ago had resonated with her. As soon as the moment was right, she'd tell him that she would like to make plans with him for the weekend away that he wanted. She appreciated being given the time and space to arrive at that conclusion herself.

Now she had no trepidation, only eagerness, and anticipation.

The remainder of the week was busy with Ronnie, Rickie, and Jackie all showing property to prospects. Jackie had been slammed with paperwork in the two days they were gone. Andee was helping Geri schedule appraisals and building inspections for the four offers that had been written, as well as entering two new listings into the MLS, and sorting through the myriad of other details that must be attended to in a busy real estate office. This uptick in sales could bode well for the future and translate into sales for their own development.

On Wednesday, Rickie asked, "Are we ready to discuss our recommendation for an architect? I want to have our answer ready for the Westlakes. I expect them to call any time now."

"Charles has medical appointments tomorrow, doesn't he?" Ronnie asked. "I would guess that Chip will be the one doing the calling."

"Charles is apparently having a liver function test, which is just bloodwork," Rickie replied. "And an MRI. Both procedures are noninvasive, but he'll be tied up most of the day on Thursday; you know how that goes. Chip and Lucinda are leaving on Friday for parents' weekend at Pemberton. Chip wasn't sure they should go, but Julia insisted. They'll take Charles's plane, and it will be on standby in Trenton. The airport is less than ten miles from Pemberton so they can be back in Maryland quickly if they need to."

"I didn't know Trenton had an airport," Andee commented.

"According to Chip, it takes small jets and has been used for things like, you know, major airlines' commuter flights."

"We're all here; why not now? Seems like as good a time as any to discuss this," Ronnie said.

Once they were seated in her office, Rickie asked, "Ronnie?"

"I'd say Lily, hands down. I really like Aaron, and they're probably equally competent, but she seems to really understand horses in ways he doesn't. I think she'd bring more ideas to the table than he would, in the long run."

"I agree with that, but my concern is—and I hate to say this—whether a woman would be able to interface as well as a man with a construction foreman. You know what macho assholes construction workers can be," said Andee.

"There is that," Rickie said. "I thought of that too, but I think Lily can handle it. She'd probably have those guys eating out of her hand on day one and falling all over themselves."

"All right then, we agree," Rickie summed it up. Later that day, when Chip called, it was unanimous.

"As satisfied as we all are with the decision, I don't envy you having to make the call to Quality. I wish we could have good news for both of them." Rickie told him.

"Firms bid and don't get contracts all the time; it goes with the territory. However…" Chip let the sentence hang, drawing out the suspense.

"However, what?" Rickie demanded.

"However, I might have some good news on that front. I'm waiting for the other shoe to drop with regard to my dad's tests. I think there's something really wrong and he knows it. Mom suspects it, and now I do, too. You saw him in Houston. I think I'm going to need to spend a lot more time here in the immediate future and can't be in two places at once. I can't leave Luc to deal with the Pittsburgh debacle alone either, so I'm going to propose we hire Aaron Marks to step in and work with Luc to get that back on track. We think we've figured out what the money problems are, and, once that's resolved, Aaron can manage the construction end. He'd have to do some re-prioritizing and re-scheduling to make up for lost time, but we have our anchor tenants committed and don't want them to go elsewhere because we can't deliver on time."

"I'm going to call both Lily and Aaron now," Chip said. "I'll call Lily first to be sure I have her acceptance before I call Aaron. Fingers crossed because this would be win/win."

The following evening, Ronnie didn't hear from Luc until almost eleven. She'd gotten home late and, after feeding the horses, watched the weather and the news with a glass of wine at her elbow and a hastily-microwaved dinner on the low table in front of her. After channel surfing for a while and finding nothing that captured her interest, she began turning off lights in preparation for bed. Purrl had preceded her upstairs fifteen minutes earlier, preferring an earlier bedtime. Ronnie was in the bathroom, washing her makeup off when her cell rang, and Luc's name appeared on the screen.

"Sorry it's so late," he apologized. "Long day!"

"I just had one of those myself, but not as long as yours."

"I won't keep you. I just wanted to touch base, say hello, and see how you are," he said.

"The office is a madhouse, so busy I forgot to eat lunch. But busy in a good way. I talked to Lily for quite a while this afternoon. Needless to say, she's thrilled that her firm got the contract and is excited about working with us. She already has her assistant researching the permits needed for the Emery Pond project and compiling lists of potential subcontractors. As soon as she can wrap up the work that's nearing completion, she'll plan another visit to Tennessee. Then I guess she'll roll up her sleeves and start the design process. What about Aaron? Have you talked to him?"

"Yesterday. No, wait, it must have been the day before. As Chip said, it turned out to be win/win. Aaron's firm has agreed that he will remain on-site in

Pittsburgh for us and travel from there to oversee projects that he has in various stages of completion in Massachusetts and Indiana. Essentially, that project is under control, but I have no idea when I'll get to see you."

Luc and Ronnie talked on the phone each evening, but it was some time before he got any kind of a break.

Chapter Fifteen

Three weeks later, on a sunny Friday morning, Ronnie turned right out of her driveway rather than left and headed for the airport in Oneida instead of going to the office. Things could have gone either way as the weather forecast for the weekend had been iffy, but the front had moved through the southeast sooner than predicted.

Now the air was warm, and the skies were clear. Ronnie's worries had dropped away like the ground beneath the wings as Luc's plane banked eastward and gained altitude.

"Oh, Luc, this is lovely! I've been so looking forward to this weekend."

"You can thank Lucinda. I was going to take you to a resort in West Virginia because it's not too far, and I didn't want to spend half the time just getting somewhere. I could easily fly into the regional airport, and I wanted to take you somewhere to be waited on hand and foot and pampered at the spa. But Lucinda got online and looked at the pictures of the rooms and told me you would hate a place with seven hundred rooms and 60s décor. She said it was pretentious and outdated, even with a recent refurbishing, and it's overpriced. Not what I had in mind at all. So I did a little research myself and found that I liked the sound of a resort that's about sixty miles north of Atlanta. I thought that distance wouldn't take too big a bite out of our weekend but, again, same thing. Good dining and it has a spa, but then I looked at the pictures of the rooms online. They're attractive, but the décor is country, which is pretty much what you all have at home. I wanted something different and elegant and special."

"Where *are* we going?" Ronnie slipped her left hand into Luc's right as he lifted it from the trim wheel between the seats.

"You'll see when we get there," he teased.

The three-hour flight time passed quickly, as Ronnie and Luc caught each other up on the events in their daily lives and dissected and discussed various aspects of the Tennessee real estate venture. The Emery Pond development should be pretty straightforward, once the necessary permits were in place, and bids had been accepted for assorted phases of excavation, site prep infrastructure, and construction.

"We need to come up with a catchy name," Ronnie told him. "We need to start our advertising campaign so we can offset the start-up costs by pre-selling. With the right name, it should sell itself."

"Maybe we should use one of those random name generators," Luc joked. He scanned the gauges, made a slight adjustment to his trim wheel, and asked, "How are things going with the bill to privatize the park? Anything new? CW is a bold thinker but conservative financially, his maxim is to invest fully in a project and see it through to completion before undertaking another. When you ladies walked him through the possibilities Emery Pond presented, he wasn't happy with the timing but recognized this as an opportunity to be snatched or missed altogether, irrespective of the privatization issue."

Rickie had carefully and methodically approached local landowners, executing private sales in a seemingly-random pattern so as to draw the least amount of attention to the Emery Pond project and the unwelcome attention of the anti-development contingent. CW's attorneys had created a couple of holding companies with innocuous names, and the deeds were recorded at intervals so anyone reviewing the registry would not perceive a series of purchases by a single buyer.

Ronnie had encouraged Stephanie to participate by entering the sales information in a spreadsheet and keeping a map up to date. They'd gotten off to a rocky start, but Steph soaked up the attention like a sponge and had morphed from surly to spirited in the space of a few weeks. Wanting the girl to become emotionally involved, Ronnie had done some rearranging at the office, carving out a space for her and a new identity as Stevie, the newest member of the unofficial Boys Club.

Steph had grudgingly allowed her father to enroll her in an after-school weight-loss program. Initially, she'd been mortified at the thought of exposing her flab for water aerobics and had vociferously and steadfastly refused to shed her clothes until she realized that her fellow participants were in no position to ridicule. It was slow going and wouldn't happen overnight, but she was smart enough to see the benefits and committed herself to a goal to be reached eighteen months out. Ronnie and Lucinda had both taken an interest in her progress. Ronnie had told her that women who wanted to appear slimmer wore black. "That's too harsh for you, though, at your age, but I think navy would accomplish the same thing."

"I'd love to take her to a good salon," Ronnie had commented during a recent conversation, one day when Lucinda had called. "A good haircut and maybe some highlights would work wonders, but I'm afraid her mother will get her back up if she perceives that some other woman is interfering with her daughter."

"I'm not sure she'd even notice!" Lucinda scoffed. "But I see your point; that would certainly make things worse. Steph would be caught in the middle, so it might sit a lot better if it came from me. If I took her, I don't think Kelli would feel threatened."

"I don't know what I'd do without Lucinda," Luc told Ronnie. "She's been such a good influence on Steph. She's such a wonderful role model, in all respects. You are too. You have no idea!"

"All compliments gratefully accepted."

Now Luc addressed the air traffic controller.

"Good morning, Charleston." He gave the tower his call sign and stated that he was following visual flight rules, descending through nine thousand feet, and was approaching the executive airfield.

"Ah-ha!" Ronnie crowed. "Well, cowboy, you made a wonderful choice. You might not believe it, but this little ole' Yankee has never been to Charleston."

The ground, which had been a checkerboard of fields and trees resolved into individual fields and houses, cars on roads, and, in the distance, the airfield came into view. Receiving clearance to land, Luc aligned the small jet with the runway, lowering the flaps and maintaining a gradual descent. Ronnie watched with fascination as he managed the yoke, rudder, and throttles to control the jet's flight path.

The runway filled the windscreen as it rose to meet them, and then, with dual chirps, the tires kissed the concrete. Luc retarded the throttles to idle, gently easing the brakes until the aircraft gradually slowed to a full stop. Ronnie was awed by his skill. He seemed to do everything well, and she shivered in anticipation of the night ahead.

The hotel had sent a courtesy car to pick Ronnie and Luc up at the nearby airport. He'd done his research thoroughly, planning the entire weekend well in advance and had engaged a suite in a historic mansion. It had two bedrooms, two baths, and a comfortable sitting area.

"We've never actually been on a date, so I thought you'd like your space and some privacy to dress for dinner. Check-in isn't until four, but we can drop our bags at the desk, and they'll put them in our rooms."

Luc handed Ronnie a flier, showing a horse-drawn carriage touring the historic district. "There are several carriage companies, but Palmetto Carriage Works is the oldest and encourages customers to visit their Big Red Barn. I was sure that'd be right up your alley. I made a reservation for two o'clock. We can walk to the carriage barn from here. It's about twelve blocks, so maybe a mile. There are lots of little bistros and pubs, and I thought we'd find a place for lunch along the way. I wanted to start with a carriage tour so we can figure out the layout of Charleston and get our bearings. We'll have a private carriage so we can stop. I know you'll want to get pictures of homes, doors, windows, gates, flower boxes, and whatever else to show Andee and Rickie. We may get some ideas for Emery Pond, too, so keep that in mind," he said.

Luc had told Ronnie to dress casually for the afternoon and to wear comfortable shoes. She hadn't known their destination and had no idea what to expect, but her definition of comfortable shoes was her Ariat trail boots. She had polished them for the occasion and saw now that they were an excellent choice, as they started walking east on Wentworth

Street. The afternoon was an absolute delight, and Ronnie fell more in love with Luc as the hours passed. She took picture after picture, hardly knowing where to look, as their carriage rolled slowly through the cobblestone streets. Charleston was a visual feast, and their driver was very knowledgeable about the area's past, drawing their attention to points of interest and skillfully weaving a narrative to bring the city's history to life.

Luc had arranged for the tour to end back at the hotel. Ronnie caught the look of surprise and delight on the coachman's face when saw the fifty-dollar bill Luc had slipped into his hand. Luc was generous in all respects, with his emotions, his intellect, his time, and his wealth. Ronnie wondered, not for the first time, if he was a generous lover. She thought he would be and knew that she would soon have her answer.

"We'll eat here at the hotel this evening," he said, after the bellman had shown them to their suite. "I made a reservation for eight o'clock, which gives us plenty of time for a couple's massage in the spa at five-thirty and maybe a power nap before we dress for dinner."

Ronnie was speechless, amazed by how thoroughly Luc had planned this weekend getaway.

"Happy?" he asked, pulling her into his arms and smiling down into her upturned face. He kissed her gently and reluctantly released her. The spa was cleverly tucked away in the former stables, a detail Ronnie would appreciate.

"Let's take the stairs down and stop in the parlor on the way. They offer complimentary wine and hors d'oeuvres from five to six."

"I could use a little something," Ronnie agreed.

Forty-five minutes later, they lay side by side in a dim, elegantly-paneled room. A white sheet and a lightweight blanket were folded at Luc's waist, and his lean muscles gleamed with oil in the lamplight. Ronnie could smell the tang of the ginger and lemongrass wrap-and-rub that he had selected. She closed her eyes in pure bliss as her therapist smoothed lavender and tangerine scented oil across her shoulders and began to knead with long, smooth strokes.

"I'll pick you up at seven forty-five, Ms. Chandler," Luc said, as they walked back into their suite. His eyes went automatically to the phone in his hand. "You can take a nap for about a half-hour, if you want, but you'd better order a wake-up call if you feel as relaxed as I do right now. I could fall asleep standing up!"

At seven-forty-five on the dot, Luc tapped lightly on Ronnie's bedroom door. She was ready to leave.

"You look beautiful! You didn't buy that in Jamestown," he said, admiringly.

"Not hardly! It's not new, though. I bought it several years ago, for an evening wedding, and haven't had an occasion to wear it since."

Ronnie wore a timeless velvet suit, with a narrow pencil skirt and a fitted short jacket. It was a deep midnight navy, with a long row of closely-spaced rhinestone buttons. Deciding jewelry would distract, she let the suit speak for itself. Her only accessories were a simple pair of suede pumps in the same shade with a matching unadorned clutch. Her silver hair was striking on her worst day, but this evening she'd put a glaze on it after shampooing so it shone, and she'd created a smoky eye with a much darker shade of shadow than she customarily wore.

"I've never seen you dressed up," she commented, eyeing Luc. She was impressed. Luc's charcoal suit was clearly custom-tailored. With a pinpoint white Oxford and a silk foulard tie in a complementary dark blue, they made a very attractive couple as they wended their way through the gardens behind the mansion and entered the on-site eatery, one of the more popular restaurants in Charleston.

"You look almost as good as Zachary Day," Ronnie teased, knowing that when Luc watched network news, it was his favorite anchor's channel. He had commented more than once on the man's impeccable dress.

"I wonder what's going on at home," Ronnie said idly after they'd ordered. She picked up her wine glass and took a sip of the excellent Merlot Luc had ordered.

"I feel like I'm a million miles away, having an out-of-body experience."

"That's the whole idea. This weekend is just for us. By the way, just so you know, I intend for you to have an in-body experience," he joked.

The waiter then quietly placed a narrow box next to her plate.

"What's this?" she asked, delighted.

"Open it, and you'll see," Luc said.

She untied the ribbon, lifted the lid, and unfolded the tissue to reveal a silver necklace. It was a long rope with a tassel, almost identical to the wrapping from Evan's ill-fated birthday gift that she'd taken such a liking to. Her mouth literally fell open, so great was her surprise. Luc laughed aloud because her reaction was so classically comical.

"How did you know? I mean, how did you find—"

"Andee emailed me a picture, so I had a lot to work with. There are a lot of artisans in the DC area, and it wasn't hard to find a jeweler who could make exactly what I wanted. Actually, it was probably pieced together more than made as there are so many countries that are known for silversmithing. The rope-y thing is from Tibet, and the tassel is Mexican. I wanted to give you something you would really enjoy and use."

"I love it!"

"I love you, Ronnie," Luc said simply.

They'd lingered over a delicious dinner, despite Ronnie's eagerness to be lying together in Luc's big bed, and savored every mouthful and every minute, not wanting the evening to end. Hotel staff had performed turn-down service in their absence, and now only one small table lamp glowed in the living room and in each bedroom. Ronnie had hung her beautiful suit on a padded hanger and drawn the whisper-thin nightgown from her suitcase. It fit her perfectly, and the sleek lines molded her slim body. Tying the matching robe's belt around her waist, she was already moving toward Luc's bedroom, toward Luc's embrace.

Luc was waiting for her, wearing only pajama bottoms. His breath hitched as she walked in and stopped before him. Looking up at him, she saw the love shining in his eyes and on his face. He bent his head and slowly pressed his lips to hers. She opened her mouth, and his tongue touched hers as his hands eased the robe off her shoulders. It slid silently to the floor, forgotten.

Taking her hand, he drew her into the bedroom. He tugged on the drawstring at his waist, and the pajama bottoms pooled at his feet. In almost the same motion, he reached for her hips and grasped her gown. One minute she was wearing it and then—it was gone. He pulled her to him, and they stood for a moment, pressing the length of their bodies together.

He kissed her voraciously, his erection rock hard between her legs.

She was burning up, her entire body was on fire with need, with wanting. She felt herself grow wet and wetter. Luc's hands were cupping her face one minute, then the next, they were cupping her breasts. He rolled his thumbs back and forth over her nipples. They had never been so hard, so sensitive.

"*Luc,*" she groaned his name. Now his hand moved to the apex of her thighs, and he cupped her—there. "Ohhh! Ohhh! Ohhh!"

Slowly he eased her onto the bed, covering her body, sliding into her. Her fingers gripped his shoulders as she arched upward, wanting him deeper—more!

He drove himself into her so deep. His release burst from him in a heated spurt, then another and another as her body convulsed, gripping him, squeezing him. He rolled off her but held her close, cupping the back of her head as she buried her face in his shoulder.

"Luc?" she whispered.

"I love you, Ronnie," he told her, his voice hoarse.

They'd made love over and over, exploring each other's bodies. She stroked up and down the length of him, had taken him into her mouth, licking and sucking. He had spread her knees wide and buried his face between her legs, licking and sucking. He had taken her, again and again, and she had given herself to him, again and again. When they woke, their bodies came together again. No words were needed, and none were spoken.

Just before dawn, Ronnie fell into a deep sleep, still wrapped in Luc's arms.

The next morning, the soap smelled wonderful as Luc passed it back and forth over Ronnie's skin. In the huge glass-walled shower, steam billowed and swirled as he lathered her slick body and washed her hair with the matching shampoo. She reciprocated, slipping her hand between Luc's muscular legs.

"I can't get enough of you," he moaned, as Ronnie put her arms around his neck and wrapped her legs around his waist. "I didn't think I'd be able to do this again so soon," he panted as he slid into her.

Ronnie's eyes were closed. Luc gazed intently at her face, watching her as her body responded, tightening around him as her excitement grew. Waves of pleasure rushed through him as he skillfully thrust into her body. Suddenly, she stiffened in his arms, her head thrown back, swept up in her tumultuous shattering orgasm. Luc let himself go seconds later, groaning with the sheer pleasure of his own release. After unlocking her ankles from his hips, Ronnie slowly lowered her legs and sagged against him. His own legs felt too weak to support them both. He reached for the control and turned the water off.

"We'll run out of hot water."

"*Way* too late for a cold shower," she agreed.

A few minutes later, room service delivered a sumptuous breakfast, and they sat facing each other at a small table in front of the windows, each wearing the hotel's thick terry robes. Luc poured steaming hot coffee from an insulated carafe. "You'll need caffeine; there's some serious shopping still ahead."

Ronnie bit her lip.

"What a fabulous weekend." She sighed. "Good company, good food, great sex—shopping…"

"A plane ride, a present…" Luc offered, teasing. Ravenous, he eagerly lifted the domed lids, revealing fluffy scrambled eggs, crisp strips of bacon, and paper-thin raspberry blinis.

"Eat up," he ordered. "You'll need your strength, and you'll walk off all these calories."

An hour later, they strolled hand in hand along King Street, enjoying the eclectic mix of nationally and internationally recognized names interspersed with the charming, locally owned-and-operated businesses. Ronnie's eye was caught by a window display, and they stepped inside. She was immediately drawn to a pile of cashmere long-sleeved tees.

"These are single ply, so they're really thin," she exclaimed. "They'd be perfect under a vest or a shirt. I love the satin binding around the neck and the sleeves." Her enthusiasm was contagious.

"What color do you want?" Luc asked.

"Oh, no! I'm buying this. What color *do* I want?" The price tag was discreetly tucked inside the folded garment, and she turned it over.

"Wow! For ninety-nine dollars, I have to get one for Rickie and Andee. And Mindy." Within twenty minutes, she'd chosen a soft raspberry for herself, a dusty olive for Rickie, a dramatic deep pomegranate red for Andee, and a rich tobacco brown for Mindy, and had proffered her debit card to the sales assistant.

They wandered in and out of shops and galleries until Luc asked, "Are you hungry? Let's just get ice cream or something now because we're going on a sunset sail in the harbor in a couple of hours, and we'll have a snack then."

Ronnie's attention was caught by something in the window of Croghan's Jewel Box, and they stopped again.

"I want to go in and look at those sapphire earrings."

"Do you want to try them on?" Luc asked after a clerk had taken them out of the window for Ronnie's inspection.

"Oh, no, they're not for me. They're for Stephanie," she explained. "You should bring her a gift, and it should be something she'll keep and treasure. She's a little young for these, but she'll be thrilled with such a grown-up gift."

The earrings were simple ovals, dark blue stones, cabochon cut, set in a narrow rim of eighteen-carat gold.

"You'll probably melt the numbers right off your credit card, but she's working really hard to lose weight, and she's doing such a great job. I think a reward will go a long way."

"What happened to bringing souvenirs back for your friends and family?" Luc laughed. "You know, stuff like key chains and ashtrays." He was teasing, but Ronnie's thoughtfulness and generosity of spirit made his heart squeeze.

By the time they'd made their way to lower King Street and wandered through several of Charleston's world-renowned antique shops, they were tired and footsore.

"Let me find a cab," Luc suggested. "We'll stop at the hotel to drop these bags; the cabbie can wait, and then we can continue on to the harbor. It's almost four, and our cruise leaves at five."

Once they stopped at the hotel, Luc directed the driver to their next destination.

"I originally envisioned us on a schooner," Luc told her on the way to the dock. "Sailing past Fort Sumter on a tall ship seemed more historic. There is one, Echo. It's a reconstruction, of course, but you get the look and feel. But I didn't want to do one of those two-hour sunset cruise things with a lot of strangers. I could have chartered it for a private sail, but that seemed like overkill. Then I decided I wanted something smaller and more intimate, something elegant, so I read some reviews, and we're going out on a fifty-footer called Maestro.

Luc and Ronnie sat side by side in comfortable deck chairs, holding hands again, as the yacht motored out of the slip and past the jetties into open water. The breeze was slight but steady as the boat surged ahead when the mainsail unfurled and filled.

Luc had planned the excursion carefully, ordering a light meal of barbecued shrimp from the charter company's caterer. He had perceived them drinking a cold beer but learned that one of the boat's owners bottled a crisp Chardonnay, and it was available for purchase prior to sailing. With Maestro's private label, he thought Ronnie would like to take the empty bottle home.

When they got back to the hotel at about seven-thirty, Ronnie went to her own room to take a shower. They had a full day and, rather than dress for dinner and venture out, they agreed to order room service and have a quiet dinner in the suite, grateful for the opportunity to spend uninterrupted time together.

Luc 's eyes lit up when he saw Ronnie in the lovely chrysanthemum robe, which she'd slipped on over the matching gown and left unbelted. He pulled her close, smiling down into her upturned face. Slowly he trailed his index finger from one side of her collarbone to the other, and then his hand moved into the deep vee of the gown's neckline and cupped her breast. Her arms went around his neck, and they stood like that for a moment, savoring each other's closeness. Luc placed a tender kiss on her forehead and took a step back. She understood the unspoken reluctance in his face, that if he put his mouth over hers, dinner would be forgotten.

"You're so good to me," she whispered.

Overcome by emotion, her eyes filled, but Luc stroked his thumbs over her cheeks, wiping the tears before they could fall. She had thought she'd put Evan Parker firmly in the past where he belonged, but she recognized now that these emotions had lain dormant for a decade. She hadn't thought of Evan in so long but obviously seeing him so unexpectedly and recently had resurrected all the longing for love.

"Did you pick this set out yourself, or did you have—help?" she asked, determined not to let thoughts of what might have been intrude on what was.

"What do you think? Of course, I picked it out myself."

"Really? And you knew just where to shop for ladies' lingerie?" she teased.

"Busted!" Luc laughed. "Lucinda took me to her favorite store, but this ensemble had your name on it the instant I saw it."

"Well, I thought I'd wear it two nights in a row," Ronnie said. "It's hardly ready for the laundry. I only wore it last night for about—mmmm—ten seconds."

Just then, there was a discreet knock at the door. When Luc opened it, a tuxedoed waiter wheeled in a table and rolled it out onto the balcony, into the warm night air. He was followed by an assistant who lit a dozen tiny tea lights and expertly uncorked a bottle of Merlot, setting it on the table to breathe. Wrapping a napkin around the champagne bottle, he tilted it and removed the cork, filling their flutes before placing the bottle in a silver ice bucket to the left of Luc's chair. After removing the domed lids from their dinners, the waiters withdrew.

"Every second of this weekend has been a dream," Ronnie said.

Chapter Sixteen

While Ronnie had gone straight to the airport on Friday morning, the day had been largely uneventful for those at Horse Country Real Estate until about three-thirty, when the sky darkened, and the wind picked up. Everyone could feel the tension as the barometric pressure dropped.

"Wow! Is it windy!" Rickie shrugged one arm out of her jacket and grabbed the edge of the door before another gust could slam it back against the wall. "What's up?"

"You have a visitor." Andee nodded in the direction of Rickie's office.

"Hey, Pee Wee!" Rickie broke into a grin when she saw who it was. But, Deputy Pete Walton didn't return her enthusiasm.

"I'm here to serve a summons, Rickie. It's not a social call." Rickie had gone to school with Pete all her life and always been pals with his wife, Christine. He held out an envelope.

"What's this about?" Rickie was puzzled.

"I'll need a signature," he'd said simply, holding out a clipboard and a pen.

The letter was addressed to Erica Ahlers, Managing Broker, Horse Country Real Estate. Rickie didn't have a clue as to what the missive might contain, but she certainly knew it wasn't good news. The deputy nodded to Rickie and then to Andee as he passed, letting himself out of the building silently. Andee stood in the doorway. Rickie could feel Andee's stare boring into her as she'd scanned the document.

"Christ on a crutch!" Rickie swore. "You won't believe this! We're being sued—the agency, me as the managing broker, and Jacqueline Slaven, Affiliate Broker."

"Sued?" Andee said. "For what?"

"Misrepresentation," Rickie said, her voice flat. "Remember those people from Louisville who bought a cabin several months ago? It was Jackie's listing. Well, they're claiming that she didn't tell them there's a 'bear problem' here, and now they claim they're afraid to ride in the woods or go hiking. They never would have bought property here if they'd known, and Jackie was negligent in not disclosing a material defect blah, blah, blah. So they say."

She closed her eyes. She felt like she'd been punched in the solar plexus. She and her partners all loved living in Tennessee and extolled the area's appeal with genuine enthusiasm. Their customers had become clients, many had become neighbors, and some had become friends.

Jackie would be particularly devastated to learn that the Crosses had turned on her. They were her first sale, and she had especially enjoyed researching the possibilities and finding them the *perfect* cabin. They had gotten to know each other through frequent emails. When Melody and Jason Cross came to look at property, Jackie had taken Rickie's suggestion to pack a picnic lunch and plan the itinerary so they would arrive right around noon at the cabin she thought they would like best. As the couple had relaxed and munched their sandwiches on the porch, they'd begun to appreciate the ambiance of the setting and started imagining themselves living there.

The Crosses had come with a lender's commitment letter and knew exactly what they could spend. They made a fair offer and accepted the seller's reasonable counteroffer, the cabin appraised for more than the purchase price, and the closing was conducted smoothly as a mail-out to both parties. Jackie's commission split was generous, and she was thrilled with her first check, realizing for the first time how much you could earn when you sold your own listing and didn't have to co-broke with another agent.

Melody and Jason both had high-pressure careers, so they didn't get here often, but when they did, it was quality time. Jackie had chosen a soft chenille throw for the couple's living room, and they were very touched when she stopped by to present her housewarming gift. If Rickie had to guess who might have initiated a lawsuit, the Crosses were the last ones she would have thought of.

"Now that I think of it, it makes perfect sense," Andee muttered. "She's some sort of ombudsman; she does something with long-term care and patient's rights. You know, grievances against nursing homes and assisted-living facilities. And he's a lawyer. Worse! And not just any old lawyer," she continued. She hadn't wasted any time in trying to determine how serious their adversary was.

"I ran a search on him and then looked him up in a legal directory. He's a consumer fraud trial attorney."

"Jesus!" Rickie swore. "They're both in the mindset to think about people getting screwed. I hope he doesn't decide to spearhead some sort of class-action suit."

"Isn't this why realtors have errors and omissions insurance?" Andee asked rhetorically. "I've always had it, but I've never even thought about how it works."

"They'll probably file a complaint with the Tennessee Real Estate Commission and pull out all the stops," Rickie said. "If they haven't already. I don't understand this." Rickie was thoughtful. "It's the woods! The park service always says the bears are just part of a natural migration from surrounding states."

"I'm thinking about the investors," Andee said. "We're too far down the road for them to pull out now, so I'm not worried, exactly, but we need to tell them we're being sued and why."

"I hope the Crosses don't plaster this on a few internet sites and make it go viral. I wouldn't want social media to sink its teeth into this." Rickie was thinking aloud.

She glanced at Andee, who nodded to indicate she caught the pun. "And generate a lot of bad press."

"We'll just have to deal with it, if or when it happens. We'll just have to put a spin on it, so it doesn't depress sales," Andee said. "You know, there's a whole contingent who are in favor of the bears, who actually want them here. You've heard them, they moved here to enjoy nature and they like to see wildlife blah, blah…"

They agreed that they'd table the discussion until Monday.

Julia had set out CW's orange juice and placed the Sunday paper next to his plate, folded, just as he liked it. It was their custom to read the paper over a leisurely breakfast, swapping sections, and discussing a range of topics. She slid poached eggs onto two perfectly toasted pieces of wheat bread and brought the plate to the table. *CW must have overslept.*

She went to make sure he was up, not wanting his food to get cold. She was surprised to see him still sleeping, facing away from her. He was unresponsive when she put her hand on his shoulder and shook him. Alarm coursing through her, she tugged his body to face her and was horrified to see his face, and his eyes were a hideous shade of yellow.

A rescue unit had arrived within minutes of Julia's frantic 911 call. Julia was too distraught to phone Chip.

"It's not a heart attack, Mrs. Westlake," the paramedic assured her as he placed an oxygen mask over CW's nose and mouth.

"You'll be most helpful by remaining calm," the female attendant told her. "Is your family's information in your cell phone? Would you like me to call someone for you?" Wordlessly, Julia pulled her phone from her pocket and handed it to the woman. Expertly, she pulled up Julia's list of contacts and was gratified to see that her son was identified as ICE, In Case of Emergency, which this certainly was, in her professional opinion.

CW was placed in intensive care, and the decision made to perform immediate surgery when a CT scan revealed a blocked bile duct. That was all Julia had been told, although Chip now knew that the colon cancer had metastasized to his father's liver, and they would most likely be in a hospice situation. Julia clung to her daughter-in-law's hand, grateful for her comforting presence, her lips moving in prayer.

It was several hours before CW was out of recovery. Once he was back in ICU, Chip had gone to his parents' home to pack a change of clothes for his mother as well as her cosmetics and some toiletries. Julia wouldn't leave the hospital, and Chip wanted her to be as comfortable as possible while she held vigil. She was allowed a few minutes at CW's bedside, once an hour.

As soon as he exited the hospital building, Chip took the opportunity to call Andee, to update her.

"You'll call Rickie?" Chip had asked.

"Of course. What about Luc? Have you called him?"

"No, and I don't want you to call Ronnie, either. There's nothing they can do right now. Luc will come right home if he knows, but they might as well enjoy this weekend."

They agreed that there was no need to impart this sad news on Sunday evening. Monday morning would be soon enough.

Rickie's car was in the small gravel parking area behind Horse Country Real Estate when Andee pulled in on Monday morning, although it was only seven-fifteen. She hadn't slept well, and what little sleep she did get was fitful, as her mind refused to rest. She sure hoped Rickie had been there long enough to start the coffee.

"How is he? Any word?" she demanded, without preamble, as she pushed through the door. Rickie's face was a white, frozen mask, and she clearly had had little or no sleep herself. "He's not dead, is he?" Her voice trailed off to a strained whisper.

"No. No, he's not. It's not that. It's something else. Something not good."

An hour and a half later, Andee's cell rang, and she glanced at caller ID. It was Mindy. If it had been anyone else, she would have let the call go to voicemail. Ronnie had not yet appeared, and she didn't want to risk ignoring the call if Mindy was calling on Ronnie's behalf. She hit 'Send' to connect and pressed the speakerphone button so Rickie could listen in.

"Mindy," she acknowledged.

"Hey, good morning," Mindy greeted her. "I'm sorry to bother you so early, but I've left several messages for Ronnie and haven't been able to reach her. I was wondering what's going on?"

Andee and Rickie exchanged looks, clearly not pleased to have a third party involved in their professional crises. They liked Mindy and knew that she and Ronnie were very good friends, as well as neighbors, but they'd hardly had time to absorb the news themselves.

"How did she find out?" Rickie mouthed.

"Ronnie's not even here yet," Andee told her. "She was away for the weekend, and we haven't seen her or talked to her since Thursday. Can I have her call you as soon as she gets in?"

"Well," Mindy faltered. "Dixie called me yesterday—you know Dixie—well, her name is Ro Ann. Well, actually her name is Roberta Ann, but everybody calls her Ro Ann. It's one of those double Southern names, you know? But we always called her Dixie at school because she was from the south.

Wait! I'm babbling. I think I've had too much caffeine. Dixie called yesterday to ask if I'd seen the paper. She said, 'What in hellevah's goin' on up theah?' I told her our paper is a weekly so I wouldn't have seen whatever it was she was talking about. She told me to look above the fold on the first page of the real estate section in the Atlanta paper. She said it read 'Tennessee Land Grab' all in caps, and the article said realtors had been buying up land because the national park was about to be nationalized—no, privatized—and that it was like insider trading because they knew it in advance."

Andee and Rickie stared at each other in disbelief. "*What?*"

"It's true!" Mindy confirmed. "I looked it up online. There's a map with the pieces colored in, and a chart that shows how much was paid for each piece. Since Ronnie is a real estate agent, Dixie just thought she'd be interested. She said she probably even knows the realtors who were doing it."

"Wow. That is interesting," Andee said, noncommittally. "I'll have her call you, okay?"

Rickie had vanished and was already in her office, booting up her computer.

"Take a look," she said, glumly, turning the screen so Andee could see the map of Emery Pond. "There's only one way I can think of as to how this information got out. Who's the weak link in the chain?"

Andee closed her eyes, her head starting to pound. Friday was bad, she thought. Sunday was very bad. It wasn't even nine o'clock; could this day get any worse? Of course, it could, and it probably would!

Geri's car wouldn't start, so she called the office to say she'd be late. She'd caught Jackie just as she was leaving her house and arranged to have her pick her up and to have the car towed into town. The car had been having problems lately, and she was told it was probably the alternator. That was a quick, easy fix, if not inexpensive, but it could be worse, she told herself.

As the two women pulled into the parking area at the office in mid-morning, the mail carrier's car was just pulling away. Jackie went inside while Geri walked out to the mailbox. She was sorting through the mail as she came through the door. There wasn't a whole lot of actual mail these days, with email having largely taken over that function. She handed copies of *Today's Realtor* magazine to Andee and Rickie, although she knew Andee would probably dump hers right into the wastebasket.

There was a card for Ronnie from someone in New Mexico and a reminder about the continuing ed courses she would need to take before her license renewed. They all considered CE as unpleasant as having a colonoscopy, but it wasn't anything an agent could get out of doing. Andee hated having it hang over her head, so she ordered correspondence courses at the outset of each licensing period and got it over with. Rickie methodically did some each month, making it just part of her routine, while Ronnie dragged her feet and usually had to blast through online courses at the last minute. They laughed about being the ant and the grasshopper. Jackie had briefed Geri on their habits as well as the requirements so she could stay on top of it.

"Where's Ronnie?" Geri asked now, ducking into her office and laying the mail on her desk. "I hope she's not sick; she's not usually this late." As she spoke, she handed an envelope to Rickie. It had a law firm in Cookeville as the return address, but that was nothing unusual as attorneys regularly performed title work and conducted closings, so Geri didn't think anything of it. Rickie tore open the flap and skimmed the cover letter.

"Shit!" she swore, handing the letter to Andee.

At that moment, Geri realized that something was very wrong. The tension in the room was palpable, and she looked from Rickie to Andee and back again.

"What's wrong?"

"What isn't?" Andee muttered under her breath.

"CW is in intensive care at Jones Hutchins," she told the latecomers. "The cancer has spread to his liver, and it's probably only a matter of weeks now. And..." Andee extended the letter to Jackie. "Your listing file for the Cross sale has been subpoenaed. They aren't wasting any time."

Jackie blanched. Her eyes filled, and she tried to blink away tears.

"I'll try to get your name removed from the suit because the broker has the responsibility for affiliates," Rickie said. "But you actually took the listing so they'll probably want to go through it with a fine-tooth comb, looking for any shred that might help them with an award for damages resulting from incompetence. Or negligence."

Jackie hadn't spoken. Her eyes went from Rickie's face to Andee's, trying to read their expressions.

"You can't help but be worried," Rickie said. "But I went thought all the paperwork before the closing, and there is absolutely nothing that they can use. There's going to be a lot of saber-rattling, but our best position is to cooperate and let it run its course. My concern is that they'll want publicity and turn it into a class action as other buyers say, *Yeah, me too*. We just need to hope that doesn't happen. That could really be ugly."

"So, they get a copy of the file…" Jackie's voice quavered. "Then what? Will I have to give a—what do you call it when you have to give them a statement?"

"A deposition." Geri heard the anger in Andee's voice. "Even if you do, you can't be expected to disclose the presence of bears in an area as a material defect. People have lived here all their lives and have never seen a bear. That's like disclosing that there might be a—a sinkhole—that might open up and half a house, four cars, a pickup, and twelve cows fall into it."

"I need to think this through," Rickie said. "I don't think we're going to get anything done today. Let's just put a 'Closed' sign on the door and let the phones go to voicemail. I'd like to use the rest of the day for a closed-door session, but not here."

When Ronnie got home on Sunday night and settled in after checking in on her animals, she hadn't bothered to set her alarm, figuring she would wake up at the usual time. So when Purrl reached out a dainty white paw and tapped her face, Ronnie opened her eyes, and her gaze went straight to the clock. *Holy crap! It's nine o'clock!*

She had thought she'd be up, out, and in the office by now. *Fifteen minutes!* She pulled on jeans, t-shirt, and stepped into clogs. Shirt—which one? Never mind, any one would do. She shoved her arms into the sleeves of the first shirt she grabbed, splashed water on her face, and quickly brushed her teeth and her hair. She could take her cosmetic bag with her and put makeup on when she got there. Kibbles for Purrl, make coffee before she fed the horses, then take it with her…

The phone rang just as she picked up her car keys. It was Luc. He spoke brusquely, without preamble.

"CW is Hutchins. He's alive, and he's stable now, but it's bad. Chip called me first thing this morning, and I went straight to the hospital."

"Oh, Luc. I'm so sorry! I overslept. I just woke up."

"I wish that was all, but there's more. All of the confidential Emery Pond information has been leaked. CW and Julia usually read the Baltimore paper over breakfast on Sunday mornings. Luckily, Julia had folded the paper next to his plate, but he never got a chance to see it, which is just as well. Lucinda saw it in the Washington paper because someone had left a copy in the waiting room at the hospital. It's exactly the same information that's on Stephanie's computer. I looked. There's no doubt in my mind that that's where it came from. I'm just sick about this."

"Did you ask her?" Ronnie demanded. "What did she say?"

"She stayed at her mother's last night, and Kelli took her to school this morning. I haven't seen her, so I haven't asked. Yet."

"It's my fault," Ronnie said slowly, trying to absorb this information and assess the damage it could cause. "I got her involved and provided the information. Do you think she did this out of spite?"

"I wish I knew."

Ronnie's cell rang, and *Rickie* came up on caller ID.

"Rickie's on the other line," she told Luc. "I'll talk to you later, probably tonight. Give Julia a hug for me."

"Hey," she greeted Rickie. "I overslept. I just got up. I'm sorry. I just got off the phone with Luc. I heard." The words tumbled out.

"We have a lot to talk about. Why don't you just stay where you are, and Andee and I'll come over there. We'll pick up something for lunch because I think it's going to take most of the day to prioritize and game plan. The office will just have to take the day off."

"I wish we were sitting around, salaciously lapping up every detail of your big weekend, but we have a lot of ground to cover, so we're going to have to put that on the back burner. On a scale of one to ten, though, I'm guessing it was a ten," Andee whispered an hour later.

"It was off the scale altogether, if you must know! I'm glad I didn't know about CW until today. It would have totally destroyed the weekend, and there's nothing any of us can do."

Jackie and Geri came through the door together and nodded, hearing the tail end of that interchange.

The five of them sat around Ronnie's kitchen table. Coffee was poured and, after a few minutes, Rickie pushed her mug toward the center of the table and pulled her notepad toward her, picking up her pen. "We need to make a list of the issues and discuss them, one at a time. It's hard to know where to begin."

Ronnie was overwhelmed by the magnitude of the weekend's events and the ramifications for all of them on so many levels, both professionally and personally.

Purrl settled herself in Andee's lap and began to knead her knee. Andee was a cat lover, and she absentmindedly stroked Purrl's back. Ronnie shook her head. It was just like a white cat to choose the one person wearing black jeans, and she knew from experience how much loose hair would end up on Andee's clothes.

"CW," Rickie continued. "There's not much we can do about that except be as supportive as we can. The next several weeks are going to be stressful and sad for Julia, Chip and Lucinda, and Luc. I don't think CW's illness or his subsequent death will affect the viability of the project here in Tennessee because he's groomed Chip to step in and take over as CEO. It's just really unfortunate timing that the Senate hearing is coming up so soon when their attention needs to be elsewhere."

Ronnie saw the puzzled looks on both Jackie's and Geri's faces but relaxed as she knew Rickie would bring them up to speed.

"There's a bill in Washington concerning the privatization of national parks. You know what that means?" Geri shook her head, and Jackie's eyes were glued to Rickie's face, waiting for her to continue.

"It's happening with state parks all over the country, where the state doesn't have the revenue to run them, and the operation is turned over to private companies, which operate them as a business. It's pretty much win/win because the state gets those line items out of their budget, but they aren't forced to close the parks. The proposal is to do the same thing with national parks, but politics on Capitol Hill makes it a lot harder to get bills through both houses of Congress.

The swing vote rests with the junior senator from Vermont who, you might have guessed and might as well know, is Ronnie's ex-husband—known none too affectionately around here as that rat bastard."

Jackie's mouth fell open in shock, but Geri immediately connected the dots.

"Didn't he visit Big South Fork a while back?" she asked.

"His background is environmental law. He decided he wanted to come here for a first-hand, fact-finding mission before casting his vote, which he did," Rickie continued her explanation.

"His vote is critical to our project with the investors from Virginia. We originally courted them to underwrite a planned equestrian community in Emery Pond. Andee walked them through the unfinished part of the master plan for Big South Fork and showed them the potential. To that end, I have quietly approached landowners and carefully selected sites in the area, and we, that is, our investors, have been buying up options on the prime pieces of property that will be needed to make that happen."

Andee picked up, "That's if Senator Parker votes 'yes' for privatizing. The hearing is this Thursday, and we need to be there. It would still be do-able on a much smaller scale if the bill doesn't go through, and the park isn't privatized. But the Westlake Group could possibly pull out because the project would be too small for them, and there wouldn't be enough return. I'm sure we could find another backer, but it would take time, and it might fall apart in the meantime."

"Here's where it gets complicated," Rickie said ruefully. "God, no good deed goes unpunished! Luc's daughter, Stephanie, you've met her. Well, she's a mess and Ronnie—wait, I need to back up. Ronnie and Luc Deschaines, one of the investors, have gotten involved. That's where Ronnie was this weekend. She and Luc went away together for a couple of days alone, for the first time."

Jackie was nodding her approval.

Rickie grinned in spite of herself .

"It doesn't take a genius to figure out that Luc will be spending a lot of time here over the next couple of years and that things would go a lot more smoothly if the daughter was on board and not fighting him every step of the way. To that end, Ronnie carved out a niche for her, letting her enter landowner purchase data for us and keep a map up-to-date on what's been optioned and which parcels still need to be locked up. Our acquisition needs to be done quietly and tactfully, and we succeeded in keeping that part of the project under wraps—until now. Someone leaked it to the press, and all of the major metropolitan newspapers picked it up. The story was probably syndicated or something." She sucked in a deep breath and blew it out.

"So now the whole world is outraged and up in arms about the unscrupulous realtors and their land grab, blatting about how the locals are getting screwed over. It's still a pretty sore subject around here about the government exercising eminent domain in order to create the national park which displaced families that had been on their land for generations. Our friend, Sara's, family is a prime example; there are still really hard feelings to this day, and that was a couple of decades ago."

"Oh, my God!" Jackie brought up a point that would give everyone more than a few sleepless nights. "If the locals think we screwed them out of their land, no one will ever trust us again. We'll be the most hated realtors in the history of the universe! No one will ever list with us again," she wailed, as it dawned on her how this would affect her new-found career.

"Who did this?" Geri demanded.

Ronnie looked down at her hands, clenched in her lap.

"Stephanie." Ronnie's voice was cold and flat. "It had to be."

"Why? To hurt her dad?" Geri gasped.

Her question was almost unheard as Jackie blurted, "Because she's jealous of you!"

"I don't know what her motives were, but she's the only one who had the information, so it had to have been her," Ronnie said. "I'm just sick about this, and so is Luc. She was at her mother's last night, and she's in school today, so he hasn't had a chance to talk to her."

"I think…" Ricky said, crossing that item off her list and moving swiftly to the next topic. "I hate to bother Chip at a time like this, and there probably isn't going to be a good time any time soon, but we need to tell him about the lawsuit. It's only fair that our investors understand the ramifications for our project. It's a fact that black bears were reintroduced into the national park here, and they have thrived, so there have been bears sighted on horse trails. While there hasn't been an actual bear encounter, people could start to get worried. I'm no math major, but anyone can see, with the population increasing, it's just a matter of time. The National Park Service is on record as having stated, 'Bears are now found throughout the area. As the numbers continue to expand, it is necessary that residents learn to live in bear country.' You know, there never used to be those plaques about securing food items, wiping grease off grills, and not throwing leftovers in the trash, but now there's one on every picnic table in the park."

"Last week Maureen Briggs said she saw four bears when she was on her way home from Oneida; you know, she works there," Geri said. "She said it was a momma bear and three cubs. She thought they were cute and wished she could have gotten a picture."

"Well, you know what, people?" Andee burst out. "Those cubs are three more bears in Big South Fork than there were last year. It's not going to do this project or any of us any good if people are afraid to move here."

Ronnie covered her face with her hands.

"We seem to be up shit creek without a paddle," Jackie summarized succinctly.

Chapter Seventeen

Luc was waiting when the doors opened, and students poured down the steps. Stephanie had been a student at Horizon Academy since enrolling there in the third grade. According to their mission statement, the school prided itself on teaching personal responsibility not only for learning but also behavior. Grooming its elite cadre of students for academic and social success, was one of the primary reasons Luc had chosen it for his only child.

He'd been trying to marshal his thoughts and not spend the day stewing. He was angry, hurt, disappointed, frustrated, bewildered, discouraged—and more. Obviously, the school had failed her. No, that wasn't fair. He had failed her. He and Kelli, her parents.

He'd been so grateful when Ronnie had taken an interest in his daughter, sending a warm and thoughtful note to Stephanie after she'd made a horrifyingly embarrassing scene at the airport and had not accompanied him to Tennessee that long-ago weekend in the spring. He'd been more so when Ronnie's interest continued even after meeting her, knowing that Stephanie could, would, and had been as rude to Ronnie as humanly possible. She had behaved appallingly—as usual—and had done everything in her power to frighten Ronnie away. In addition to being perceptive and kind, Ronnie was such a good role model when Stephanie needed one most.

But this—his stomach heaved. Chip and Lucinda, and Julia especially, had enough on their plates without having to deal with this particular piece of bad news. Chip and Lucinda knew that the Big South Fork information was now prematurely in the public domain, but they were too preoccupied, spending their time in the windowless tenth floor medical ICU waiting room, even to think how the information had fallen into the hands of the media. Lucinda had thrown the newspaper into the trash before Julia could see the article, so she and CW were both unaware that they'd been betrayed, seemingly from within.

It was up to Luc to get to the bottom of it, and he knew just where to start. He'd sent Stephanie a text, telling her that he would be picking her up from school. Lost in thought, he hadn't seen her approach the car, and he looked up, startled, as she opened the door and heaved her bulk up into the passenger seat. She seemed genuinely glad to see him, basking in his unexpected attention. She had lost some weight. He could see that she already looked much better. The school's dress code was casual, and she had obviously taken Ronnie's advice to dress simply in dark solid colors for a slimming effect.

Stephanie had had her heart set on attending Marden as a day student when it came time for college prep and, although McLean was only twenty miles away, the commute was incalculable, time-wise, in DC's congested environs. Both Luc and Kelli felt strongly that she should remain at Horizon and, given the problems that had developed, Luc was very glad she was in such a nearby and nurturing environment. The head of the school was a psychologist. In addition, Horizon also employed a director of counseling and had a licensed registered nurse on-site full time who provided not just nursing care but health education. Together, they had addressed Stephanie's burgeoning weight and arranged her enrollment in a weight-management program for teenage girls.

Hers wasn't the usual anorexia/bingeing so common in that age group; there were underlying psychological issues that were also addressed by the professionals entrusted with his daughter's well-being. Luc was aware that she felt abandoned by her mother after her remarriage, so the last thing he wanted to do was to become increasingly involved with Ronnie, leaving Stephanie even more disenfranchised. He'd seen the positive changes in her attitude as she'd been given a role in the Tennessee project and an alternate persona as *Stevie*. In her newfound desire to emulate Ronnie, she'd embraced the weight-loss regimen with alacrity, and Luc could see it paying off week by week.

He was shocked and deeply troubled to think that Stephanie would knowingly and calculatedly undermine their efforts, and mortified beyond words that he was responsible, however indirectly, for the damage she had done.

"Daddy, where are we going?" It was clear that Luc had no intention of dropping her off for her after-school session.

"I need to talk to you; we need to go somewhere quiet." Stephanie didn't respond, and, a few minutes later, he pulled into a pocket-sized park and cut the engine.

"Look at me," he directed. "I want to see your eyes when I ask you why in hell you did what you did." He had promised himself that he would discuss the matter rationally, and he had to suck in a deep, cleansing breath to calm himself.

"What?" Stephanie was shocked by his vehemence, and it was written all over her face. Her mouth dropped open, and her eyes filled with tears.

"Did what? What did I do? You're mad at me!" Her lower lip quivered, and the tears rolled down her cheeks as she stared at him, uncomprehending.

"Stephanie," he started over. "You can't deny it. I saw the paper. The information could only have come from you, but I don't understand why you would do such a hateful thing. You have no idea how much damage you've caused, and I'm sick over this. I can't face Chip, and I can't face Rickie, Andee, or Ronnie."

"Daddy, I *didn't do* anything!" Stephanie gulped, her face a mask of misery.

"Don't even try to deny it." Luc's tone was stern and unrelenting. "What I want to know is why you would deliberately hurt the people who love you and are trying to help you? I also want to know who you gave the information to."

Stephanie dragged her sleeve across her face, to try to stem the tears. Mucus streamed from her nostrils, and, as it ran over her lips, she swiped it away with her fist.

"I didn't! I don't even know what you're talking about!"

"So, that's it? Deny, deny? Okay, fine. When we get home, you'll go straight to your room. No TV, no music, no computer. When you're ready to talk, you let me know. I can promise you one thing; this isn't going away. You'd better come up with one hell of a good explanation."

They drove home in silence, and Stephanie disappeared, slamming her bedroom door. Luc poured two fingers of single-malt scotch into a tumbler and took a restorative swallow, sinking into an armchair and closing his eyes. His head was pounding.

Stephanie sat sullenly at the kitchen table the next morning, mutely stirring her cereal around and around but eating only a few mouthfuls. They made the drive to school in silence, and when Luc pulled up in the drop-off lane, she got out of the car without a backward look, slamming the door with considerable force. It was clear that she, too, was furious. Had she honestly not known what he was talking about? No, the information had to have come from her. That's the only explanation. But when? Where? Why?

In the time it took to drive to Baltimore and find a parking place outside Jones Hutchins, Luc had asked himself the same questions twenty times. He was no closer to having an answer.

Don't ask, he mouthed and rolled his eyes, signaling his distress, when Lucinda sent him a questioning look.

He had his answer the next day when he drove Stephanie to water aerobics. She stared out the passenger window, her arms folded, and her body rigid, still silent. Again, she slammed the door when she got out of the car. He watched in dismay as she stalked into the building because he was at a complete loss. He sat in the car, reading a prospectus that Chip had passed on to him for his opinion. Well, more accurately, he was attempting to read it. He couldn't concentrate on anything while this whole Stephanie mess was unresolved. After putting the file back into his briefcase, he went into the building and nodded to the receptionist as he passed the information desk and entered the pool area.

It took a few minutes to get accustomed to the humidity, and he felt queasy. Was it the temperature, or was it anxiety, he wondered. Probably both. Eleven girls were clad in identical swimsuits, carefully chosen with a draped bodice and a short skirt rather than the typical tight-fitting tank. It took a moment to pick Stephanie out of the group, but there she was, clutching the coping at the edge of the pool and kicking vigorously, her mouth set in a grim line.

Luc wished he had an outlet to work off his hostility and envisioned himself on a horse at the ranch in Texas, galloping, with the wind in his hair. He knew that the general manager, Teodor Sauseda, would be looking over the current crop of yearlings and deciding which would be sent to the fall sale, assessing the current crop of colts approaching two years of age and deciding which would be gelded. And he also knew that the ranch needed no oversight from The Westlake Group, not under Teddy's efficient stewardship. He wished he were there, but that was hopeless; the last thing he could do at this critical point was leave. His daughter needed him, and his best friend needed him.

He closed his eyes and was lost in thought when he felt someone sit next to him. He'd chosen a seat toward the top of the bleachers, intending to avoid small talk with the handful of parents present. His heart sank when he saw his companion. *Aw, crap! I should have waited in the car*. It was Helena Harkness, the absolute last person he wanted to see.

"Luc," she purred in her low, sultry voice, laying a hand on his arm.

It was all he could do not to shudder and shake off her unwelcome touch. This was a man-eater, if ever there was one, and he was in no mood for her company. Not that he'd ever be in the mood, but she did not deter easily.

She did not deter easily. *She did not deter easily.* He frowned. *Oh, my God!* He knew, with sickening clarity, how the Tennessee information ended up in major metropolitan newspapers. He wasn't sure how the file had fallen into her hands, but he knew what she'd do with it when she got her mitts on it. What she *had* done with it! She was an investigative journalist, prying, digging, and assembling discrete pieces of information. She was focused, she was intuitive, and she was relentless. Stephanie was naïve, no match for her. *Oh, my God!*

Helena Harkness specialized in undercover reporting and published under the byline Jeneva Weatherford. She had two Pulitzers under her belt, was nominated for a third, and Luc did not for one instant underestimate her. Her appearance was deceiving, and she used it to her advantage, engaging her subjects and encouraging their confidences.

"Helena." He smiled warmly but shook out his cuff, turning his wrist and looking at his watch. "I was lost in thought and lost track of time. I need to make an important call at four, so you'll have to excuse me. Let's catch up next week, shall we?" She swiveled her knees to the side to let him pass, affording him a deliberate eyeful of her long legs as her skirt rode up. As if, he thought, utterly revolted.

After the girls had parted on the sidewalk an hour later, and Stephanie had settled herself in the car, he conversationally asked, "You really like Hailey, don't you?"

"She's cool," Stephanie agreed. "Her mom is way cool. She said to ask you if I can sleep over on Friday night. She wanted me to come before when I stayed with you, remember, but I told her we were going to Tennessee so I couldn't. She wants you to call her."

I'll bet she does!

"Or am I grounded?" Stephanie queried.

"Steph, where's your tablet?" Luc asked. "Is it in your backpack?"

"Why? Are you taking it away?" She turned to him, her distress evident.

"No. I'm not," he said, still thinking. "I think I may have misjudged you, and I may owe you an apology. You keep your tablet in your backpack, right? You haven't misplaced it?"

She shook her head.

"Have you loaned it to anyone?"

"No."

"Has anyone else used it?"

"Why?" Stephanie was confused by this line of questioning. "Is something wrong?"

"Something is very wrong, and I'm trying to figure out how it could have happened," Luc explained. "I was hoping you could help me. You've been working with us on the Tennessee project—Ronnie is sending you data to enter, and you're updating the spreadsheet with the purchases of land, right?"

She nodded, looking confused.

"Then you update the map, right?"

She nodded again.

"Has Mrs. Harkness ever used your computer? Have you ever left it somewhere where she might use it?"

"No," she replied. Luc was surprised. He thought, surely, he'd stumbled on the answer and was disappointed to find himself at a dead end.

"She's getting Hailey one for her birthday but told me not to tell."

"When was that?" Luc asked.

"About two weeks ago. She asked if she could look at mine so she could get her the same kind of cover."

"Were you there when she looked at it?" Now Luc was sure he was on the right track.

"Yes. I showed her; then I put it back in my backpack."

"Did you tell her you were helping Ronnie?" Luc asked.

"I—uh—I guess I did. Kind of."

"What do you mean by kind of?"

Oh, boy, here we go.

"Well, I started to tell her, but then I remembered it's a secret, so I told her I couldn't talk about it."

By itself, it wasn't that big a story, but Luc had the sick feeling that Jeneva Weatherford was going to parlay it into a series of articles on releasing federal land and the implications thereof. He'd just read an article in a national paper about the federal government opening up thousands of acres of public land in Colorado for oil and gas drilling in an area renowned for its organic farms, leasing it or auctioning it over the protest of the local populace. 'We're unbelievably blessed in this place here,' one Colorado resident was quoted. 'But we could be unblessed really quickly.' That could easily be a Tennessee resident talking, Luc thought.

Because of the quirks of mineral ownership, one party can own a piece of property, and another own the subsurface rights. You have only to spend an hour in the registry of deeds to realize how many parcels have the mineral rights assigned, and Luc feared that Helena Harkness would be making a trip to The Volunteer State in the not-too-distant future. She would look around Big South Fork, and it wouldn't take her long to see the natural gas wellheads. She'd already made a trip to North Dakota and California and had written a lengthy piece about hydrofracking the Bakken Shale and the Monterey Shale. She would turn this into a series, whipping her readers into a frenzy over the rape-and-pillage mentality. 'Land grab' would be her byword, and she'd be writing with the next journalism award firmly in her sights.

She'd used Stephanie as a pawn. The minute the words *realtors* and *investors* and *privatizing* and *secret* entered her word hoard, she knew she was on to something. She was a formidable opponent. Luc needed to warn Ronnie, Andee, and Rickie—and have them warn Mindy—that they should be expecting a visit and to avoid Ms. Harkness like the plague. With her sniffing around, who knew what tidbits she'd turn up, or what she'd turn them into.

He had no doubt that Helena had helped herself to the contents of Steph's backpack, with the girl totally unaware. Stephanie had been falsely accused, and he needed to make this up to her. As bad as it was, with worse undoubtedly yet to come, Luc was profoundly relieved to know that Stephanie had not acted out of vengeance.

Chapter Eighteen

Rickie, Ronnie, and Andee spent Wednesday night at an airport hotel in Nashville. They took an early-morning flight to Washington Thursday morning for the senate hearing on the privatization bill. They arrived at the committee room where the hearing was being held just minutes before two metal stanchions with a velvet rope blocked the hallway.

Luc had called Ronnie to say he and Stephanie arrived early and intended to save seats, but the rows had filled quickly, and that proved impossible. He'd been looking around for them, and Ronnie gave him a little wave once they were seated near the back. They'd probably all have lunch together and could discuss the proceedings then.

Ronnie turned her attention to Evan, impressed in spite of the many times she'd observed him in court, filleting his hapless opponent.

"Lucinda stayed with Julia so Chip could come," Luc explained when they gathered in the hallway during a break. "He thought the session on privatization was entirely germane to our interests. And I allowed Stephanie to miss school today," he continued. "I thought she'd be interested in the hearing on privatization since she's been involved in our project. It's somewhat of an apology, after the way I treated her when her information inadvertently blew the lid off."

"I'm starving," Ronnie whispered to Luc two hours later as they filed out. "Breakfast was a long time ago!"

"I grabbed a muffin and downed a cup of coffee on the way," he replied. "I've been hungry for the last hour, but I forgot all about it because I got so engrossed in the proceedings."

"I thought Evan—Senator Parker—was brilliant," Ronnie said. She kicked herself mentally for the slip and hoped Luc hadn't noticed how easily Evan's name rolled off her tongue. She was going to have to confide her status as his ex-wife very soon and wished she'd done it before the trip to Charleston. Evan had made it clear with his over-the-top birthday present that he wanted her back and was pursuing her. She'd closed her mind and her heart to that idea and had seen no need to bring it up with Luc. Evan was the past, and that's where she'd intended he remain. Was Luc the future? After Charleston, it looked like things might be heading in that direction. Did she owe him total honesty, or was the unpleasant past best buried?

"Ronnie? Ronnie!" Rickie waved a hand in front of her face. "You were a million miles away!"

"Evan Parker must have been hell on wheels in a courtroom." She heard Chip say.

"I've done some research online about where we should eat," Andee broke in, deflecting the subject. "There are restaurants near Capitol Hill, of course, and they're categorized as house side or senate side. I thought one called Janus sounded good. I looked on a map of the area; we're in Dirksen, and it's on D, one street over. We can easily catch a cab."

She eyed Ronnie's footwear, a pair of high-heeled stilettos she'd bought online at Rue La La, and smirked.

"You're not walking in those shoes. Anyway, it's a classic Washington political restaurant, you know, 'a long-time favorite hangout of senators, lobbyists, and staffers,' " she paraphrased. "Complete with requisite marquee."

"Clever name for a restaurant where politicians and lobbyists hang out, those two-faced bastards, most of them," Rickie commented.

In the moments before the elevator arrived, Senator Parker and his colleague, Senator Dave Strickland, rounded the corner. Evan clearly recognized the women, and he halted in mid-sentence.

"The contingent from Tennessee!" he greeted them. "Ms. Ahlers, Ms. Barton, and—ah—Ms. Chandler."

Introductions were performed all around, and then Dave said, "Evan and I have another hearing this afternoon, so we're headed to the Senate dining room. It's a lot more convenient when you're sandwiching a meal between back-to-back sessions."

Ronnie and Rickie's mouths twitched as they looked at each other, suppressing a grin, knowing Andee had caught Dave's unintentional pun.

"Please join us," Evan said smoothly, glancing from Chip to Luc to Andee and to Rickie but not meeting Ronnie's eyes. Ronnie froze, expecting one of her partners to come to her rescue, but, to her horror, no one demurred.

"You'll have to have a bowl of bean soup," Evan told Stephanie, adroitly including her in the conversation.

As the group entered the elevator, Dave explained the reference for the benefit of the uninitiated.

"The menu changes every day and features food products from different states on different days, but bean soup is on the menu every day and has been for over a hundred years. It's a senate tradition."

Without delay, they were ushered into an alcove containing one large round table. It was elegantly set with a heavy white cloth. Sparkling stemmed goblets held clear, cold water, and Ronnie gratefully lifted hers to her lips as soon as she was seated. She and Rickie both ordered medallions of beef with shitake mushroom sauce and new potatoes in a lemon sauce. The meat was cooked to perfection, and Rickie did justice to an excellent meal. Ronnie couldn't taste the food and couldn't swallow past the lump in her throat.

She forced herself to eat a few small bites as the conversation flowed around her; her ears were ringing so loud she wasn't listening.

Thankfully, the lunch break came to its conclusion, and she lifted the heavy cloth napkin from her lap, placing it on the table. Luc and Evan were in earnest conversation.

"Actually," she heard Luc say, "I'm going to be taking a page out of Senator Parker's book. I wanted to observe today's hearing before making a move, but I've come to a decision. I'm going to call a press conference for Stephanie and let her tell the world how she was used by an unscrupulous reporter to do damage control for the whole 'land grab' mess. It's the last thing Ms. Harkness would expect, and I'd love to give that lousy bitch a taste of her own medicine."

When they parted and were standing on the sidewalk, Rickie whispered to Ronnie, "Your ex couldn't take his eyes off you at lunch. Do you think Luc noticed?"

"God, I hope not. I never imagined the three of us in the same room at the same time!"

"Have you told Luc that you were married to Evan once upon a time?"

Ronnie was saved from answering when a cab swerved to the curb, and Andee reached for the door handle. Chip hadn't stayed for lunch. He'd left when it became clear that the session was finally wrapping up, eager to get back to his father's bedside.

In other circumstances, Luc would have taken Ronnie somewhere elegant for a quiet dinner, but he didn't want Stephanie to feel that she'd been ditched, and he wasn't sure it would be fair to Rickie and Andee to leave them alone to order from room service.

"It's a school night for Steph, and you three will be up at dawn to get through airport security and onto an early flight, so why don't we have an early dinner somewhere and brainstorm my idea for a press conference."

Stephanie was thrilled to be included in the adults' evening and delighted to find herself part of the planning.

"Wear what you have on now," Ronnie told her as they hashed out a plan. "It's absolutely perfect!" Stephanie, Luc could see, was morphing into Stevie, well on her way to becoming an attractive, poised, tastefully dressed, expensively-educated, and articulate young woman.

Rickie was making a list of *talking points* for her as they refined their strategy. Helena Harkness would be blindsided—gobsmacked—attacked from the rear where she was least expecting it, and Luc relished the thought of her comeuppance at the hands of his teenager. He vowed to himself to make it happen, outraged on Stephanie's behalf and Rickie's as well. Helena Harkness had no idea what hell she'd unleashed. Between them, he and the Westlakes knew a lot of powerful people who knew a lot of powerful people, and it wouldn't take long before they secured a spot on TV, probably not something nation-wide but surely something credible.

Stephanie still had a long way to go, weight-wise, but she'd begun steadily shedding pounds and looked, now, just very, very heavy instead of unhealthily obese. She wore tapered navy pants with a long matching tunic, both of which had a slimming effect. Lucinda had proven an excellent mentor, helping Steph accessorize. The wedge heel on her smooth navy shoes gave her a bit of height, and the long strap on her navy shoulder bag mimicked the tunic's long lines.

Lucinda had encouraged her to wear the lovely scarf Ronnie had chosen for her in Charleston, loosely tucked into the neck of her top, to draw attention to her face and away from her body. She had booked a Saturday at a day spa a few weeks earlier and had treated Stephanie to her first makeover, where a skilled colorist wove several shades of blonde highlights and lowlights through the girl's own unremarkable hair, giving it both depth and body. A skilled cut worked wonders, framing her face in layers, and showcasing the new sapphire earrings that would always be treasured. A makeup technician had spent another forty-five minutes in a booth with her, teaching her how to apply a little eye shadow, a little mascara, a little blusher, and a lipstain only a few shades darker than her own lip color so the finished product was subtle and age-appropriate.

Luc would be eternally grateful to the women in his life, Ronnie and Lucinda, so kindhearted and generous with their skills and sophistication. He felt a familiar flash of anger at Kelli and determinedly put those negative thoughts out of his mind. It was what it was. It certainly wasn't what he would have chosen for his family, but with hindsight, it was apparent to him that, in closing one door, she'd inadvertently allowed others to open. What did the future hold? He frowned. Evan's attentiveness at lunch hadn't escaped him. If no explanation manifested itself, he would ask Ronnie if that had just been his imagination or if there actually was an undercurrent between them.

When Rickie, Ronnie, and Andee returned to their hotel suite, the red message light on the living room phone was flashing. Andee said she was tired after getting up so early and went into the bedroom without even glancing at it.

Whenever the three had to make a minor decision, doing 'Rock/Paper/Scissors' was the way they always jokingly resolved it. When Andee prevailed, she claimed the single room for herself.

Retrieving the message, Rickie said, "It must be for you or Andee; there's no actual voicemail, just a callback number I don't recognize. I'm not expecting any calls." She brought up the feature for her phone's alarm clock.

"What time are we getting up?" She kicked off her shoes and dropped her shoulder bag on a chair before disappearing into the bathroom.

Ronnie heard water streaming into the tub and thought how good it would feel to relax in a hot bath, wishing she'd gotten there first. It had sure been a long day!

"Early," Ronnie called, but Rickie had already closed the door. She keyed the unfamiliar number into her cell phone, realizing with a jolt it had a Washington prefix and could be only one person. She was tempted to hang up, but her momentary indecision had cost her that choice.

The call connected, and her past and her present collided.

"Are you alone? Can you talk?"

She opened her mouth, but no sound emerged.

"Ronnie," Evan Parker said into the silence. "I want to see you before you leave town. I'm downstairs in the bar, and I'm not leaving until you talk to me. Will you give me fifteen minutes?"

His mellifluous voice poured over her, mesmerizing as always. No wonder he'd had one jury after another eating out of his hand. No wonder he'd controlled the outcome of the hearing today; the naysayers hadn't stood a chance. She hadn't stood a chance, until the day came when she'd simply had enough of being relegated to second place, waiting for the leftover crumbs of his time and attention. She'd recreated herself, made a new life for herself.

What could he possibly have to say that would make a difference?

Absolutely not! her mind screamed. "Fifteen minutes," she said.

Two hours later, she and Rickie lay in their beds. Rickie had the covers pulled tightly under her chin, and she was sound asleep. Ronnie lay awake, wishing for dawn so she could get up, get dressed, get to the airport, and get home. Home to Purrl, home to Cash and Black Jack, home to Mindy, to Horse Country Real Estate, and to all else that was familiar. She felt like she was on quicksand. If she gave Evan even half a chance, what would be different? Leopards don't change their spots; she knew that. Different state, different job, but—same person, right? It would look safe, and she'd step out, just as she had once before, trusting and unsuspecting.

Well, no; not exactly. This time she wouldn't be either trusting or unsuspecting. So, there was the answer, clear as it could be. Why was she even thinking about this? She rolled over, turned the pillow over, and scolded herself to get some sleep.

She wished she hadn't seen him, not that day at The Hungry Horse and not today on Capitol Hill because—she had to admit—the physical attraction was as strong as it had ever been. It was easy to hate him when he was out of sight and out of mind. Yes, he was ambitious. Yes, he was driven. Yes, he was brilliant. But was he bad? No, just bad for her. He'd said all the right things an hour ago. He hadn't realized how much he'd loved her until she'd left him. Hadn't understood how much he'd hurt her. He'd taken both of her hands, looked deep into her eyes, and humbly asked for a second chance. She was speechless for the second time that evening—not angry, not upset, simply at a loss for words.

But Evan had fooled her once when she was Vee, and there would be no second chance for him, now or ever. Absently, she'd fingered the silver tassel on the silver chain Luc had given her in Charleston. Her fingers closed around it, and the contact gave her courage as they talked.

"I can't, Evan. It's so over," she had said, sadly. "I'm not the person I was, the person you think I am, and I don't want to go back to the life I had. I'm in love with someone else now."

"Luc. The man who was with you at the hearings. I met him at lunch."

"Yes," she'd replied and knew it was true. That knowledge notwithstanding, she remained sleepless. Her mind roiled with all the loose ends. Should she tell Luc about Evan? Yes? No?

Could Stephanie pull off a press conference, carefully coached, or was she simply too young and inexperienced to stand up to a self-serving stainless-steel bitch like the formidable Ms. Harkness? What would happen when CW died, which appeared to be imminent? How would that affect Luc? And poor Julia. She, Rickie, and Andee would be back here for the funeral, and what a sad occasion that would be.

Ronnie thought room service had arrived when she cracked the door at dawn. Rickie was in the shower, waking herself up, and hadn't heard the knock. They would be leaving before the hotel's continental breakfast was available and, in the interest of time, decided to have a carafe of coffee and some croissants sent up.

Ronnie had belted the hotel's thick terry robe over her nightie and opened the door, leaving the chain engaged. Her mouth fell open in shock when she saw Evan standing before her, inches away.

"I have something more to say to you, Vee; it will only take a moment. Can you step outside?"

"Please make it fast. Rickie's in the shower, but Andee could wake up and wonder where I am any time now," she whispered. She released the chain and opened the door wider, standing in the doorway.

"I'm not willing to leave things between us this way," he informed her in a low, controlled voice. "Everyone deserves a second chance, and I want the opportunity to try to win you back. You're not going to grant that, and you've left me no choice but to play hardball, so here it is. You decide how important your project is and how important your investor friend is. If my proposal is more important, I swing this bill your way. If not, I have second thoughts, recommend further study, etc. etc., and the vote goes down in flames after I quietly make a few strategic phone calls."

Ronnie's eyes widened, and angry tears spilled over her lower lashes. She made no attempt to wipe them away.

"You lousy son of a bitch!" she hissed, feeling outmaneuvered and trapped. "You wouldn't!"

"I will," he said calmly, holding her gaze for a moment. She closed the door in his face but, having delivered his ultimatum, he had already turned to walk away. She was shaking like a leaf with shock and disbelief. She sank onto the end of the bed a moment before her knees gave out and pressed a fist to her trembling lips. "Oh, my God!" She had just moments to compose herself before Rickie emerged and saw her white face. So many futures now depended on her. She needed time to think things through. She told Rickie she'd had a bad dream, a nightmare. That was the truth, all right. She was having a recurring nightmare.

All three dressed mostly in the same clothes they'd worn the day before. None of them checked luggage when they flew and, knowing they'd be going straight from the airport to the senate building, they'd worn business attire en route.

As dressed up as she ever got, Andee looked very attractive in a black turtleneck with pleated-front khakis, a black and white herringbone wool blazer—one of her late mother's expensive tweeds—and her hair in a neat single braid. Ever practical, Andee wasn't willing to endure the discomfort of fashionable footwear; on her feet were her practical go-anywhere black lace-up Ariat trail boots.

Rickie's former mother-in-law had taught her well, and her sense of style was effortless. Whatever she wore, whatever the occasion, was exactly right. For the trip to Washington, she'd chosen a wrinkle-free gabardine trouser suit in understated olive. With a crisp white shirt, expensive loafers and belt in tan harness leather, small gold hoop earrings, and a plain gold bangle, her streaked blonde hair just grazing her shoulders, she was stunning in her simplicity.

Ronnie loved clothes and had a closetful of seldom-worn but classic wardrobe staples. She'd chosen one of her favorite suits, a dark-brown lightweight wool with a faint black pinstripe. Her black silk shirt was the perfect complement, and the long silver chain with the silver tassel was exactly the right length for the jacket's elongated line. Unable to resist the opportunity to wear something other than her trail boots, she'd debated the wisdom of wearing the high black heels but gave in. Her silver cuff and the oversize silver studs in her ears completed her outfit. She remembered wearing almost the same thing the day she defended her doctoral dissertation. She loved the suit, but not even one of her favorite outfits could make her feel better.

Chip had commented, when he saw them, that they both looked like senators themselves. They all laughed, but Andee had laughed the hardest. There had been some exceptionally gratifying moments during the hearing, and, on the whole, they all felt that it had gone very well. But there was still a long road ahead of them.

The bill had passed in the House without fanfare and should now pass in the Senate when the roll was called and a vote taken, thanks to Senator Parker's oratory. If either chamber did not pass a bill, then it died, so the outcome would signal a new beginning or, quite possibly, the beginning of the end. But Senator Evan Parker was a powerful voice despite being a relative newcomer, and it was understood that, with his influence, the bill would soon be sent to the president to be signed into law.

Evan's affirmative vote would literally pave the way for Andee, Rickie, and Ronnie, the three realtors, and for CW, Chip, and Luc, the investors. They looked forward to their association and to their creation, although they all sadly acknowledged they would forge ahead without CW's guidance. Rickie rejoiced for the people of the counties surrounding the national park who would, she hoped, soon share in the stewardship of their beautiful home. And a lot of people who had never paid much attention to Tennessee, one of those states in the middle of the country that wasn't really north, south, east or west, would be considering it with new interest.

Contingent on whether she, Veronica Chandler, made the right decision. The only decision, as far as Evan Parker was concerned. He didn't often lose, and he wasn't one to accept defeat graciously. Ronnie knew this as well as she knew it was Friday. Pleading a headache, she stayed silent during the trip back to Tennessee. She couldn't hide much for long though, and, in the end, she would have to confide in her closest friends.

Chapter Nineteen

The next morning, Ronnie bunched the covers under her chin and created a cocoon with the down-filled duvet, trying to get warm, to comfort herself. Her mind roiled, and so did her stomach. Oblivious, Purrl slept soundly, tucked tight against Ronnie's torso, and quite comfy under the covers. The sky was still black as ink at this hour, more night than morning, but there was no point in lying there any longer. Purrl wouldn't be happy, but Ronnie decided to get up. She hadn't slept at all, and both her body and mind felt leaden. She needed a hot shower, fleece-lined jeans, and a steaming cup of hot coffee. Then she would do what she had decided to do.

She'd thought it all through, from the very beginning, up to this moment, and far into the future. She knew she couldn't do this alone. In early April, the details of her past were still a secret, held close, and shared with no one. No one's mouth had yet dropped open when they learned who her ex-husband was. Eleven years ago, she had moved halfway across the country and had planned never to see him again. Now, not only was he back in her life, he was back in a big way, holding her future hostage unless she made the right decision. Her relationship with her colleagues, with Andee and Rickie, would implode and, with it, her career. Would she sell them out and sell her soul in the process? Could she, even if she wanted to? There were the moral implications, but, logistically—could she get away with it, even if she tried?

Charles Walker Westlake had hidden his condition from his family until he no longer could. Always in control, he no longer had had control over his own body, and now he was close to death. She had come to respect and admire him, and she felt very close to him and Julia. She wished she could go to him now with her terrible burden, but he kept slipping in and out of consciousness, and, on this dark morning, he was unable to help her. She would call Chip, that was a given, but he wouldn't—couldn't—be her first call. Her hand trembled as she held the phone, and her voice was shaky.

"Rickie," she whispered.

"Ronnie? What's wrong?" It was still early, only five-thirty, but the shakiness in her friend's voice snapped Rickie fully awake in seconds.

"I…" Ronnie didn't know where to begin.

"Are you hurt? Sick? Is Purrl okay? Is one of the horses hurt?" Rickie didn't waste time and demanded answers.

Ronnie took a deep breath, sucking in the soothing aroma rising from her cup. She tried again.

"I need to talk to you. All of you. But you first. And Andee first, too."

"What the hell? What is going on? Are you okay?"

"I'm not hurt, and I'm not sick, but I'm not okay. Ohhh, Rickie…" she trailed off in a wail of despair.

"I'm coming over. As soon as I can get there. I'll call Andee." Rickie was nothing if not decisive, and relief washed over Ronnie. Her knees were weak, and she sank into a chair at the kitchen table.

"Yes. Please," she whispered and disconnected the call.

It had been twenty-four hours since Evan had detonated his bombshell. Twenty-four very long hours. Evan Parker, United States Senator from the great state of Vermont. Evan Parker, environmental activist. Evan Parker, brilliant former litigator. And so much more. So, so much more.

Suddenly, Ronnie's stomach roiled again, and the coffee that had been so welcoming now tasted bitter at the back of her throat. She had no idea how long she'd been sitting at the table, shivering, lost in thought. Lost in memories. The back door banged open, and Rickie burst into the kitchen. Her eyes flicked left, and right and a frown creased her forehead.

"Ronnie? What is it?" She pulled her friend up and into a hug. "You're freezing! Your hands are like ice!" She darted into the living room and returned with a soft wool throw from the arm of the couch.

She draped it over Ronnie's shoulders and pushed her gently back down onto the chair. “Andee is feeding your horses. I'm going to make us some scrambled eggs."

"Holy shit!" Andee exclaimed, when Ronnie had run out of words, the tale told.

"Yeah, that sure sums it up," Rickie agreed. The three women sat in silence, at a total loss for words.

"We need a council of war." As usual, Andee, the planner, had speedily assessed the situation and taken charge. "Chip," she decreed. "Luc. Lucinda. I'll call and tell them we're on our way." Noting the expression of alarm on Ronnie's face, she continued, "We can't just sit here all day, Ronnie; you'll go crazy! At least if we're driving, we can talk on the way, and we'll be getting on with it."

Rickie nodded agreement.

"We'll be in northern Virginia by late afternoon if we leave in about an hour," Andee continued.

Was it only yesterday morning they'd been in Washington? It seemed like a million years ago! Like everyone else in that crowded Capitol Hill hearing, they'd watched Evan in action, wide-eyed and rapt. But shock and horror were what Ronnie was feeling now. How would she face Luc when she hadn't had a chance to tell him about Evan? She closed her eyes, her despair deepening. What a frigging nightmare! It would all come out.

Seeing that Ronnie was in no shape to pack an overnight bag, Rickie went upstairs to get a few essentials together for her. Andee's husband, Frank, would take care of their animals overnight, but she'd volunteered to call Mindy and ask her to look after Purrl and Ronnie's two horses again when she made arrangements for her own animal care.

Andee dispatched the two phone calls to Chip and Luc, saying only that they had an urgent issue that had arisen unexpectedly, and they needed a face-to-face brainstorming session with their investment partners. After they picked up their own luggage, she pulled in for a few minutes at the Horse Country Real Estate office and made sure that Jackie and Geri knew that she, Ronnie, and Rickie would be out of town and they could reach her on her cell, although she had complete confidence in both of them. The agency had run like clockwork since Jackie had gotten her license and had found Geri to come in as office manager. They took Ronnie's SUV, although Ronnie was in no condition to drive and would remain in the back seat while Andee and Rickie took turns at the wheel.

Ronnie stared out the window, remembering the day she'd met Charles and Chip and Luc. Lucinda came later. Then Stephanie. So much had happened in less than a year.

So curious that Evan, the secret from her past, was here again, the soon-to-be-revealed secret right here in the immediate present. So, was that one secret or two? How ludicrous! She almost laughed aloud, absently fingering the silver tassel she wore around her neck like a talisman. If she could turn the clock back, what would she have done differently?

As it happened, the clock wouldn't be turned back but forward. As the miles rolled by, she was able to think more clearly, and by the time the group was seated in the Westlake living room, her mind was clear. She felt strong, focused, and filled with a sense of purpose. Evan had Ronnie, and all of them, over the proverbial barrel. Infuriating as it might be, they grudgingly admired his cunning. She had no choice but to capitulate, and so she would. Not at first, and not easily. But, in the end, she would teach him a lesson he'd never forget.

Charles drifted in and out of sleep as the group sat around his hospital bed. He had rallied somewhat in the past day or so, and his mind was still remarkably lucid, during his periods of wakefulness. He had immediately grasped the problem, and it was he who proposed the plot.

Ronnie had balked at having any further contact with Evan. It took some persuading to get her to see how revenge would be exacted, how the tables would be turned. She recoiled from the idea that she would have to talk to him, play a part, to string him along. Now, she was on board with the concept but was having trouble with the mechanics.

"He's going to expect you to sleep with him…" Lucinda spoke slowly, letting that reality sink in.

Ronnie blanched. She sat silent, unable to meet Luc's eyes. He, too, was silent.

"No way!" Andee exploded. "She can't do that!"

"Of course, she can't." Julia's voice was quiet, her tone measured.

Before she could complete her sentence, Lucinda interrupted. "I didn't say she should, or would. I said he'll be expecting her too. We have to have a strategy for that."

"No," Ronnie croaked, her voice thick. Rickie slipped her hand into Ronnie's and squeezed.

"Well," Lucinda continued. "She can make plans with him and then get the flu. Or have one of the horses colic. Or have car trouble. Or have to take Mindy to the emergency room in the middle of the night and stay with her. How long can it take to vote on this bill? Don't we just have to drag this out for a few weeks, maybe a month or two at the most?" She turned to Ronnie, her head cocked, waiting for a response. "Once the bill passes, we're home free!" she insisted.

But Ronnie's attention was caught by the small group gathered at Charles' bedside. Chip saw that Charles had awakened, and he'd taken the chair at his father's bedside. In a moment, Chip caught Luc's eye, and he joined them. Ronnie had the feeling they were discussing her. She strained to hear what they were discussing, without appearing obvious.

"That's the only way I could stomach this plan," Luc agreed. "It's not the way I had intended to do this but, the more I think about it, the more I like it. The satisfaction will be that much sweeter. We'll be laughing up our sleeves the whole time!"

He crossed the room in several quick strides, standing in front of Ronnie and taking both of her hands in his.

"I want you to marry me, Ronnie. Monday. I don't want to wait. I love you with all my heart. Will you be my wife?"

Now, you could have heard a pin drop. Ronnie, Rickie, Andee, Lucinda, and Julia stared at Luc, their eyes wide.

"Marry me, Ronnie," Luc repeated. "Now, before we get started with this thing. He can't have you; you'll be mine. We'll pull this off. We'll just be playing him for the fool he is. He should never have let you go."

"Marry you? Here? Now?" She must sound like a complete idiot. Then his words sank in.

"Oh, yes, Luc. I will." She threw her arms around his neck and burst into tears of relief and happiness.

"It's a sting!" Andee crowed.

"We can have the wedding here," Julia said, pragmatic as always. "Charles would love to give you away if he's able and, if not, Chip will. Rickie and Andee can go with you in the morning to buy a dress. I wish you could wear mine, but it would never fit.

Lulu and I will arrange for some flowers and some food."

"I guess it will be just us," she continued. "Luc, your family won't be able to come from New Hampshire." Luc's sister had just given birth the week before to her second child, and his own parents were staying with her family for a few weeks to help.

"It's just as well," Julia admitted. "Given the circumstances."

Andee had said Frank would fly to DC and she'd pick him up at the airport. He'd called back to tell her their usual dog sitter wasn't available, and he didn't want to board Luna.

"What about driving up and bringing her?" Andee asked. "We can probably fix up a bed for her in the garage. I'm sure that would be okay with Julia. Let me ask her, and I'll call you right back."

Julia rejected Andee's suggestion immediately when the subject was broached.

"She can't stay in the garage!" she exclaimed. "Do you think my two grandsons haven't made many a mess in this house? Luna's entirely welcome to stay with us. She's a member of your family!"

Frank laughed when Andee called to relay the good news.

"I love that woman!" he said.

By Monday evening, the living room and dining room had been transformed, with yards of white tulle and candles on every surface. The caterers had brought a portable arch that they set up facing Charles' bed. Chip would be Luc's best man, with all of the women as Ronnie's attendants.

Ronnie wore a slim strapless satin dress, in a color called moonlight, that hugged her body and flared in graceful folds at her feet. Her silver hair gleamed in the candlelight. She wore no veil but had one perfect gardenia anchoring her hair back on one side. Julia's borrowed pearls were as elegant and understated as the dress itself.

Julia and Lucinda both had closets full of beautiful clothes, and each looked lovely, Lucinda in apricot chiffon and Julia in a dressy full-length lightweight wool dinner suit in palest blush pink.

Andee wore a newly-purchased long velvet dress in a deep carnelian, with high-heeled satin sandals in the same deep red. Both the dress and the shoes were a departure for her, but she admitted she looked, as Rickie put it, like a million bucks.

Rickie herself looked as chic as she always did in deep bronze satin, a dress Julia had worn several times to the performing arts center and had loaned Rickie for the occasion, after paying the local dry cleaner a king's ransom to tack up the hem and steam it.

Stephanie had spent the night at her mother's and was away on a class trip that she'd been looking forward to for months, but she would have been heartbroken not to have been included in the ceremony. Luc had had a car waiting for her when she returned to Horizon Academy, and she joined the group at the last minute. Without the opportunity to take her shopping, she wore the same tailored navy pants and tunic that she'd worn to the hearing, but Julia had produced from the depths of her closet something called a 'Shoulder Show Off,' a cleverly-cut piece that lay over the shoulders, transforming the everyday into the elegant. It was velvet, an abstract swirl of deep jewel tones, accentuated with metallic thread that gleamed in the candlelight. She'd added a gold bangle on one of Stephanie's wrists and a wide band of dark red jade on the other. Even Luna sported a dressy bandanna for the occasion, fashioned from one of Julia's many silk scarves.

Each woman wore a lush corsage to compliment her dress, and Ronnie's bridal bouquet was a combination of colors and textures that echoed all of theirs. When Julia placed calls to the florist and the caterer she usually used and explained the urgency, both had refused to add a surcharge for rush service. Luckily, it was a weekday, and both were able to accommodate her requests. In an hour, it was over.

And, in that moment, it was all beginning. So many thoughts crowded into Ronnie's mind as the magnitude of what this would mean washed over her. Where would she and Luc live, with his business in Virginia, his daughter in school there, and the soon-to-be-widowed mother of his best friend needing him? Her own work, her friends, her life was in Tennessee; how would they mesh their households?

What about Stephanie? Would she be the meat in the sandwich, her loyalties torn between her biological mother and her new stepmother?

And Evan? Sweet Jesus, she hoped that damn bill passed and soon! What would the repercussions be when he learned he'd been played for a fool? He couldn't hurt her any more than he already had. But could he hurt Luc? He would certainly try, that much she was sure of.

Ronnie closed her eyes. She didn't see Luna move to her side, sensing her unease, but she felt the dog's soft tongue lick her hand. She reached to stroke Luna's head and saw the wide platinum band gleaming on her fourth finger. Looking up, she saw love shining out of Luc's eyes and on the beloved faces of her dearest friends. Suddenly, she was infused with a sense of joy and hope, and she knew that whatever was around the next corner, they would meet the challenges together.

ABOUT THE AUTHOR

Linnhe McCarron is the pen name for Leslie Helm who lives in an equestrian community near Big South Fork National Park in Jamestown, Tennessee. Originally from Connecticut, she lived in Maine for 15 years and Vermont for 10 but she has had horses most of her life, wherever home might be.
She rides gaited horses now, a black Tennessee Walker named Luc, and a buckskin McCurdy Plantation Horse called Jax.

If you enjoyed this book, please support the author by leaving a review.

Made in the USA
Coppell, TX
07 March 2022